# BOX SOCIALS

# BOX SOCIALS

# SOCIALS

A NOVEL BY

# W. P. KINSELLA

BALLANTINE BOOKS • NEW YORK

Library of Congress Catalog Card Number: 91-58628

ISBN: 0-345-37749-4

Text design by Debbie Glasserman

Manufactured in the United States of America

First American Edition: May 1992

10  9  8  7  6  5  4  3  2  1

*For my daughter, Erin Irene.*

"We cannot let go the need to bear witness . . ."
—*Patty Lou Floyd*

# Contents

# BOX SOCIALS

# TRUCKBOX AL'S BIG BREAK

# Chapter One

This is the story of how Truckbox Al McClintock almost got a tryout with the genuine St. Louis Cardinals of the National Baseball League, but instead ended up batting against Bob Feller, of Cleveland Indian fame, in Renfrew Park, down on the river flats, in Edmonton, Alberta, summer of 1945 or '46, no one can remember which, though the date in question has brought on more than one disagreement, which turned first to a shoving match, then to an altercation, and finally a fist fight, though not a brouhaha, the general consensus in the Six Towns area being that it takes more than two people to staff a brouhaha, the fist fight though, usually resulting in bent cartilege of someone's proboscis, and blood spots on a Sunday shirt.

I was young and pretty small at the time, not much taller than my dog, Benito Mussolini, who, when he stood looking sorrowful, if the light was right, appeared to have a long, bald head, though in reality he was just a plain old soup-hound of unknown but varied ancestry, with whiskers that stuck out like a cat's and bad breath.

"We're hillbillies," my mama said, on more than one occasion, "only difference is we know we're hillbillies, and we won't always be that way, unlike some we know." Mama hailed from South Carolina, and though she'd grown up prosperous, with a daddy who was a mining engineer, had had at least a passing acquaintance with hillbillies, up until the time she met Daddy.

The *unlike some we know* at one time referred specifically to three families, the Venusberg Stevensons, the more-or-less-Doreen Beach Sigurdsons, and the Red Sigurdsons, who were also known as our Sigurdsons because they lived in the general area of Fark, which was also the town my family lived in the general area of. Fark was about nine miles as the crow flies from New Oslo, a little further than that from Sangudo, and exactly eleven miles from Doreen Beach, which wasn't a resort or even on a lake, as many surprised visitors found out each summer. Fark wasn't big enough to be a town, and it was, Mama said, a cruel punishment for anyone to have to live in the general area of a town called Fark, the naming of which I'll get around to later.

My family, the O'Days (my father was John Martin Duffy O'Day, my mother Olivia), had been forced into unsuccessful farming by the Depression. One of my grandfathers was an engineer, not the steam-engine kind, but the coal-mining kind, and a great-grandfather had owned a winery in the old country, and my daddy, John Martin Duffy O'Day, built fine houses, only there weren't any fine houses to build during the Depression, so he sold his property in the city of Edmonton, Alberta, and bought a farm sixty miles more or less west of Edmonton, Alberta, which in the mid-1930s might as well have been six thousand miles more or less west of Edmonton, Alberta, because folks around the Six Towns area in general and around Fark, in particular, traveled by horse and wagon, or horse and buggy, or just plain horse.

The summer of 1945 or '46 Truckbox Al McClintock garnered a certain amount of attention, which without too much exaggeration could be construed as notoriety, when at a sportsday, while playing right field and batting cleanup for the New Oslo Blue Devils against an all-Indian team from the reserve at Lac Ste. Anne, the game being played on a newly mowed field on the banks of the Pembina River, Truckbox Al managed to come to bat five times, and five times he hit the ball about fifty yards beyond the centerfielder, which meant that the ball landed in the yellowish and murky water of the Pembina River, where it bobbed away downstream getting smaller and less white as it did so. In his fifth and final at-bat it is said that he hit the ball clean across the Pembina River. That mammoth blow caused the game to be called though it was only the fifth inning, because the Indian team was out of baseballs, and as home team they were obligated to supply them.

Outfielders who could hit five home runs in a game were in short supply, not to mention outfielders who could hit five consecutive baseballs into and across the Pembina River, so because of his prodigious feat that afternoon Truckbox Al was seduced into playing the remainder of the summer for the Sangudo Mustangs. What the Sangudo Mustangs used to seduce Truckbox Al was the fact that Bear Lundquist, the self-appointed coach and general manager of the Sangudo Mustangs, knew a man in Calgary, Alberta, a brother-in-law by marriage, once divorced, a man who hailed from Oklahoma and had played semi-pro baseball in his younger days; and that selfsame brother-in-law by marriage, once divorced, had an uncle in Pasadena, California, who, when he had last visited Calgary, Al-

berta, in the summer of 1937, said he was a speaking
acquaintance of a scout for the genuine St. Louis Cardinals of
the National Baseball League.

What Bear Lundquist promised was that if Truckbox Al would
play the rest of the summer for the Sangudo Mustangs, Bear
Lundquist, who was at the sportsday and witnessed Truckbox
Al hit five home runs, four into the Pembina River and one
clean across it, off a skinny Indian pitcher named Eddie Grassfires, whose only saving grace was a passable pickoff move to
first base, was that he would write to Calgary, Alberta, to his
brother-in-law by marriage, once divorced, who would pass the
information about Truckbox Al's baseball prowess along to his
uncle in Pasadena, California; who, if he wasn't a liar, and the
general consensus was that he was, would pass on the information of Truckbox Al's baseball prowess to the scout for the
genuine St. Louis Cardinals of the National Baseball League
with whom he was a speaking acquaintance.

Bear Lundquist's Sangudo Mustangs were not in the tourna-
ment that sportsday because no matter how hard they tried they
could only raise seven players, which included Bear Lundquist
who was sixty-two years old and arthritic, playing catcher, and
his wife, Mrs. Bear Lundquist, who wasn't arthritic but moved
like she was, playing first base. Bear Lundquist explained to
Truckbox Al that mighty oaks from little acorns grow, and that
once the scout for the genuine St. Louis Cardinals of the National Baseball League heard about his hitting prowess, playing
major league baseball for the genuine St. Louis Cardinals was
only a matter of time.


Truckbox Al's mother was a Gordonjensen, the bulldog-faced
daughter of Banker Olaf Gordonjensen of New Oslo, about nine
miles as the crow flies from Fark, a little further than that from

Sangudo, and exactly eleven miles from Doreen Beach, which wasn't a resort or even on a lake, as many surprised visitors found out each summer. When there had been a railroad, Doreen Beach had been named by an employee of the railroad, R. Ebeneezer Beach, for his daughter Doreen.

The family name, Gordonjensen, came about because of a misunderstanding with immigration, or at least an incompetent government official, who may or may not have been with immigration. When Gordon Jensen, newly arrived from Norway, was asked his name, he remained silent until someone behind him who understood more English than he did said in Norwegian, "Name?"

"Oh, Gordon Jensen," was his reply.

The government official wrote, O. Gordonjensen.

"What does the O stand for?" asked the official.

The newly christened Gordonjensen and his more comprehending friend behind him discussed the matter. They knew from their experience in Norway that all government officials were fools.

"O often stands for Olaf," they told the bureaucrat.


Olaf Gordonjensen established the Bank of New Oslo in 1900 and raised three bulldog-faced daughters, the youngest and most bulldog-like of whom, Gunhilda, he was marrying off on a spectacular fall day in 1929, when the groom, already dressed in the striped wedding trousers his future father-in-law had purchased for him, walked eleven miles cross-country through stubble fields, cow pastures, and blueberry muskegs, afraid to be seen on the main roads such as they were, to the Edmonton-Jasper Highway, where he used the last of his ready cash to buy a one-way ticket to Edmonton on the Western Trailways bus that stopped once a day at Bjornsen's Corner.

The groom was never heard from again. Besides the striped trousers and frock coat, he carried away with him, carefully pinned in an inside coat pocket for safekeeping, the diamond-encrusted wedding ring, and a pearl necklace, his present to the bride, both items provided by his future father-in-law. The groom rode out the Depression in a room above a Chinese café on 101st Street in Edmonton, and when times began to pick up, he sold the ring and necklace and went to attend chiropractic college in Davenport, Iowa, where at the age of thirty-nine, he was just about to graduate at the head of his class, when his jilted sweetheart's firstborn was about to face Bob Feller, of Cleveland Indian fame, in Renfrew Park, down on the river flats, in Edmonton, Alberta, summer of 1945 or '46, no one can quite remember which.

It was a classic mixture of Norwegian and Irish stock that made Truckbox Al McClintock the baseball player he was.

"Sort of like mixing straw and manure," my daddy said. "They seem an unlikely combination, but chink up the cracks in your house or barn with the mixture and it'll withstand sixty below or a hundred above."

The wedding took place in New Olso, at the Christ on the Cross Scandinavian Lutheran Church, also founded by Banker Olaf Gordonjensen who figured his customers would save more money and pay their loan installments more promptly if they were soundly chastised every Sunday by a God-fearing, guilt-spewing pastor of his own choosing.

Banker Olaf Gordonjensen, who wasn't really a banker, because the government wouldn't allow just anyone to own a bank in Alberta, though he did anyway, because the closest bank was forty miles away in Stony Plain, and things in general were a lot less sophisticated in those days, personally paid the Reverend Ibsen's first yearly stipend at the Christ on the Cross Scandinavian Lutheran Church. In return all he asked was that every one of Reverend Ibsen's sermons deal in some way with the virtue of saving money, and that Reverend Ibsen point out with equal frequency and fervor that those who did not repay their debts promptly were doomed to eternal damnation.

Curly McClintock, Truckbox Al's father, came from a long line of black Irish mechanics, self-taught mechanics, who would have looked down on and failed to heed the advice of anyone who had formal mechanical training. It was possible, my daddy speculated, that Curly McClintock wasn't even black Irish, though no one could tell, for the McClintocks, male and female, had an inordinate affinity for grease and oil.

Young Curly, who was slow-moving and slow-thinking, grew up lying on his back under a dripping differential. He wore a green Allis-Chalmers Farm Equipment cap, backwards, because on weekends at baseball tournaments, sportsdays, and picnics he was catcher for the Fark Red Sox, Fark being the town in the Six Towns area that the McClintocks lived closest to. Curly McClintock just couldn't see the wisdom of turning the cap around between sportsdays. That green Allis-Chalmers Farm Equipment cap, and Curly's striped railroad overalls, if they'd still been around in 1974, could have solved the world oil shortage all by themselves.

Curly's daddy, and Truckbox Al's granddaddy, Black Darren McClintock (as opposed to his first cousin Red Darren McClintock who had gone off to fight in the First World War and been reported missing in action), was a sometime dealer in used automobiles, buggies, farm equipment and horses, an occupation that just naturally followed his inordinate affinity for grease and oil, an affinity that he had inherited, and passed to his son, and would pass to his grandson. Black Darren McClintock had sold the Reverend Ibsen a Model T Ford, at a clergyman's discount, even though the Model T Ford was paid for by Banker Olaf Gordonjensen, and Black Darren McClintock had never heard of a clergyman's discount until Banker Olaf Gordonjensen brought the subject up.

That Model T Ford which the Reverend Ibsen used to visit his parishioners in and around New Oslo, so as to enjoy an afternoon snack of Norwegian fruitcake and perhaps a piece or two of cold fried chicken, and, if it was offered, a glass of dandelion wine, while he impressed on them the biblical virtues of saving money and paying loan installments on time, was a car that simply refused to keep its oil pan on.

Because that Model T Ford refused to keep its oil pan on, young Curly McClintock was dispatched by his daddy, Black Darren McClintock, to New Olso, on a brilliant October day in 1929, where he found himself in his usual and familiar position of lying on his back with oil dripping on his face. On this brilliant October day, Curly McClintock found himself lying on his back with oil dripping on his face in the driveway of Reverend Ibsen's parsonage next to the Christ on the Cross Scandinavian Lutheran Church in New Oslo, Alberta, at a time when Banker Olaf Gordonjensen was marrying off his youngest and most bulldog-faced daughter, Gunhilda.

The youngest and most bulldog-faced daughter of the banker was being married off to the local schoolteacher, a Mr. Perry Wyandotte, all the way from Edmonton Normal School, who figured rightly that marrying the banker's bulldog-faced daughter beat hell out of teaching forty-five hard-headed little Norwegians their ABCs for twenty dollars a month in a one-room schoolhouse, where before class each day he had to chop wood for the big, blue, pot-bellied stove that sat in the middle of the classroom.

Mr. Perry Wyandotte's one vice was that he had brought with him from Edmonton a battery-powered radio from which he could, on clear nights, pick up KSL Salt Lake City, and other exotic radio stations, sometimes being able to hear Gene Austin croon "Ramona," or Jimmie Rodgers sing "Moonlight and Skies."

It was while Mr. Perry Wyandotte was lying on his cot in the one-room teacherage, next to the one-room schoolhouse in New Oslo, the night before his wedding, that he heard on his radio that the stock market had crashed, and stockbrokers and bankers in various cities across the continent were leaping to their deaths just like they were lemmings driven by instinct, and the concrete below them was ocean water.

The news of the stock market crash hadn't reached New Oslo yet. Banker Olaf Gordonjensen did have a telephone, one of only three in the Six Towns area, but local partridge hunters couldn't resist the green glass insulators on the makeshift telephone poles, so the line was out of service fifty percent of the time all year 'round, and one hundred percent during hunting season, which late October was.

Three days after the wedding, Banker Olaf Gordonjensen found out he was, like everyone else in North America, more or less insolvent, and he came to understand why the young schoolteacher, Mr. Perry Wyandotte, had taken off cross-country rather than marry his bulldog-faced daughter.

There is a saying in and around New Oslo, actually it is a joke: "How do you stop a Norwegian wedding?" is the question. "You can't," is the answer. It loses a lot in translation. You'd have to be Norwegian to appreciate the nuances.

But on that brilliant October afternoon in 1929, when the bride, the youngest and most bulldog-faced daughter of Banker Olaf Gordonjensen, had been waiting at the Christ on the Cross Scandinavian Lutheran Church going on to four hours, and one of the Skalrud boys, Little Ole, who was probably but not certainly Flop Skalrud's nephew, had just reported to Banker Gordonjensen that one of the Bjornsens (the guitar player in the Bjornsen Brothers Swinging Cowboy Musicmakers who played at barn dances, box socials, whist drives, sportsdays, and ethnic weddings) had seen Mr. Perry Wyandotte sneaking onto the eastbound Western Trailways bus that stopped once a day at Bjornsen's Corner on the Edmonton-Jasper Highway.

It was about that time that Curly McClintock pulled himself out from under the Reverend Ibsen's Model T Ford, a Model T Ford that refused to keep its oil pan on, and wiping the oil off his face and hands with his green Allis-Chalmers Farm Equipment cap, returned it to his head, backwards as always. Curly McClintock then dripped his way over to the steps of the Christ on the Cross Scandinavian Lutheran Church, where what was left of the wedding party, and the Reverend Ibsen, were enjoying the Indian summer sunshine.

"She's in A-1, tip-top shape, Reverend," Curly said, wiping the last drop of oil off his nose with his sleeve.

"Thank you, young man," the Reverend Ibsen said.

"Excuse me," said Gunhilda Gordonjensen, touching Curly's sleeve, "but you wouldn't be interested in getting married, would you?"

Curly wiped his face and forehead on his other sleeve, the one that the bulldog-faced banker's daughter had just touched, while he eyed the people on the church step, especially the bulldog-faced Gordonjensen girl, as he tried to determine if they were making fun of him. He scuffed one of his oilstained boots on the brown October grass as he surveyed the solemn faces in front of him.

"Who to?" he said.

"Me," replied Gunhilda Gordonjensen.

"You the banker's daughter?"

She nodded.

While Gunhilda Gordonjensen was proposing to Curly Mc-Clintock, the thoughts going through Curly's mind concerned something his uncle, Red Andrew McClintock, manager and first base coach of the Fark Red Sox baseball team, often urged on his players, between innings or at their rare practices.

"Want you boys to try as hard as a homely girl on her honeymoon," Red Andrew McClintock would say, as he slapped ground balls at the infield, or when he had the Fark Red Sox practicing rundowns between first and second base.

Curly McClintock, at twenty years of age, still wasn't too sure what it was that a homely girl tried hard *at* on her honeymoon, but he knew when he looked at Banker Olaf Gordonjensen's youngest and most bulldog-faced daughter, that he was staring at a homely girl. But dressed up in her cream-colored lace wedding dress, with the long sleeves that hid her muscles, her face screened by a little veil freckled with seed pearls, Gunhilda Gordonjensen looked less bulldoggish than she would ever look again, and, Curly recalled, Banker Gordonjensen owned an eight-room house with a cistern and indoor plumbing.

Only indoor plumbing Curly had ever seen was on the rare occasions when his father, Black Darren McClintock, allowed him to go along in the dump truck, on the twice-weekly jaunts to Edmonton for groceries, and then the only indoor plumbing he had encountered was in a tiny room at a truck stop on the edge of the city. A truck stop where the bowl and basin were so covered in grease and the smell was so strong Curly didn't see a lot of improvement over the two-holer behind Mc-Clintock's garage-house. The McClintock's garage-house had at one time been the station house, when the railroad used to run by Fark, where the living room was now full of stripped-down motorcycles, and a couple of dozen generators sat around on the kitchen floor like patient cats waiting for supper.

Curly removed his oil-soaked Allis-Chalmers Farm Equipment cap, just long enough to turn it around and place it formally on his large, round head, crown forward, before he said, "By golly, let's do it."

Considering the circumstances of the marriage, Curly McClintock and Gunhilda Gordonjensen were said to have been as happy as any, and happier than most.

"You can't stop a Norwegian wedding," one of Gunhilda Gordonjensen's aunts said, as Reverend Ibsen lined up Curly McClintock and Gunhilda Gordonjensen on the steps of the Christ on the Cross Scandinavian Lutheran Church.

Curly and Gunhilda McClintock (*née* Gordonjensen) borrowed Banker Gordonjensen's open-topped touring car, and drove west on the Edmonton-Jasper Highway, stopping for the night at a town called Entwistle, at the Hide-A-Way Tourist Court, where they got a granary-sized tourist cabin all to themselves for two dollars, and where Curly sure enough discovered what it was a homely girl tried hard at on her honeymoon. Curly became quite fond of his discovery.

When Curly and Gunhilda got back from their honeymoon, having driven as far west on the Edmonton-Jasper Highway as Edson, where they stayed in a granary-sized cabin at the Bide-A-Wee Tourist Court for two dollars a night, they moved into Banker Gordonjensen's eight-room house with a cistern and indoor plumbing, and learned that the banker, along with almost everybody else in North America, was more or less insolvent.

Alvin Olaf McClintock was born nine months after the night at the Hide-A-Way Tourist Court in Entwistle, Alberta, where Curly McClintock discovered what it was homely girls tried hard at on their honeymoon. And about two years later, as one of Curly's brothers was watching Alvin Olaf toddle across the floor of the kitchen at Banker Gordonjensen's eight-room house with a cistern and indoor plumbing, the baby wearing only a diaper and a smile, the brother said to Curly, "By golly, that baby's built just like the box on Daddy's dump truck."

And Curly looked close at Alvin Olaf, toddling across the floor, wearing only a diaper and a smile, and said he had to agree, "That boy is built like the box on Daddy's dump truck." A dump truck that was soon to become Curly's, because only a few months later, Black Darren McClintock pushed back from the table after a feed of partridge parts and fried turnips, unbuckled his belt and passed away.

The McClintocks held a family meeting, where it was decided that since Curly was the only one married, and since his father-in-law, Banker Gordonjensen, knew how to handle money, even if he didn't have any anymore, that Curly should inherit the dump truck and the twice-weekly run to Edmonton to take the cream cans full of cream to the dairies, and bring back supplies from the grocery wholesalers to the towns in the Six Towns area.

"Hiya, Truckbox," Curly McClintock and his brother said several times to the baby, who grinned back like he understood, as he walked face-first into a wall.

# Chapter Two

Alvin Olaf McClintock was blessed with the best, or if not exactly the best, the most noticeable qualities of both his parents; he was squat and bulldog-looking like his mother, and he had an affinity for grease and oil that even surpassed his father's. One odd thing was that no one ever called Alvin Olaf McClintock *Truckbox* to his face. As he grew up squat and bulldog-looking and covered in grease, people would say, "Yonder goes Curly and Gunhilda's boy, Truckbox Al."

But if they met the boy coming out of the Fark General Store, or at a sportsday at Doreen Beach, they'd say, "Howdy, Al, how are you keepin' these days?" Truckbox Al would stare at the questioner like they'd asked him to write an essay on a subject unfamiliar to him, pull the visor of his oil-stained Allis-Chalmers Farm Equipment cap low over his wide, bulldog-looking face, and stalk away, swinging his right leg in a wide arc as he did so.

It wasn't until Truckbox Al McClintock reached sixth or seventh grade in the one-room schoolhouse in New Oslo, where a teacher named Miss Quick had replaced Mr. Perry Wyandotte, after Mr. Perry Wyandotte had walked cross-country for eleven miles through stubble fields, cow pastures, and blueberry muskegs in order the catch the eastbound Western Trailways bus at Bjornsen's Corner, leaving behind, forever, the Six Towns area, and the bulldog-faced Gordonjensen girl who would become Truckbox Al's mother, that anyone noticed that beyond being bulldog-looking and oil-covered, Truckbox Al had quick wrists and a certain amount of eye-hand coordination that made him able to hit a baseball with great frequency, and further than a fair distance.

Actually it was Miss Quick who noticed, on a day when Truckbox Al McClintock hit both of the school's baseballs over the side-by-side boys' and girls' outhouses, deep into a slough full of tall grass, bullrushes and swamp willow clumps, the baseballs, like the long departed Mr. Perry Wyandotte, never to be seen again. That evening, Miss Quick passed on what she had noticed concerning Truckbox Al's hitting prowess to her brother-in-law, the infamous Flop Skalrud, who occasionally played third base for the New Oslo Blue Devils.

Miss Quick, though she had been teacher at the one-room schoolhouse in New Oslo for nearly fifteen years, and had been married for twelve of those fifteen years to Einar Skalrud, the infamous Flop Skalrud's older brother, was still known as Miss Quick, not only at school, but everywhere else, something the women of the Six Towns area regarded as peculiar, abnormal, unnatural, and, some said, a crime against nature. *Some*, being primarily the widow, Mrs. Beatrice Ann Stevenson, Mrs. Edytha Rasmussen Bozniak, and her mother, Mrs. Irma Rasmussen.

So it didn't come as any particular surprise to the widow, Mrs. Beatrice Ann Stevenson, Mrs. Irma Rasmussen, or her daughter, Mrs. Edytha Rasmussen Bozniak, that while Einar Skalrud was off working in a logging camp up near Whitecourt, the infamous Flop Skalrud, as my daddy called him, spent many an evening, after the children were safely in bed, at the home of his brother Einar, and his brother's wife, Miss Quick.

"We all know what Flop Skalrud is interested in," the widow, Mrs. Beatrice Ann Stevenson, said one evening as she was drinking tea at our kitchen table in our house at the end of Nine Pin Road.

There was a rumor, I had heard my mama say, unsubstantiated, but a rumor nevertheless, that the widow, Mrs. Beatrice Ann Stevenson, had intimate knowledge of what it was the infamous Flop Skalrud was interested in, and what it was made Flop Skalrud interesting, or infamous as my daddy referred to him, that knowledge having, according to the unsubstantiated rumor, not all been acquired after the widow, Mrs. Beatrice Ann Stevenson, had become a widow. Mama, of course didn't mention *that* rumor to the widow, Mrs. Beatrice Ann Stevenson, and she delicately guided the conversation away from the infamous Flop Skalrud (the naming of, and what it was that made Flop Skalrud interesting, or infamous, I'll get around to later) and his sister-in-law, Miss Quick, to the fact that she had heard my daddy and Earl J. Rasmussen discussing the possibility that Truckbox Al McClintock might have some genuine potential as a baseball player.

The area we lived in was vaguely known as the Six Towns, though that designation never showed up on a map, and almost everyone lived near a town, not in a town. The Six Towns, New Oslo, Sangudo, Fark, Venusberg, Magnolia, Doreen Beach, and Bjornsen's Corner, which, if you count carefully, was seven, though Bjornsen's Corner was just a place, not a town, or even a post office, so didn't officially count, were all too small to be towns anyway; they were also too small to be villages, but any place that was officially named and had a post office wasn't too small to be a hamlet.

So where we lived became known as the Six Towns area, an area made up of six hamlets, though each and every one of them called itself a town. Each of the six towns had a grocery store of varying degrees of splendor, where the grocer-postmaster and his family lived in the back, or in the case of Fark, upstairs, or in the case of Magnolia, next door. The grocery in Doreen Beach was brick with big glass windows in the front, and a cement walk, which as far as I can recall was the only concrete in the Six Towns, while the grocery in Venusberg was in a log cabin with no windows on the front side at all, while inside, coal-oil lamps burned all year round.

The Venusberg grocer-postmaster did have a glass window in his living quarters, which was a lean-to, more or less attached to the back of the store. The Swangards, who owned the Venusberg store, were very old, and their personal smell, of liniment, pipe smoke, and herbal tea, permeated the whole store.

Each of the Six Towns also had a gas pump, but at the worst of the Depression only the ones in Fark, where Curly McClintock began his twice-weekly run to Edmonton, and New Oslo, where Curly McClintock finished his twice-weekly run to Edmonton, held gas. The remainder stood tall and skeletal, like weathered but empty thermometers; the glass got broken in some, so that rust and general dilapidation set in. By the time Truckbox Al got his big break, the economy had improved enough that gas was for sale everywhere in the Six Towns area except Venusberg and Magnolia.

Most of the Six Towns had, as well as a grocery store, a community hall, where occasional box socials and whist drives, community dances, or ethnic weddings, were held often enough that something happened at one of the community halls every second Saturday all year round. Even more occasionally, a farmer who had lived long enough to retire, moved to his favorite hamlet, in order to be close to the hustle and the bustle. Hamelts south and east of the Six Towns had elevators, and most of the towns that had elevators had the railroad, but there was no grain raised in the Six Towns area, mainly because the land was a kind of ash-gray and full of rocks, ranging from rice-gravel to some big as dump trucks.

So there were no elevators in any of the Six Towns, which weren't big enough to be called towns anyway, and because there were no elevators, the railroad had been discontinued several years before I was born. Fark, and Venusberg, and Magnolia, and Doreen Beach had all, at one time, been on the railroad, and now, in all except Doreen Beach, where the station house had burned down, somebody lived in the station house, because railroad station houses were solid-built buildings, and became free housing once the railroad abandoned them, just as the railroad grade, once the ties and tracks had been hauled away, became a road of sorts.

Churches in the Six Towns area were few and far between, in fact the only town that had a church was New Oslo, and that had been built by Banker Gordonjensen with an eye to keeping his neighbors in line. About five miles east of Fark, just off the railroad grade in a little grove of trees, there was a small log church that didn't have a name, and folks couldn't seem to recall who had built it in the first place. Before the Depression, a circuit rider used to come through every third week of summer, and as the weather would allow in the winter, and he was a generously liberal fellow, my daddy said, a man who preached a nondenominational service where Catholics, and Protestants, and Holy Rollers, who liked the smell of varnish and sitting on hard benches in a room that had bird nests in three of its corners, and evidence of mice everywhere underfoot, could rejoice at whatever those type of people rejoiced at, sing a hymn or two, and be properly slathered with guilt.

The Holy Rollers were more inclined to sing the hymns loudly, creating what they called a joyful noise, the Catholics took the generous supply of guilt to their hearts, while the Protestants preferred a large helping of fire and brimstone, which fit right in with the guilt and hymn singing, so all three groups left happy.

Truckbox Al's grandfather, Banker Olaf Gordonjensen, eventually died, something most everyone gets around to sooner or later, and he was hardly cold in the ground before it became apparent that Gunhilda Gordonjensen McClintock must have had a smattering of grease and McClintock inclinations in her blood even before she proposed to Curly McClintock.

Gunhilda's mother had been a Badke girl from over near Cherhill, and her branch of the family, the Wolfgang Badkes, as opposed to the Adolph Badkes who were relatively prosperous, prosperity being relative, lived over near Bjornsen's Corner. The Wolfgang Badkes were dirt poor and, if you checked back far enough, were shirt-tail cousins of Black Darren and Edina McClintock, Curly's parents.

Banker Gordonjensen, about the time he started his bank, which wasn't a bank at all, because private banks weren't allowed in Canada, but since there wasn't a bank within forty miles in any direction, it wasn't likely anyone was going to complain, decided that an enterprising young banker, even if he wasn't really a banker, but just a businessman who loaned money, and stored money, if somebody had enough that they needed to store some, should be married. With marriage foremost in his mind, Banker Olaf Gordonjensen attended a box social at Magnolia one summer night, where he met Gerta Badke, of the Wolfgang Badkes, who was squat and bulldog-faced. Immediately after a short courtship, and an almost formal wedding at the Christ on the Cross Scandinavian Lutheran Church, a wedding which was the social event of the year in the Six Towns area, Gerta Badke Gordonjensen produced, at nine-month intervals, three daughters in her bulldog-faced image, before she succumbed to something mysterious, known vaguely as woman troubles.

As soon as Banker Gordonjensen was safely buried, launched from the Christ on the Cross Scandinavian Lutheran Church, officiated over by the Rev. Ibsen, suitably eulogized by Torval Imsdahl, Earl J. Rasmussen, and several other people who owed him money, Curly and Gunhilda McClintock began to let the eight-room house with a cistern and indoor plumbing go to rack and ruin. The banker, in his economically imposed exile from banking, had been a great one for shutter painting, step repairing, and flower planting.

Curly and Gunhilda proved to be determined, and what with the Gordonjensen house being bigger than most, the average house in the Six Towns area was two rooms with outdoor plumbing, there was more to go to rack and ruin, and even after the house and grounds had got to rack and ruin, they were still more prosperous than most. But, my daddy said, the car parts, and machinery parts, and motorcycle parts, just crept into that big old house, like mice into a home without cats.

And Banker Olaf Gordonjensen hadn't been dead even ninety days, when the telephone service was cut off for non-payment, never to be reinstated, leaving only two telephones in the Six Towns area, so when the big day came, when the phone call from John "The Raja of Renfrew" Ducey, came long distance all the way from Edmonton, to let Truckbox Al McClintock know he'd been chosen to play for the Alberta All-Stars against a team of genuine Major Leaguers, including Bob Feller, Hal Newhouser, and Joe DiMaggio himself, that long-distance call had to come, not to the Old Gordonjensen home at New Oslo, but because the old Gordonjensen home had been allowed to go to rack and ruin, and have its telephone service cut off, never to be reinstated, that call had to come to the McClintock home place, where the window of Black Darren McClintock still lived in the old station house, just east of Fark, with what was left of the McClintock clan, knee deep in grease and auto parts, in established rack and ruin, as opposed to newly acquired rack and ruin, which was what Curly and Gunhilda were enjoying in the old Gordonjensen house at New Oslo.

When Truckbox Al's grandmother, Edina McClintock, accepted the long-distance call from John "The Raja of Renfrew" Ducey, and learned that her grandson had been chosen to play baseball against a team of genuine Major Leaguers, including Bob Feller, Hal Newhouser, and Joe DiMaggio himself, she promised to deliver the message as soon as humanly possible, which meant that early the next morning when Curly McClintock came rumbling down the railroad grade, which was the closest thing to a real road in the Six Towns area, gunning his dump truck so it spit white gravel out behind him, and pulled into the yard of his old home place, Edina McClintock was on the platform of the old station house, among many years' accumulation of auto parts, machinery parts, and general unsaleable second-hand merchandise, waving a blue polkadotted handkerchief, just in case Curly wouldn't see her in among the debris.

When Curly heard the news, he decided to postpone his trip to Edmonton long enough to gun the truck back down the railroad grade, which was fairly straight and smooth except for a couple of spots where there used to be small bridges, bridges that the railroad people tore out when they removed the tracks and ties in preparation for abandonment. In those places Curly had to gun the dump truck through ankle-deep water, except for one spot between Magnolia and New Oslo where there had been an honest-to-god trestle that the railroad people hadn't bothered to salvage, but which eventually fell down of its own accord, and lay like a dinosaur skeleton, its timbers bleached gray as owl feathers, in the swamp it once crossed over and above.

To get by that swamp Curly had to gun the truck over a two-and-a-half-mile detour of corduroy road that invariably shook a few parts off the truck every time he drove it. Luckily, Curly was mechanically inclined and had a plethora of spare truck parts at the old home place just east of Fark, and now, since Banker Gordonjensen was dead, in and at the old Gordonjensen place at New Oslo.


Truckbox Al McClintock was enjoying his new-found fame as a home-run hitter. Since the afternoon at the sportsday on the banks of the Pembina River, where in five times at bat he hit five home runs off a skinny Indian pitcher whose only saving grace was a passable pickoff move to first base, four home runs going into the Pembina River and the fifth clean across it, Truckbox Al was attempting to take every advantage of the situation that he possibly could. Until the afternoon when he hit the five home runs, Truckbox Al McClintock, being squat and bulldog-looking like his mother, and covered in grease and motor oil like his father, and as my daddy said, being dumber than a salt lick, and both his folks put together, had never been a favorite with the young ladies.

The week before he hit the home runs, at a box social at Doreen Beach, Truckbox Al spent his total savings of thirty-five cents to buy the box lunch he was certain belonged to the second-youngest Tomchuck girl, of the Venusberg Tomchucks, having to top a bid of thirty cents from her first cousin, Billy Steve Tomchuck, of the prosperous Nikita Tomchucks, who lived near Bjornsen's Corner, because he had heard the rumor that the second-youngest Venusberg Tomchuck girl was hot-blooded.

Unfortunately, by the time he paid the thirty-five cents, picked up the box lunch, which was a Paulin's Soda Cracker box covered in white tissue paper with pink tissue paper rosettes on each corner, the second-youngest Venusberg Tomchuck girl had disappeared in the company of her first cousin Billy Steve Tomchuck, something they'd been known to do at other box socials, whist drives, sportsdays and ethnic weddings, in spite of severe criticism that their interest in each other was unnatural, not to mention peculiar, irregular, and downright bizarre, not to reappear until the Bjornsen Bros. Swinging Cowboy Musicmakers had announced that "The Red Raven Polka" would be the first number after intermission.

When they reappeared, the second-youngest Venusberg Tomchuck girl's lipstick, blouse, and skirt were all a little ruffled looking, which only intensified Truckbox Al's conviction that she was hot-blooded, besides, he had thoroughly enjoyed the double portions of roast pork sandwiches, and rhubarb pie, in the box lunch, in spite of the fact he had to eat alone, although he had paid thirty-five cents for the privilege of eating lunch with the second-youngest Venusberg Tomchuck girl.

What he didn't like was that Billy Steve Tomchuck was standing right behind the second-youngest Venusberg Tomchuck girl, with his own shirt only half tucked in, and a lot of the second-youngest Venusberg Tomchuck girl's lipstick on his sunburned face.

What he said to Billy Steve Tomchuck, which Truckbox Al believed thoroughly put him in his place, was, "How many home runs have you hit recently?" A query that Billy Steve Tomchuck didn't attempt to answer; he simply put one of his large, farm-boy hands on the nearest hip of the second-youngest Venusberg Tomchuck girl, and winked at Truckbox Al, a gesture which only further intensified Truckbox Al's conviction that the second-youngest Venusberg Tomchuck girl was hot-blooded.

Truckbox Al McClintock being invited to Edmonton to play against a team of genuine Major Leaguers, which included Bob Feller, Hal Newhouser, and Joe DiMaggio himself, had what my daddy called a trickle-down effect, in that it provided good fortune, temporary employment, and exposure, if not notoriety, for several residents of the Six Towns area. Good fortune was what it provided for Earl J. Rasmussen.

It was because of Earl J. Rasmussen that everybody in the Six Towns area, and everybody who came to one of the box socials, whist drives, or community dances in one of the Six Towns, knew "Casey at the Bat." Earl J. Rasmussen, a bachelor who lived in the hills south of New Oslo with about six hundred sheep, loved to recite "Casey at the Bat," at the top of his lungs, at every box social, community dance, whist drive, and, if given the opportunity, at ethnic weddings. Earl J. Rasmussen, who had emigrated from Minnesota, had been raised near Norseland, Minnesota, but had played baseball as a boy somewhere up in the Iron Range, my daddy thought it was Buhl, or Hibbing, or maybe even Chisholm, but never remembered to ask for certain, though he knew it was a place where it gets fifty below in the wintertime.

In Minnesota, just like in Alberta, there was about nine months of wintertime, followed by three months of poor sledding, and people in both places took to memorizing poems in the cold months, which, if you combined wintertime with the cold months and poor sledding, pretty well took up the whole year in both Alberta and Minnesota.

There was a custom at box socials, community dances, and whist drives, whist being a card game my daddy said was bridge for people who couldn't regularly recall how many suits there were in a deck of cards, that while the band, the Bjornsen Bros. Swinging Cowboy Musicmakers, were taking their break, anyone and everyone was not only allowed, but encouraged, to come forward and contribute an *entertainment*. There was always some question as to how much entertainment was involved when Earl J. Rasmussen, who was about forty-five years old and lived alone in the hills south of New Oslo with about six hundred sheep, recited "Casey at the Bat" at the top of his lungs, but speculation of that nature never stopped Earl J. Rasmussen from reciting.

Earl J. Rasmussen had been unsuccessfully courting the widow, Mrs. Beatrice Ann Stevenson, who also recited poetry, and claimed her deceased husband to be a second cousin, once removed, of the famous Icelandic poet, Stephan G. Stephanson, her husband's family name having been altered by an incompetent immigration official so the spelling was no longer the same as that of the famous poet. But entertainment or not, Earl J. Rasmussen was always the second person to come to the front of the community hall, when the Bjornsen Bros. Swinging Cowboy Musicmakers were taking their break, the first always being the widow, Mrs. Beatrice Ann Stevenson.

The widow, Mrs. Beatrice Ann Stevenson, was a Sangudo Stevenson, as opposed to the Venusberg Stevensons, a group that often lived in tents along the road allowances just like Indians, and couldn't have recited their ABCs without cursing fit to curdle the moon of a clear night. The Sangudo Stevensons, on the other hand, owned their own land, occasionally wore store-bought clothes, and somewhere in her life Mrs. Beatrice Ann Stevenson had come in contact with some poems by a woman poet name of Emily Dickinson.

To solidify her position as *the* artistic person in the Six Towns area, a position temporarily challenged by Mrs. Edytha Rasmussen Bozniak the time she instigated, bulldozed through, and more or less organized, a Little Box Social for the children of the Six Towns area, a story I'll get to a little later, the widow, Mrs. Beatrice Ann Stevenson, not only claimed to be a second cousin by marriage, once removed, of the famous Icelandic poet, Stephan G. Stephanson, but she claimed, and with some truth, to have been before her marriage a Birkland, from Camrose, a town south and east of Edmonton, big enough to actually be called a town; a town where there was an actual college, called Camrose Lutheran College, where Miss Beatrice Ann Birkland had actually attended through tenth grade, and where she may well have been exposed to the poetry of this woman poet, Emily Dickinson.

As soon as the intermission break was announced at a box social, whist drive, or community dance (Mrs. Beatrice Ann Stevenson considered it inappropriate to perform at ethnic weddings), the master of ceremonies or the members of the Bjornsen Bros. Swinging Cowboy Musicmakers would barely be off the stage before the widow, Mrs. Beatrice Ann Stevenson, would be at center stage performing an *entertainment*, which consisted of reciting three Emily Dickinson poems complete with gestures.

It was my daddy, who had no small ear for music, especially after a slug or two of Earl J. Rasmussen's raisin wine, or a nip or two of chokecherry wine, dandelion wine, or Heathen's Rapture, logging-boot-to-the-side-of-the-head homebrew, the self-same combination of ingredients that caused Earl J. Rasmussen to recite "Casey at the Bat," at the top of his lungs, who caused the widow, Mrs. Beatrice Ann Stevenson, to switch from three Emily Dickinson poems complete with gestures, to Lord Byron's "The Destruction of Sennacherib's Host at Jerusalem," with considerably fewer gestures, though on the line "And the sheen of their spears was like stars on the sea," she did raise her right hand as if she was about to launch a spear into the wild blue yonder.

It was Daddy, who, humming along with, and tapping his foot to, the widow, Mrs. Beatrice Ann Stevenson's, recitations, discovered quite by accident, that everything she recited by the woman poet, Emily Dickinson, could be sung to the tune of "The Yellow Rose of Texas," which, he pointed out on the way home that night, took away a bit of what he called the artistic integrity of both the poetry, and Mrs. Beatrice Ann Stevenson's performance.

At the next box social, when the Bjornsen Bros. Swinging Cowboy Musicmakers took their break, and the widow, Mrs. Beatrice Ann Stevenson, took to the stage, for what Daddy said was, approximately, the two-hundred-and-fiftieth time, Daddy just sauntered along behind her, and sat himself down to the open-topped piano that had only one key missing, the piano having been vacated by Arne Bjornsen. Arne was not a Bjornsen brother but a Bjornsen cousin, though a Bjornsen all the same, and not a very good piano player, often tending to lose his place, especially in the middle of "Wildwood Flower," but he was kept around, first, because he was family, and second, because he was a good square-dance caller in both English and Norwegian.

That particular night, as the widow, Mrs. Beatrice Ann Stevenson, was reciting and gesturing, her eyes dewy with emotion, Daddy began to two-finger "The Yellow Rose of Texas" on the cousin Bjornsen's piano.

Now it was plain from the first note that a little two-finger piano playing immeasurably improved the quality of the widow, Mrs. Beatrice Ann Stevenson's, recitations. Usually, people tried to get out of the community hall during Mrs. Beatrice Ann Stevenson's recitations, and Earl J. Rasmussen's shouted rendition of "Casey at the Bat," and, if there was time, the performance of Little Grendel Badke, of the prosperous Adolph Badkes, who would sit at the piano that had only one key missing, and play "Alice Blue Gown," while she sang the words in a whisper no one could hear.

But this particular night, it was about fifty below, and whenever the back or front door of the Fark Community Hall was opened, a blast of steam and deathly cold air filled the little hall. So by mutual agreement, instead of going outside for a drink, the men went behind the ragged blue curtain at the back of the stage to sample the dandelion wine, raisin wine, chokecherry wine, homemade beer, and Heathen's Rapture, or bring-on-blindness, logging-boot-to-the-side-of-the-head homebrew. The young people who were dying to get their hands on each other's bodies did their body touching in the coat closet, which was just like a cloakroom at Fark schoolhouse, mainly because the school and the community hall had been built by the same carpenter, the infamous Flop Skalrud by name.

At first, as Daddy played the piano that had only one key missing, people just tapped their feet, while the more musical ones snapped their fingers, but in the middle of the second poem a few people began to hum, and by the time the dewy-eyed widow, Mrs. Beatrice Ann Stevenson, began the third poem everybody was ready to sing along, and did.

"Oh, I love to see it lap the miles and eat the valleys up . . ." sang about seventy people and a couple of dogs, including my old soup-hound, Benito Mussolini.

As my daddy said on the way home, the widow, Mrs. Beatrice Ann Stevenson, didn't know whether to pee or go blind. But when she was finished, instead of two or three of her friends from the Fark Sewing Circle and Temperance Society applauding, the whole seventy people burst into applause, cheers, and whistles, while Benito Mussolini and his friend howled along.

The audience, for the first time in history, demanded an encore, and when the widow, Mrs. Beatrice Ann Stevenson, repeated her performance, they sang along lustily, to all three Emily Dickinson poems, which, though they hadn't realized it, they knew by heart from hearing them so many times. Then everyone called for an encore of the encore, and all seventy people sang louder and stomped their feet harder, and even the young people who had been engaged in serious body touching in the cloakroom, stuck their heads around the corner to see what was going on, while Daddy played the piano more emphatically but with no more ability, and the widow, Mrs. Beatrice Ann Stevenson, eventually stopped reciting altogether, and just stared at the audience in a truly bewildered manner.

When the Bjornsen Bros. Swinging Cowboy Musicmakers emerged from behind the ragged blue curtain at the back of the stage, fully fortified with raisin wine, dandelion wine, homemade beer, and Heathen's Rapture, they had their work cut out for them to recapture the stage from Daddy, and the widow, Mrs. Beatrice Ann Stevenson; Earl J. Rasmussen and Little Grendel Badke having completely missed their turn to provide an entertainment.

Sixty miles away in Edmonton, though my daddy said it might as well have been six thousand, there lived a mythical man named John Ducey. John was pronounced Jawn, and rhymed with yawn, and he was an American, and a promoter of baseball, known to one and all as "The Raja of Renfrew," because Renfrew Park, down on the river flats, was the place in Edmonton where professional baseball was played. John "The Raja of Renfrew" Ducey, while not a wealthy man, had more money than most, because he had married into money.

John Ducey, before he was known as "The Raja of Renfrew," had married into a family who owned a successful inn, known as the New Edmonton Hotel, located on 97 Street in Edmonton, a section of the city my daddy said could not be compared with Fifth Avenue in New York City, or with any street in North America where rich society types might meet.

"During a depression, cash is king," my daddy often said, and, immediately after he said it, lamenting his own lack of cash, often for a considerable length of time. The New Edmonton Hotel, which was not large, three stories of red brick, and had never been elegant, was successful because it had a very large bar, which was patronized almost exclusively by Indians, who, even at five cents a glass, consumed enough beer to keep John Ducey, and John Ducey's in-laws, in money through the Depression. And there was even a fair amount of money left over, with which John Ducey promoted baseball in Edmonton, and thus became known as "The Raja of Renfrew," Renfrew being the name of the baseball park down on the river flats.

On a Sunday afternoon in 1945 or '46, no one can remember which, John Ducey took his wife, the wealthy hotel owner's daughter, on a drive into the country, where they stopped for a few minutes at a sportsday at a town on the banks of the Pembina River, where they watched a few innings of the final game of the day between the New Oslo Blue Devils and an all-Indian team from the reserve near Lac Ste. Anne, where they saw Truckbox Al McClintock hit three of his five home runs, two into, and one clean across, the Pembina River.

Most of the years while I was growing up, there was a war on, and all of us knew it, though it was about as far away as it could be, Europe and the South Pacific and all. Europe and the South Pacific and all, being several thousand miles away, one in one direction and one in another, were pretty hard for folks in the Six Towns area to visualize, for about two-thirds of the folks in the Six Towns area had never been as far away as

Edmonton, which was approximately sixty miles, but might as well have been six thousand.

Several, four I believe was the exact count, boys from the Six Towns area had joined the Canadian Army, and one, a Rose from near Sangudo, was rumored to be fighting in Italy, which most all of us knew was shaped like a boot and was where the pope and the real Benito Mussolini lived, but not much else. And, we all knew, the orphaned genius electrical engineer, Arthur Bozniak, who was married to a local girl, Edytha Rasmussen, had been one of the first Canadians killed in World War II, a story I'll get around to later.

The reason I mention the war at all, is that it turned out to be the underlying reason for the baseball game between the Alberta All-Stars and a team of genuine Major Leaguers, featuring Bob Feller, Hal Newhouser, and Joe DiMaggio himself, at Renfrew Park down on the river flats, in Edmonton, Alberta, summer of 1945 or '46, no one can remember which. The Americans were building something called the Alaska Highway, which I guess ran from Edmonton to Alaska, though I wasn't much good at geography then, and have never bothered to improve myself on the subject. To this day, I don't understand why they were building it, or what it had to do with the war in either Europe, or the South Pacific.

But build it they did, and there were many thousands of American soldiers stationed in Edmonton during the war, which was exceptionally good for the economy, because American soldiers had money and were willing and eager to spend it on almost anything, no matter the price. The city of Edmonton took on itself a nickname: "The Gateway to the North," it called itself, a nickname that stayed around until oil was discovered south of Edmonton at a place called Leduc, which translated from the French, means The Duke, and Edmonton decided to call itself "The Oil Capital of Canada," a nickname it still uses.

Apparently the Americans thought it was important to build the Alaska Highway, so it didn't matter what anyone else thought about it, and to build that highway they sent thousands and thousands of troops to Alaska, and all of them, at one time or another, passed through Edmonton.

There was something else that the Americans thought was just as important as building the Alaska Highway, or winning the wars in Europe and the South Pacific, and that was entertaining the troops. Apparently American troops didn't build good highways, or fight successful wars, unless they got frequent and good quality entertainment.

Many names, that those of us who had radios, would readily recognize: Bob Hope, Jack Benny, Phil Harris, Dennis Day, the McGuire Sisters, The Ink Spots and The Mills Brothers, to name a few, were flown into Edmonton, some on more than one occasion, to entertain the troops.

There was usually some spillover. Those stars, after they had entertained the troops sufficiently, so the troops could go back to building good solid highways, and fighting successful wars, would often put on a show in the city of Edmonton itself, having performed the original entertainment in a hangar at Namao Airport, north of Edmonton.

There was a place, which my daddy had seen, called the Edmonton Arena, sometimes called the Edmonton Gardens, which the radio said could hold five thousand people. I liked the name Edmonton Gardens better, because I could picture marigolds, petunias, red geraniums, and tall hollyhocks surrounding this white frame building, where five thousand people could go to hear Bob Hope, Jack Benny, Phil Harris, Dennis Day, or the McGuire Sisters.

My daddy said that the year after I was born, he traded a calf and two suckling pigs to an itinerant peddler for a radio, and, once word got around, our house was overflowing for several weeks, as everyone who didn't have a radio, which was most of the people in the Six Towns area, came by to stare at the large, cathedral-shaped box and the yard-long battery that powered it. There were many dire predictions concerning the radio, not the least of which was that God would strike radio owners dead on some preordained day; some of the old-timers, especially those from Europe, believed it a tool of the Devil, and that the voices that came out of it were actually demons. The widow, Mrs. Beatrice Ann Stevenson, said she thought the radio contributed to the general moral decline of the twentieth century, and that the radio almost certainly had something to do with a horrendous increase in teenage pregnancies, and may even have affected the weather in some mysterious way—just look at how late spring was, and hadn't a robin turned up frozen to death on her lawn in February, poor demented thing—and that she certainly wouldn't be caught dead with such a contraption in *her* house. She then settled in to enjoy four hours of Sunday night radio, beginning with "The Jack Benny Show," and promised to return the next night to hear "Lux Presents Hollywood," which was featuring "Captain Blood," with Errol Flynn recreating his original movie role.

The radio was around from my earliest days, so I wasn't awed by it, though I do remember considering it somewhat magical, as it brought in an occasional Major League baseball game from St. Louis, and minor league baseball from Kansas City, on clear nights in the spring and fall. The radio would also broadcast events that, when I look back, seem inconceivable.

There was a show originating from "the beautiful Trocadero Ballroom in the heart of downtown Edmonton," a show which consisted of the announcer simply introducing the orchestra, Mart Kenney and his Western Gentlemen, naming each song they were about to play, then describing the dancers: the beautiful women in their silks and furs, and the handsome men in their tuxedos, which, I guess, was a large enough dose of vicarious living to keep the show on the air for several years.

And, once a year, something called The Fun Parade came to the Edmonton Gardens, where a crowd of five thousand people would fill the place to *watch* a radio show. The master of ceremonies was named Roy Ward Dixon, and he would do real fun things like send two men, tied together like Siamese twins, out to ride the bus with just one bus ticket, and if they could convince some poor bus driver that the two of them, tied together like Siamese twins, should ride for the price of one, they got to bring the bus driver back to the stage at the Edmonton Gardens, where Roy Ward Dixon awarded everybody chintzy prizes.

It was because the American troops stationed in Edmonton needed, in order for them to build good solid highways, and fight successful wars, to be entertained with great frequency and regularity, that John "The Raja of Renfrew" Ducey was able to arrange for a group of Major League baseball players to come to Edmonton on a summer Sunday afternoon in 1945 or '46, no one can remember which.

This group of Major League baseball players were doing a stint in the service, neither building good solid highways nor fighting successful wars, but in their own way entertaining the troops just as if they were Bob Hope, Jack Benny, Phil Harris, Dennis Day, or the McGuire Sisters; their stint in the service involved them mostly going from military installation to military installation, playing exhibition baseball games against pick-up service teams.

Since Edmonton, "The Gateway to the North," was a place most of the troops just passed through, on their way to build the Alaska Highway, and didn't spend all that much time in, it was decided that the troops would be flown in to Edmonton in flying boxcars for that special Sunday afternoon of baseball. But since it was going to be difficult, if not well nigh impossible, to get together a team to challenge these Major League All-Stars, which included Bob Feller, Hal Newhouser, and Joe DiMaggio himself, John "The Raja of Renfrew" Ducey decided to stimulate local interest by having the Major League All-Stars play a local team to be named, with a genuine lack of originality, the Alberta All-Stars.

It was because of baseball and a train wreck that my daddy met my mama, and because of baseball and a train wreck that two people from South Carolina, my daddy and my mama, met in South Dakota, ended up getting married and eventually found themselves farming unsuccessfully in Alberta during the Depression.

Mama was born in Charleston, S.C., just a few days after her parents arrived there from the country of Colombia, where my grandfather had been working as a mining engineer in an emerald mine. My grandfather went back to the emerald mine, and to diamond and coal and copper and zinc mines at various places around the world for the next twenty years, while Mama and my grandmother remained in Charleston.

Daddy, himself, admitted to being born in South Carolina, about a hundred miles, geographically, and two hundred and ten, socially, from my mama. They never did come even close to meeting while they were growing up in South Carolina.

When Mama was twenty years old, my grandfather decided to settle down and bought himself a permanent position as a part owner of a copper mine in Butte, Montana, and decided that if he was going to live there forever he should have his family with him. Forever to my grandfather only lasted ten years and when last heard from he was supervising the installation of diamond-mining equipment near Cape Town, South Africa.

My mamma gave up her job at an art gallery in Charleston,

located on Calhoun Street, not far from the statue of John C.
Calhoun, who, she said, was famous for a number of things, the
oddest being that he was supposed to be the true father of
Abraham Lincoln, and caught a train which in several days
would deliver her to Butte, Montana.

As the train was traveling across South Dakota, where Mama
said the prairie was like green ocean in every direction and the
tall buffalo grass swayed down as the train passed just like a
wind sweeping over water, the track gave way and the engine
plowed off through the tall, green buffalo grass, more-or-less
parallel to the direction it had been running in, until it bogged
down with its wheels buried in the prairie. The derailment had
been so gentle that most of the passengers didn't realize what
had happened, Mama said. The crew were very polite and they
suggested that the passengers might like to have a picnic out on
the sunny prairie while they waited for a repair crew to arrive,
and as the passengers sat in little groups on the grass the white-
coated waiters from the dining car passed among them handing
out sandwiches and cool drinks.

Daddy, who after the First World War had traveled about
considerably, playing baseball in Florida and California, though
I could never establish who he played for, or who with, or for
how long, had been living in a town almost in the shadow of
Mount Rushmore, playing baseball on weekends and working
for the railroad during the week. Daddy was on the crew sent
to put the train back on the track.

Daddy readily admitted that he didn't know a whole lot about
putting a train back on the track, his paramount skills being to
charge in from third base and field bunts barehanded, and
hammer a double down the right field line about every third
time he came to bat, but his eyes sure did recognize a beautiful
girl when he saw one, and his ears sure did recognize a Charleston, S.C., drawl when he heard one, and by the time the train

was back on the track, Daddy had decided to spend the last of his ready cash to buy a one-way ticket from wherever on the plains of South Dakota they were, to Butte, Montana, which he did, and Daddy and Mama were married four months later, and Daddy decided to settle down forever and apprenticed himself to a man who built fine houses for the mine owners, doctors and lawyers of Butte, Montana.

Fortunately, or unfortunately, Daddy had in his veins what he described as *wandering blood*, and, three years later, when a barnstorming baseball team passed through Butte, Montana, a team called Brother Pettigrew's Divine Light Baseball Mission, combining, Brother Pettigrew said, the two Gods of rural North America, the mysterious and sometimes troubling one in the sky and baseball, a team whose third baseman was arrested for Disturbing the Peace in Butte, Montana, by kicking out the window of his hotel room at three A.M. and singing "Amazing Grace" in an off-key, but very loud voice, a charge that would have gotten him nothing but a two-dollar fine and a lecture about disturbing the peace, except an eagle-eyed deputy leafed through a stack of Wanted Posters and discovered that the third baseman was wanted in Orlando, Florida, for Bank Robbery and Assault with a Deadly Weapon, which, my daddy said, could well have been his loud, off-key singing voice.

My daddy was called in to repair the splintered window sash, and next afternoon found himself on his way to Bozeman, Montana, where Brother Pettigrew's Divine Light Baseball Mission was scheduled to play a game against the team from Bozeman Bible College.

Daddy toured with Brother Pettigrew's Divine Light Baseball Mission for about three months; the team traveled in a circle through Washington, Oregon, and Idaho, then moved up into Canada. They played in Medicine Hat, Alberta; they played in Lethbridge; they played in Calgary; they played in Red Deer;

they played in Edmonton; well, not exactly played in Edmonton. There had been a slight misunderstanding, and they had been booked into a softball park and scheduled against a women's softball team. They agreed to make certain adjustments and play the game anyway, but only eleven spectators showed up and the game was canceled. The bus wouldn't start so the players, and Brother Pettigrew, had to take a streetcar to their hotel, and when they got up in the morning they discovered that Brother Pettigrew had absconded owing each and every one of them a full two months' wages. To add insult to injury, though it was barely Labor Day, three inches of wet snow had fallen during the night.

My daddy was down to only a few dollars and one change of clothes, his baseball uniform. He studied the ads in the *Edmonton Bulletin*, but there were no ads for South Carolinians who built fine houses, but what he did see was an ad for a mining engineer at a coal mine a few miles north of Edmonton, and using his father-in-law's name he applied and was immediately accepted. He signed on at a salary about five times as high as he earned building fine houses in Butte, Montana, and accepted the job on the condition he be assigned a talented assistant. The mine owners were delighted, they reported that the assistant mining engineer knew everything there was to know about coal mining but he didn't have his *papers*. If the assistant mining engineer had his papers, they said, they would have promoted him to mining engineer and hired an assistant instead of hiring an experienced man like my daddy.

Daddy, who admitted to being mildly claustrophobic, said he had no desire, in spite of the excellent pay, to go down in a mine. He managed to work for three months, in which he earned more than he would have in a year as a carpenter, without ever going down in the mine. His talented assistant was indeed talented, so that Daddy had only to sign his name to an occasional document and he spent his days in his office, playing cribbage with the janitor. When he resigned after three months, supposedly to accept a position with an emerald mine in the country of Colombia, he signed the necessary papers to certify his talented assistant as a genuine mining engineer.

When he got his first paycheck from the mine, Daddy, instead of returning to Butte, sent Mama the train fare to visit him. It was Mama who talked him into resigning before he got found out. They rented a little house in Edmonton, and in spring Daddy found work building fine houses and in the fall they bought the house they were living in and decided to stay in Alberta for a while.

Things had turned out just as Daddy expected them to. Daddy, much to Mama's eternal consternation, always expected things to turn out well. When Brother Pettigrew's Divine Light Baseball Mission went bankrupt, Daddy never even considered that he wouldn't find a job, either building fine houses or working as a mining engineer; it never occurred to him that it was odd for two people from South Carolina, via South Dakota and Montana, to wind up in Edmonton, Alberta, and it never occurred to him to anticipate the Depression, or to accept Relief when the Depression crashed down. It never seemed odd to him to sell his house in the city of Edmonton and buy a useless and stony quarter section of land in the general vicinity of a town called Fark, the naming of which I'll get around to later, where he and Mama, and eventually me would ride out the Depression.

"He was never any better a ball player than he thought he was," Mama said one afternoon as she was darning socks by the light of the south window. "I married your daddy because he was a nice, cheerful man who never expected to bat less than .400, never expected to lose a game, and certainly never expected a Depression."

# Chapter Three

Until shortly before John "The Raja of Renfrew" Ducey scheduled that exhibition baseball game, most of us in the Six Towns area had seen but one real live American soldier close up. Those who lived near the Edmonton-Jasper Highway had seen an occasional truck or Jeep carrying American soldiers who were maybe off to build the Alaska Highway, but more likely just sightseeing, and Bjornsen's Corner never did have a gas pump, so even if they needed gas they had to drive on to a town called Wildwood, a long ways west of the Six Towns area.

Curly McClintock and his son, Truckbox Al McClintock, had both seen, on their twice-weekly jaunts to Edmonton in the dump truck, the long convoys of camouflage-brindle trucks and Jeeps heading west on the Edmonton-Jasper Highway, toward the Whitecourt turnoff, a turnoff which, in seven or eight days, would take them to where the rest of the American troops were building the Alaska Highway.

Curly McClintock and his son, Truckbox Al McClintock, both attempted to describe what they had seen, but both were slow-talking, and slow-thinking, and covered in an inordinate amount of grease and oil, and whenever anyone asked them a question they both looked as if they'd been asked to write an essay on a subject unfamiliar to them, so the residents of the Six Towns area never got a proper description of the convoys of camouflage-brindle trucks and Jeeps, let alone of the American soldiers who manned the camouflage-brindle trucks and Jeeps.

One afternoon an American soldier, driving a camouflage-brindle, two-ton army truck, and carrying a dispatch pouch full of supposedly vital information, completely and cleanly missed the Whitecourt turnoff, and might have carried on until he traveled all the way to Jasper, and got stopped by the mountains, except that the camouflage-brindle, two-ton truck developed engine trouble and stopped dead in the center of the road, within spitting distance of Bjornsen's Corner.

The lone American soldier pushed the camouflage-brindle, two-ton truck off to the side of the road, then stood with his hands on his hips and stared all around him. What he saw to the left of the Edmonton-Jasper Highway was a lot of muskeg sprinkled with twisty tamarack trees, while what he saw to the right of the Edmonton-Jasper Highway was a lot of prairie covered in red clover, and a big, white farmhouse with green shutters, sitting well back in a grove of cottonwoods.

The lone American soldier walked the quarter mile to the big white farmhouse with green shutters, which belonged to Sven Bjornsen, of the Bjornsen Bros. Swinging Cowboy Musicmakers, clutching the dispatch pouch which contained supposedly vital information, and once he made himself understood, which wasn't easy, because he came from South Carolina, and the Bjornsens came from Norway, and what each of them called English didn't sound like English to the other one, he was able to use Sven Bjornsen's telephone, one of only two in the Six Towns area since Curly and Gunhilda McClintock allowed their telephone to be cut off for non-payment, to call the United States Army in Edmonton and let them know approximately where he was.

Approximately, because when the lone American soldier asked where he was, Sven Bjornsen said very authoritatively, "You're at Bjornsen's Corner, Alberta, Canada."

Sven Bjornsen said that so authoritatively that the lone American soldier believed him, and the United States Army believed the lone American soldier when he gave that as his location. Finding the lone American soldier proved to be quite difficult for the United States Army, because, when they copied down the information the lone American soldier gave them, they didn't know that (a) the lone American soldier had missed the White-court turnoff and was many miles west of where he was supposed to be, and (b) that as far as map makers were concerned, there was no such place as Bjornsen's Corner, Alberta, Canada.

The lone American soldier then tinkered with his camouflage-brindle, two-ton truck, enough so that he could call back the United States Army in Edmonton, the first time Sven Bjornsen's phone had been used for two long distance calls in one day, and tell them what he thought was wrong with it, and the United States Army in Edmonton told him to hold tight and another camouflage-brindle, two-ton truck would be sent to Bjornsen's Corner with replacement parts, only, they added, the parts had to come from someplace like Michigan or Minnesota, so he should hold tight for a few days.

When the lone American soldier asked about the dispatch pouch containing supposedly vital information, the party he was conversing with said he was a mechanic and that wasn't his department and what difference could it make if a few pieces of paper were a few days late getting to Alaska, and the lone American soldier said he had to agree.

That lone American soldier was an amiable sort, and the first night he was at Bjornsen's Corner, he sat right in with the Bjornsen Bros. Swinging Cowboy Musicmakers, played the spoons like he was a regular musician, and sang Jimmie Rodgers's songs in a high, sweet voice, like they were meant to be sung.

There were eleven Bjornsens in the house at Bjornsen's Corner but they made room for the lone American soldier anyway.

"Ve vill yust put anoder cup of vater in the soup," said Mrs. Bjornsen, which she did.

But when, after a week, the second camouflage-brindle, two-ton truck didn't arrive with the parts, the Bjornsens arranged for the lone American soldier to move in with the Wasyl Lakustas, who were known as the Lakustas by the lake, although Lily Lake, the lake they lived by, had dried up years earlier.

The lone American soldier was both willing and able to pay for board and room, while the Wasyl Lakustas were known (a) to be so poor their children took bacon-fat sandwiches to school, when they went to school, which was infrequently, and (b) to have two eligible daughters, at least one of whom was rumored to be hot-blooded.

Now the lone American soldier, who had a name, but who everybody, which at this point was only the eleven Bjornsens, referred to as the Little American Soldier, because of his size, which was negligible, the Little American Soldier took an immediate shine to Lavonia Lakusta who was seventeen, had dark red hair and brown eyes, and was rumored to be the hot-blooded one among the Lakusta sisters.

Two more weeks passed, and the Little American Soldier walked from the Lakustas by the lake to Bjornsen's Corner and again used the phone to call his superiors and inquire about the missing truck parts. The United States Army told the Little American Soldier to be patient, that they hadn't forgotten about him, that they had ordered parts for his camouflage-brindle, two-ton truck from Michigan or Minnesota or wherever, and that they had tracked down the approximate location of Sven Bjornsen's telephone, and that it wasn't anywhere near where the Little American Soldier was supposed to be, but since he was liable to be there for a spell, a spell being a unit of time that both the Little American Soldier and the United States Army understood, it was agreed that his pay would be sent to the post office at Fark, which was the closest post office to Bjornsen's Corner, a place which the United States Army said didn't exist. In the meantime, several of the eleven Bjornsens had towed the Little American Soldier's camouflage-brindle, two-ton truck into their yard and parked it in their machine shed.

Wasyl Lakusta, of the Lakustas by the lake, thinking of his old age, recognized good solid son-in-law material when he saw it, and did what he could to promote a match between the Little American Soldier and his daughter, Lavonia. Promoting the match mainly involved showing off Lavonia's cooking and showing off Lavonia. The oldest Lakusta girl, Sylvie, who was nineteen, took after her mother, and was as Wasyl Lakusta described her, "Not much good for look at, but pretty much good for strong."

Wasyl wasn't worried about finding a husband for Sylvie, one of the Yaremko boys from Stanger had already shown an interest, a large-bodied Yaremko with legs like tree stumps and knuckles that grazed the ground when he walked, and he was at that very moment building himself a place to live, converting a granary into a cabin, and with a wife by his side they could apply as a couple to homestead three hundred and twenty acres instead of just one hundred and sixty, which was all a single man was allowed to apply for.

But Lavonia was another matter, slim and delicately constructed, she was only good for light work around the house, weeding the garden, feeding the chickens, and for going to round up the milk cows morning and evening. So Wasyl Lakusta, thinking of his old age, arranged for Lavonia and the Little American Soldier to be left alone as often as possible, and even took his pocket knife and cut the cowbell off the neck of the lead cow, so the animals would be harder to find, and leave Lavonia and the Little American Soldier, who always accompanied her, longer to walk alone in the woods and get acquainted.

The Little American Soldier was not slow, and on these long walks he admired Lavonia's dark red hair, stared into her brown eyes, and discerned by the very act of being alone with her that the rumor about Lavonia being hot-blooded was true.

As far as Lavonia was concerned, the Little American Soldier, in his khaki-gaberdine uniform, and genuine military cap that made him look like Smilin' Jack, the hero of a Big Little Book she and her brothers and sisters shared, one of two books in the Lakusta cabin, the other being a Bible printed in Ukrainian, was just the handsomest, best-looking man she had ever seen. She particularly like the uniform. Lavonia's best girlfriend was Stevie Dwerynchuk, and one of Stevie Dwerynchuk's brothers was in the Canadian infantry, but when he came home on leave his uniform was the color and texture of weatherstripping, and instead of a genuine military cap that made him look like Smilin' Jack, he wore a turned-over-trough of a cap made of the same ugly, scratchy material as his uniform.

Mrs. Wasyl Lakusta, her first name was Rose, though no one called her Rose, except Mr. Wasyl Lakusta, thinking of her old age, immediately recognized the Little American Soldier as good solid prospective son-in-law material. She boiled up many fat pyrogies (little dumplings stuffed with cottage cheese), each one bulging with the cheese; she fried them in bacon grease and onions; she had Lavonia carry them to the table and set them in front of the Little American Soldier, and when he didn't seem to know what to do with them, she had Lavonia spoon thick sour cream over the pyrogies, sprinkle them with pepper and caraway seeds. Then Mrs. Wasyl Lakusta would appear from the kitchen, smiling from beneath her babushka, careful not to show her bad teeth, and say, "Eat! Eat! Lavonia cook, you eat!" using up four of the half dozen English words she knew. And eat he did, his brown eyes happy. And he shaved each morning using Wasyl Lakusta's straight razor, first dipping warm water from the reservoir on the cook stove and placing it in a white enamel wash basin with a scarlet line around the rim.

During the Little American Soldier's third week there, the Laukstas butchered a pig, one they'd intended to fatten until winter, but after a long conference involving the Wasyl Lakustas, Sylvie Lakusta and her oldest brother, Nestor, and Sylvie's fiancé, Pete Yaremko, the conference held while the Little American Soldier was walking with Lavonia Lakusta along what would have been the banks of Lily lake, if Lily Lake hadn't dried up several years earlier. At the conference it was decided the most important thing they could do was feed Lavonia's prospective husband, their collectively prospective son-in-law, and brother-in-law, as well as was humanly possible. That same afternoon the pig, who had expected to live at least until the first snowfall, and since the first snowfall was known to occasionally happen in August, probably long after that, was bashed in the center of the forehead by a sledgehammer with Pete Yaremko attached to the handle of it, had barely fallen to its knees when Sylvie Lakusta slashed its throat with a butcher knife, and Wasyl

Lakusta attached a rope to its left hind foot and the three of them swung it aloft from the log arch above the corral gate.

The Little American Soldier took to the Lakustas by the lake like fleas to a dog, but he especially took to Lavonia and her dark red hair, brown eyes, and delicate construction. One afternoon, he walked the four miles to the Fark General Store, where he picked up his army pay and bought for Lavonia's dark red hair a pair of barrettes shaped like everlasting daisies, white flowers with yellow centers. And he brought home a sackful of store-bought groceries, including coffee, chocolate bars, and two packs of tailor-made cigarettes.

He showed Lavonia's youngest brother how to tie string to the four corners of a khaki handkerchief so as to make it a parachute, and how to fold that parachute, and how to put a stone in the middle and toss it up in the air, then to duck the stone when it fell back down and watch the parachute float to the ground just like dandelion fluff.

Now the Bjornsen Brothers, both the ones in the Swinging Cowboy Musicmakers and the ones not, were no slouches as mechanics, so with a welding torch and the frame of a 1939 Terra-plane that had rolled in the ditch two miles west of Bjornsen's Corner the winter before and been abandoned, and a certain amount of native Norwegian mechanical genius, they constructed a part or two that made the Little American Soldier's camouflage-brindle, two-ton truck operational again.

Five weeks had passed by now, and the Little American Soldier still phoned Edmonton every week, and the United States Army still told him to hang in there, that the parts were on the way from Michigan or Minnesota or wherever, and that they hadn't forgotten him. The Little American Soldier had tucked the dispatch pouch, full of supposedly vital information, underneath the seat of his truck and more or less forgotten about it.

Once the Bjornsen Brothers, the ones in the Bjornsen Bros.

Swinging Cowboy Musicmakers, and the ones not, had used their native Norwegian mechanical genius to make the camouflage-brindle two-ton truck operational again, the Little American Soldier was able to drive around and explore the Six Towns area, nearly always taking Lavonia Lakusta with him. They'd drive up to New Oslo and buy gas, then head over to Doreen Beach, where the brick general store with glass windows had an ice house attached and, for about two hours twice a week had ice-cream cones available, the two hours being right after Curly McClintock had unloaded from his dump truck the grocery order from the wholesale in Edmonton, which included a gallon tub of ice cream.

Once word got around about the Lakustas by the lake having acquired their very own American soldier, they had an inordinate number of visitors, including my daddy and me, who just happened to drive four miles out of our way after a trip in our horse and cart to Fark General Store of a Saturday afternoon. It was, my daddy said, about as crowded at the Lakustas by the lake, as it had been years before when we acquired our very own radio, for the widow, Mrs. Beatrice Ann Stevenson, was there, as were just about every family in the Six Towns area who had an eligible daughter.

The Little American Soldier, and Victor Lakusta, Lavonia's youngest brother, demonstrated to me how to fold a khaki handkerchief the way a parachute was supposed to be folded, how to put a stone in the middle, how to toss the handkerchief and the stone into the air, how to duck the stone and watch the parachute float to earth just like dandelion fluff. I never did master folding the handkerchief, and after I got home I folded one of Daddy's red bandannas like I thought a parachute should be folded, put a stone in the middle and tossed it in the air, where the stone came out but the still-wadded bandanna dropped straight down in a soft lump. The stone hit me on the top of the head causing a small hard lump and severely damaged pride. After that I remembered to duck the stone but the parachute never opened properly even once.

When it became apparent to the families with eligible daughters, that the Little American Soldier was smitten by Lavonia Lakusta, the discovery unleashed a certain amount of jealousy. Folks in the Six Towns area, not only those with eligible daughters, for the widow, Mrs. Beatrice Ann Stevenson, who had no daughters, or children at all for that matter, and Mrs. Edytha Rasmussen Bozniak, whose daughter, Velvet, wouldn't be eligible for five or six years, depending on what age one considered a daughter eligible, were jealous that it was Lavonia Lakusta who landed the Little American Soldier, and in their jealousy began asking themselves philosophical questions like, Why couldn't the Little American Soldier's camouflage-brindle, two-ton truck have broken down a mile from their house, instead of over by Bjornsen's Corner? Or, Why couldn't the Bjornsens have steered the Little American Soldier their way, instead of arranging for him to board and room with the Lakustas by the lake?

The more outspoken asked questions like, How come the Bjornsens, who were Norwegians through and through, didn't steer the most eligible bachelor to hit the Six Towns area in ten years to a Norwegian family with an eligible daughter, instead of to a Ukrainian family with two eligible daughters? That question got asked philosophically, then got asked out loud, then got asked directly to the Bjornsens, and got asked so loudly on a couple of occasions that a shoving match ensued, though it was broken up before it progressed to an altercation, a fist fight, or a genuine brouhaha, and before any blood was drawn on either side.

The only noticeable repercussion of the question asking was that the Bjornsen Bros. Swinging Cowboy Musicmakers had an appearance, after a Saturday night whist drive at New Oslo Community Hall, canceled. Unfortunately, the only other person in the Six Towns area, other than the Bjornsens, with any real musical ability, was Little Grendel Badke, the same Little Grendel Badke who, if there was enough time left at intermission at a box social, whist drive, community dance, sportsday, or ethnic wedding, rushed to the stage, where she played "Alice Blue Gown," on the piano, and sang in a whispery voice no one could quite hear or understand.

It also turned out that "Alice Blue Gown" was the only song Little Grendel Badke could play on the piano, having, after several years' instruction from her mother, who swatted her on the side of the head with a rolled-up newspaper every time she hit a wrong note, memorized which keys to hit. So, at New Oslo Community Hall, when the dancing was supposed to begin, instead of the Bjornsen Bros. Swinging Cowboy Musicmakers playing polkas and waltzes, two steps, fox trots and Virginia reels, Little Grendel Badke played "Alice Blue Gown" seven times in a row on the piano that had only one key missing, that unfortunately being a key that was needed frequently in "Alice Blue Gown." After the seventh time, the widow, Mrs. Beatrice Ann Stevenson, led little Grendel Badke away from the piano and down off the stage, in order to get her a lemonade.

The young people who were anxious for a chance to rub their personal body parts together on the dance floor didn't mind dancing to seven straight renditions of "Alice Blue Gown," but the older people who were licensed to rub their personal body parts together any time they wanted to, and usually did after being stimulated by the Saturday night dance and whist drive, wanted something a little livelier, and looked forward to Cousin Arne Bjornsen calling a good square dance in both English and Norwegian.

The upshot was that, after enduring Little Grendel Badke's

seven consecutive renditions of "Alice Blue Gown," the question asking, whether it was philosophical, out loud, or direct, eased off some, and it was suggested by more than one person that the Bjornsens had been punished sufficiently for their indiscretion.

So the next week, when there was a box social at the Fark Community Hall, the Bjornsen Bros. Swinging Cowboy Musicmakers were back, big as life, and even the Norwegians who were mad because they didn't get a crack at making the Little American Soldier their son-in-law, were out to dance a schottische or two, a couple of polkas, a Virginia reel, and listen to Cousin Arne Bjornsen call a good old-fashioned square dance or three, in both English and Norwegian.

The Little American Soldier, once the Bjornsen brothers had made his camouflage-brindle, two-ton truck operational, even took Lavonia Lakusta to the moving picture show at the Doreen Beach Community Hall, where a traveling projectionist came by once a month, in a car with cardboard in the passenger window where the glass should be, to show a fluttery Pola Negri silent film at ten cents for adults, and five cents for children, where everybody sat on scarred yellow folding chairs and stared at the wall at the rear of the stage, because the traveling projectionist had had his screen stolen a couple of years before, after showing a movie at Stanger.

People in the Six Towns area said, No wonder he got his screen stolen, and, Lucky he didn't get his projector stolen too, or even his car, because people around Stanger were like that.

Actually, the screen didn't so much get stolen as misplaced. One night, while the traveling projectionist was showing a movie at the abandoned Stanger Methodist Church, the last Methodist having left the district several years before, the traveling projectionist took a shine to a pretty little Ukrainian girl named Cassie Novashewsky, who appeared to be unattached, but was actually married to a fellow named Big Novashewsky, who was away in the army, and was last heard from fighting in Sicily.

For that particular evening, Cassie Novashewsky acted like she was unattached, and when the fluttery Pola Negri silent film was over, took the traveling projectionist home with her. Unfortunately, Big Novashewsky had several brothers, one of whom was out hunting the milk cows at five A.M., when he saw the traveling projectionist's car parked in Big Novashewsky's yard, and calculating that, since Big Novashewsky was last heard from in Sicily, it was unlikely that the car belonged to him, and that since the cow-hunting brother had been at the movie the previous night himself, he recollected that that particular car belonged to the traveling projectionist, since it had been the only car parked in front of the abandoned Stanger Methodist Church.

Big Novashewsky's brother knocked out the passenger window with a block of wood, grabbed the movie screen, which rode catty-corner of the car, and running clear across the yard at full speed, acting as if he were chucking a very large spear, plunged the screen down the water well, the location of which had been divined by a woman named Loretta Cake, who resided in a hut about halfway between Doreen Beach and the Stanger post office, with about one hundred cats, and seemed to live off the land.

The traveling projectionist, always a light sleeper, knew the crash of glass in his very own car window when he heard it, rushed out of Big Novashewsky's house, half to three-quarters dressed, and managed to get the car started and headed for what passed for a road, before Big Novashewsky's brother could get back across the yard to do him and the car further damage.

The Little American Soldier, who had been to the movies probably a hundred times in his life, wasn't all that interested in watching a fluttery Pola Negri silent film, but Lavonia Lakusta, who had only been to a movie once before, that being a silent western movie she'd seen at the Fark Community Hall, was at that particular moment, as much interested in the film as she was in the Little American Soldier.

On days when Mrs. Walter J. Sutterman's arthritis wasn't acting up she would sit at the piano, at the side of the stage, in the Doreen Beach Community Hall, and play music to accompany Pola Negri's gestures, and the fluttering of her eyelashes, which were covered in so much mascara they each looked like a giant spider leg. However, the day the Little American Soldier chose to take Lavonia Lakusta to the movies was a day when Mrs. Walter J. Sutterman's arthritis was acting up, so she only plunked a note or two, with her one unarthritic thumb, to signal the climax of each scene.

The Little American Soldier and Lavonia Lakusta sat in the dark and kissed and touched each other, as a preliminary to driving away in the Little American Soldier's camouflage-brindle two-ton truck, to a really private place, where they could get down to serious touching, kissing, and other related activities, including much rubbing together of private and personal body parts.

Mrs. Wasyl Lakusta, whose first name was Rose, thinking of her old age, recognizing excellent son-in-law material when it was thrust in front of her nose, saw to it that a goose-down comforter and a large, hand-sewn patchwork quilt, both of which she had carried with her from the Ukraine, found their way into the back of the camouflage-brindle, United States Army two-ton truck, while Mr. Wasyl Lakusta, as his contribution, kept his mouth shut, and looked the other way.

Another three weeks passed, and the prayers of the Lakustas by the lake were answered when the Little American Soldier formally asked Wasyl Lakusta if he could marry his daughter, Lavonia.

Mrs. Wasyl Lakusta, who, though she only spoke a half-dozen

words of English, understood a lot more than she let on, let out a joyful wail when she saw, from her kitchen window, Mr. Wasyl Lakusta head across the farm yard and pull up a string from the cream well that had at the bottom end of it a bottle of dandelion wine that had been sleeping in the cool waters thirty feet below the surface of the earth. Mrs. Wasyl Lakusta knew, as she let out her joyful wail, a wail that brought her daughter, Sylvie, and her son, Nestor, running in from the north field where they had been stooking oats, that, an hour before, Wasyl Lakusta and the Little American Soldier had gone for a walk together, and that Mr. Wasyl Lakusta did not drink dandelion wine of a weekday unless there was an occasion to celebrate: a new calf born healthy, a new granary finished and painted, a Little American Soldier asking for their delicate daughter's hand in marriage.

Mrs. Wasyl Lakusta unwrapped her best handpainted plate, which she had brought with her from the old country, on which she planned to feed the Little American Soldier an engagement supper of fried chicken and sour cabbage pyrogies; she then killed a chicken, first scattering a few grains of wheat outside the kitchen door and snatching the unsuspecting bird while its head was down pecking the earth. She wrung the bird's neck with a joyful twist, and had it half plucked before the chicken even realized it was never going to get to swallow the grain of wheat it had just picked up.

It was about this same time that the phone call came, to the old McClintock place just east of Fark, from John "The Raja of Renfrew" Ducey, announcing that Truckbox Al McClintock had been chosen to play for the unimaginatively named Alberta All-Stars, against a team of Major Leaguers, including Bob Feller, Hal Newhouser, and Joe DiMaggio himself, of a Sunday afternoon, at Renfrew Park, down on the river flats, in Edmonton, Alberta.

Now, the red brick general store in Doreen Beach also doubled as the Municipal Office for the county, and the storekeeper in Doreen Beach, Mrs. Ogden Quince, a lanky woman with a nasty facial disfigurement, said to have been caused by being kicked in the head by a milk cow, was allowed to issue birth certificates, death certificates, marriage licenses, dog licenses, radio licenses, and overweight trucking permits, providing she had seen the baby, the corpse, the prospective bride and groom, or the dog; she was allowed to take the applicant's word about the radio, and the overweight truck.

The Little American Soldier and Lavonia Lakusta presented themselves to Mrs. Ogden Quince, the lanky lady with the nasty facial disfigurement, and for two dollars they were issued with a marriage license good for ninety days. They originally planned to get married the Saturday before the Sunday when Truckbox Al would play baseball in Edmonton, but had to move the wedding ahead two days, to a Thursday, so everyone would have time to celebrate and still get to the baseball game in Edmonton, a place most of the folks in the Six Towns area had never been.

Mr. Wasyl Lakusta wanted to move the wedding ahead a full week so the celebration could take its proper form, for after all this was his first daughter to get married, and he wanted to show the folks in the Six Towns area what a genuine Ukrainian wedding was like. Mr. Wasyl Lakusta had been to a number of Norwegian weddings, where everyone celebrated for one evening and went home, allowing the bride and groom to leave on their honeymoon, or at least retire unmolested to their new residence, and he had been to a couple of English weddings, where nobody celebrated much at all, and, he suspected, neither did the bride and groom, even after they retired alone and unmolested to their new residence.

"Good Ukrainian wedding go on for six days," Mr. Wasyl Lakusta announced to anyone who cared to listen. "When me and Missus get married, party six days, never sleep, nobody."

But Mrs. Wasyl Lakusta decided a three-day party would be sufficient, with the Presentation—a gift-giving ritual associated with Ukrainian weddings, beloved by some, said by others to be a barbaric rite—being held on the night of the wedding, an evening when everyone, even Truckbox Al McClintock, would still be present and maybe even passably sober.

Mrs. Wasyl Lakusta argued that Lavonia, being delicate, couldn't stand the strain of a six-day wedding, and Mr. Wasyl Lakusta finally agreed, announcing instead, to anyone who cared to listen, that when Sylvie and Pete Yaremko got married he would throw a six-day, all-out, no-holds-barred wedding. Sylvie being not much good for look at, but pretty much good for strong, would have no trouble adjusting to the rigors of an all-out, no-holds-barred, six-day Ukrainian wedding. Mr. Wasyl Lakusta also decided that the Little American Soldier, not knowing precisely what to expect, might not be able to last through the rigors of a six-day wedding, and he didn't want to do anything that would make his future son-in-law, the refuge of his old age, unhappy.

The morning of the wedding, a Jeep-load of the Little American Soldier's friends arrived from Edmonton, so at and immediately after the wedding ceremony, or wedding ceremonies as it turned out, everyone in the Six Towns area got to see their second, third, fourth, and fifth genuine American soldier close-up.

Each of the Little American Soldier's friends was decked out in his shiny gabardine uniform, and genuine military cap that made him look like Smilin' Jack. One of them, a boy who talked with an even deeper deep-south southern drawl than the Little American Soldier, stood up for him as best man. And after the wedding ceremony, or wedding ceremonies as it turned out, the Little American Soldier's friends showed that they could drink their fair share of chokecherry wine, dandelion wine, raisin wine, blackberry wine, homemade beer, and Heathen's Rapture, or plain old bring-on-blindness, logging-boot-to-the-side-of-the-head homebrew.

The eligible daughters of the visiting guests, and the partially eligible daughters of the visiting guests—those being daughters who were promised or engaged but not yet married—and there were lots of both guests and daughters, pretty farm girls named Stella, Rose, Maika, Cassie, Steffie, and Connie, let it be known that they were just wild about the Little American Soldier's wedding party. A wildness that produced much annoyance in the hearts of the sons of the visiting guests, and there were a lot of them, both guests and sons, big, strapping, sunburned farm boys named Nick, Mike, Bohdan, Wasyl, Orest, and Nestor, who as soon as the wedding ceremony, or wedding ceremonies as it turned out, were over, took off their jackets, rolled up the sleeves of their white shirts, and stood around looking uncomfortable until the first fist fight broke out.

As it turned out, within a mere three months of the wedding, three of the four members of the Little American Soldier's wedding party married eligible daughters of the visiting wedding guests, or partially eligible daughters who on seeing the members of the Little American Soldier's wedding party in the snazzy dress uniforms and military caps that made them look like Smilin' Jack, altered their status to become eligible daughters.

The fourth member of the Little American Soldier's wedding party could have found himself a wife, too, only he wasn't particularly attracted to women in general, and after a day and a half of sampling chokecherry wine, dandelion wine, raisin wine, blackberry wine, homemade beer, and Heathen's Rapture, or plain old bring-on-blindness, logging-boot-to-the-side-of-the-head homebrew, the fourth member of the Little American Soldier's wedding party, in as tactful a way as possible, let it be known to Big Wasyl Podalanchuk, who had been standing around with his sleeves rolled up looking uncomfortable for a day and a half, that he thought Big Wasyl Podalanchuk was just the cat's meow; cat's meow, being my daddy's term to describe that particular situation. Big Wasyl Podalanchuk, after it became clear to him what the fourth member of the Little American Soldier's wedding party meant by the cat's meow, coldcocked that little blond American soldier, with one blow from his big, sunburned fist, creating a momentary commotion around the side of the Lakusta's horse barn.

What had happened, I heard Earl J. Rasmussen tell my daddy a little later in the day, was simply a case of the fourth member of the Little American Soldier's wedding party being attracted to the wrong Wasyl Podalanchuk. Big Wasyl Podalanchuk had a cousin named Little Wasyl Podalanchuk, who really was little, being probably the only Ukrainian dwarf in Alberta, and Little Wasyl Podalanchuk, like the eligible and partially eligible daughters of the wedding guests, was just wild about the Little American Soldier's wedding party.

Unfortunately, Little Wasyl Podalanchuk and the fourth member of the Little American Soldier's wedding party never did get together; the fourth member of the Little American Soldier's wedding party, when he woke up face-down in the tangle grass at the side of the Lakusta's horse barn, put some ice on his bruised face, and behaved impeccably for the remainder of the celebration, even dancing a polka or two with one of the Chalupa girls, not the youngest one, who was rumored to be hot-blooded, but an older one with a mustache, who could stook grain at the same pace as her brothers.

# Chapter Four

"A Ukrainian wedding is a unique experience," my daddy said as we were getting ready to leave, "kind of a cross between a genuine speaking in tongues, Holy Roller church service, and a closing-time riot at a cowboy bar, something everyone should undergo at least once." He was hitching our old roan horse, Ethan Allen, to the buggy as he said it.

Since I had never been to a genuine speaking in tongues, Holy Roller church service, or experienced closing time at a cowboy bar, I still didn't have much idea what to expect.

The friends and relatives of the Lakustas by the lake had begun arriving three days before the wedding, and the last ones wouldn't leave until a week after the wedding was over, my daddy explained. Those relatives and friends came from all over Northern Alberta, mainly from Eastern Alberta, which was full of Ukrainian settlements; some came as far as one hundred miles, most traveled at least fifty miles, and all but the most prosperous came by horse and wagon, the wagon being loaded with children and provisions.

Each of the wagons was loaded down with smoked meat, a dozen varieties of bread and cakes, and vegetables. Most of the wagons had a slatted box full of live chickens tied to the tailgate, while an occasional one carried a pig or led a yearling calf behind it, the calf or pig to be slaughtered and cooked at the wedding celebrations.

The Little American Soldier, who was mobile, because several of the eleven Bjornsens, some of whom were members of the Bjornsen Bros. Swinging Cowboy Musicmakers, had forged the necessary parts to make his camouflage-brindle, two-ton truck operational again, drove many miles west on the Edmonton-Jasper Highway, to a town called Edson, in order to find himself a Holy Roller preacher to perform the marriage. The Little American Soldier hailed from South Carolina, where, my daddy said, Holy Roller preachers were a dime a dozen, and your run-of-the-mill Sunday morning service or Wednesday evening prayer meeting was comparable to the closing-time riot at a cowboy bar. The Holy Roller preacher's name was Brother Bickerstaff, and he was pastor of the Holy, Holy, Holy, Foursquare Brotherhood Church. He arrived at the Lakustas by the lake a day ahead of the wedding, having been advanced bus fare by the Little American Soldier.

Preachers of any ilk were a rare commodity in the Six Towns area, and church attendance was not a high priority for the residents of the Six Towns, except perhaps, for Mrs. Sven Bjornsen, who once a year, caught the westbound Western Trailways Bus to Edson, where she sang and prayed at Brother Bickerstaff's Holy, Holy, Holy, Foursquare Brotherhood Church, returning home sung out, and prayed out, and broke, but saying to anyone who happened to drop by the farm, "I feel so restored. I could yust live in shurch."

Most of the people at Lavonia Lakusta's wedding had never seen anything like Brother Bickerstaff—he was dressed in a plain gray suit, floppy gray hat, black shoes with gray spats, and a tie the color of the red carnations my mama grew in the back flower garden. He clutched a Bible the size of a *Life* magazine, and that Bible was covered in quilted white satin. Brother Bickerstaff's cheeks continually quivered, as if he was about to sneeze, but he never sneezed, just uttered the words "Praise the Lord!" which he did frequently and heartily, whether the occasion called for it or not.

The Lakustas by the lake, thinking of their old age, were so happy to have a prospective son-in-law who was clean-cut, handsome, and wore a smart military cap that made him look like Smilin' Jack; a son-in-law who was most likely destined to amount to something after the war was over, that they were willing to overlook the fact that he wasn't Ukrainian, and didn't speak Ukrainian, though Wasyl Lakusta and some of Lavonia's brothers and uncles made a valiant attempt to at least teach him a few curses. The Little American Soldier, being an amiable sort, tried hard to learn to curse in Ukrainian, but couldn't seem to master the subject matter at all, something Wasyl Lakusta blamed on the fact, that as near as he could tell, the Little American Soldier didn't speak a lot of English either, though he claimed he did.

As the guests started arriving for the wedding, and the tents started going up in the farmyard of the Lakustas by the lake, it became clear that one of the relatives had stopped along the way and picked up a Russian Orthodox priest, so as to be sure to get the job done right. The Russian Orthodox priest was tall and looked as if he hadn't had a good meal since he left Russia, if he'd ever had one. He wore a black pillbox of a hat and a black cassock that swept the ground and hid his feet entirely, so when he walked across the farmyard he looked as if he was gliding.

Though the Russian Orthodox priest didn't appear old, he had a scraggily black beard and food stains down the front of his cassock. My daddy said maybe the reason he was so thin was that when he was eating he spilled a lot instead of getting food directly into his mouth in a proper manner.

There were no formal invitations to the wedding, a single fifteen-cent phone call from Mr. Wasyl Lakusta to the Smokey Lake General Store in Eastern Alberta, the proprietor of which arranged for a message to be relayed to Mr. Wasyl Lakusta's brother Bohdan, let the relatives know of the upcoming wedding, and otherwise, anyone who lived within traveling distance of the Lakusta farm, or anyone who was even a casual acquaintance of the Lakustas by the lake, was considered to be invited. It was also all right for anyone to attend if they just knew someone who knew the Lakustas by the lake.

Consequently, the Rev. Ibsen turned up the day before the wedding, hoping that he might be called on to perform the ceremony, thus supplementing his rather meager income as a farmer. When the Rev. Ibsen had been serving as a God-fearing, guilt-spewing, financial-advising pastor at the Christ on the Cross Scandinavian Lutheran Church in New Oslo, Alberta, his salary had been paid by Banker Olaf Gordonjensen, but when Banker Gordonjensen became insolvent, Rev. Ibsen found himself out of a paying job and eventually out of a parsonage, and he had to rent himself a quarter section of stony land where he tried to farm. But once a reverend always a reverend apparently, so Rev. Ibsen still occasionally performed a marriage or said a few words over a dear departed, and a couple of times a year still preached a sermon at the now-completely-gone-to-rack-and-ruin Christ on the Cross Scandinavian Lutheran Church. The rack and ruin came on gradually, just as Banker Olaf Gordonjensen's health deteriorated gradually until his imposing form in its black banker's suit looked more like a scarecrow than a banker, and the Scandinavian Lutherans methodically moved away to better farming country, being replaced by, as my daddy said, a potpourri of humanity who cared more about cream prices and hockey than God or guilt.

The day of the wedding dawned clear and sunny, and the ceremony itself was held in the garden of the Lakustas by the lake. Mrs. Rose Lakusta, and her delicate daughter Lavonia, had planted sweet peas, and scarlet runner, both of which twined up strings covering the walls at the back of the cabin with a blaze of color. There was also a stand of plate-sized sunflowers, and several beds of pansies, marigolds, and purple petunias, outlined by whitewashed rocks, mixed in with a half acre of cabbage, cauliflower, and rows and rows of turnips.

The wedding party lined up in a row, the Little American Soldier and his best man, Lavonia Lakusta and her sister Sylvie, Mr. Wasyl Lakusta in a blue suit he hadn't worn since his own wedding in the Ukraine, a suit which gave off an overpowering odor of mothballs and camphor, and Mrs. Wasyl Lakusta in a rose-colored dress that was too small for her.

Lavonia Lakusta, while pretty, was not nearly as pretty as she might have been, because her best friend, Stevie Dwerynchuk, of the Magnolia Dwerynchuks, had brought over a dog-eared fashion magazine she had bought for five cents, a year earlier, on her one and only trip to Edmonton, and between Stevie Dwerynchuk and Mrs. Wasyl Lakusta they made Lavonia up to look like a fashionable 1945 or 1946 bride, which meant that her beautiful dark red hair, which was always worn down over her shoulders, was now piled on top of her head, and one piece of her beautiful dark red hair was made into a very weird but fashionable roll just above her forehead, a roll that looked like a mummified hand waving goodbye.

Stevie Dwerynchuk, of the Magnolia Dwerynchuks, had also talked Lavonia, in the name of fashion, into putting shoulder pads into Mrs. Rose Lakusta's ivory-silk wedding dress, carried with her when she emigrated from the Ukraine. Even being made ugly in the name of being fashionable couldn't make Lavonia Lakusta truly unattractive, and all during the wedding ceremony, or wedding ceremonies as it turned out, the Little American Soldier looked adoringly at her, while most of the female wedding guests, and the fourth member of the Little American Soldier's wedding party, got tears in their eyes as the wedding ceremony, or wedding ceremonies as it turned out, began.

The Little American Soldier, who was more interested in getting married than exactly how he was getting married, or who was marrying him, said that he didn't mind at all if the Russian Orthodox priest performed the ceremony. As long as everything was legal, he went on, it didn't bother the Little American Soldier a whit that he couldn't understand a word of what was going on. Every time the Russian Orthodox priest stopped talking, and stared intently at him, the Little American Soldier said, I do, two words that seemed to satisfy everyone involved, so the wedding ceremony was completed in short order.

But while the wedding ceremony was going on there developed an undertone of unease, which by the time the wedding ceremony was finished, was upgraded to genuine consternation, the unease being exhibited by the English-speaking people present, and the consternation being exhibited primarily by Brother Bickerstaff of the Holy, Holy, Holy, Foursquare Brotherhood Church of Edson, Alberta, which had exactly eight members, including Brother Bickerstaff, seven of whom weren't present at the wedding.

At a point where it appeared to those present who didn't speak Ukrainian, that the ceremony was over and the happy couple had been pronounced man and wife, just as the Little American Soldier was about to kiss the bride for the first time,

Brother Bickerstaff stepped to the fore and whispered a few impromptu words into the ear of the Little American Soldier, several of which were heathen, pagan, and infidel.

The Little American Soldier, who was more interested in getting married, than in how he was getting married, and who was marrying him, allowed as how it wouldn't do them any harm to be married a second time, so Brother Bickerstaff nudged the Russian Orthodox priest aside, and jowls a-quiver, married them again, with much flamboyance and praising of the Lord, and also delivered a twenty-seven-minute sermon on the sanctity of marriage, in between Do you take this woman? and For richer for poorer, with a long digression on who was going to heaven and who wasn't, the digression aimed mainly at Lavonia Lakusta and her family, and those present who weren't members of the Holy, Holy, Holy, Foursquare Brotherhood Church of Edson, Alberta, which seemed to include everyone present, except possibly Mrs. Sven Bjornsen, who attended Brother Bickerstaff's church one week a year.

When Brother Bickerstaff finally wound down, and while the Little American Soldier was kissing the bride for the second time, it was Sven Bjornsen, of the Bjornsen Bros. Swinging Cowboy Musicmakers, who stepped forward and whispered a few words into the ear of the Little American Soldier, pointing out that he was speaking as a Lutheran first, a Bjornsen second, and a musician third, and suggesting that since the Russians had had their day, and the Holy Rollers had had theirs, that it might be appropriate for the Lutherans to have a whack at the happy couple.

The Little American Soldier, who was more interested in getting married than in how he got married, and who was marrying him, beckoned to the Rev. Ibsen who had been standing like a crow at the back of the garden, and the Rev. Ibsen stepped forward and, nudging aside the Russian Orthodox priest, who was fairly easily nudged, and Brother Bickerstaff, who stood like a rock and required concentrated nudging before he reluctantly stepped aside, married the happy couple again, in a straightforward, no-nonsense ceremony that everyone, except perhaps the Russian Orthodox priest, understood. By the time the third ceremony was over, and the Little American Soldier got to kiss the bride for the third time, the female members of the audience and the fourth member of the Little American Soldier's wedding party were about cried out, and ready to get on with the celebration.

Mrs. Wasyl Lakusta said to everyone, "Eat!" and pointed the guests toward tables in the yard in front of the Lakustas' cabin, tables laden with every type of food imaginable and a few types beyond the imagination.

Mr. Wasyl Lakusta said to everyone, "Drink!" and pointed the guests toward some tables slightly separated from the food, where every kind of wine and beer and homebrew was available, along with a few cases of store-bought beer, and even a bottle or two of Liquor Store whiskey.

The Bjornsen Bros. Swinging Cowboy Musicmakers set up their instruments on a makeshift stage not too far from the food and drink and the celebration began.

Other than the bride and groom, the most important person at the wedding and the following celebration, was Truckbox Al McClintock, for everybody who wasn't dead knew that Truckbox Al McClintock was going to Edmonton that weekend to play baseball for the unimaginatively named Alberta All-Stars against a team of genuine Major Leaguers featuring Bob Feller, Hal Newhouser, and Joe DiMaggio himself.


It was at the wedding, or weddings as it turned out, and the celebration afterward, that people began to call Truckbox Al

McClintock, Truckbox Al to his face. Before the wedding, or weddings as it turned out, people always said, Yonder goes Truckbox Al McClintock, or, Truckbox Al McClintock plays right field for the Sangudo Mustangs, but if they met him coming out of Fark General Store, or at a box social at New Oslo, they said Howdy, Al; or, Howdy, Alvin.

But now, because he was going off to play baseball against a genuine Major League All-Star team partially composed of Bob Feller, Hal Newhouser, and Joe DiMaggio himself, people felt it was not only all right, but about time that he had a nickname. They felt that it was all right for a baseball player to have a nickname like Truckbox, and have it used right to his face, while it wasn't all right for a slow, husky, grease-covered boy with a bulldog-faced mama and a slow, husky, grease-covered father to have such a nickname used to his face.

Truckbox Al McClintock took readily to his nickname, in fact he thought a nickname like Truckbox gave him a certain quality of bigness, and he discovered that girls were interested in boys possessing a certain quality of bigness. In fact, he detected that the youngest Chalupa girl, even though she spent a good part of her time holding hands with Heinrick Badke, still cast a number of glances his way, glances that he interpreted as long-ing glances. And he decided that, when he hit his first home run in the baseball game at Renfrew Park, down on the river flats, in Edmonton, Alberta, against Bob Feller, or Hal New-houser, and over the head of Joe DiMaggio himself, why he would dedicate that first home run to the youngest Chalupa girl, though the notion was tentative, and Truckbox Al McClintock wasn't entirely sure how he would go about dedicating a home run, or, once it was dedicated, letting the youngest Chalupa girl know the home run was dedicated to her.

Truckbox Al McClintock, who people were now calling Truckbox Al right to his face, having been calling him Truckbox

Al behind his back for fourteen of his sixteen years, continued to fantasize about dedicating his first home run to the youngest Chalupa girl, and how when the youngest Chalupa girl found out the home run had been dedicated to her, she would be so genuinely grateful, as well as obligated, indebted, and beholden, that she would latch herself onto Truckbox Al's arm and remain somewhat attached there, warm and soft, kissable, and agreeable to the touch, for the remainder of Truckbox Al's life.

Those fantasies continued for most of the afternoon, until a time about four hours after the wedding, or weddings as it turned out, when, while Truckbox Al was leaning against the corner of the Lakustas' chicken house, eating a ham sandwich and drinking a bottle of Wynola, a kind of cherry-flavored soft drink, Louisa May Sigurdson, one of the white-blond daughters belonging to the more-or-less Doreen Beach Sigurdsons, a family that my mama succinctly said was white trash, no doubt about it, tapped him on the shoulder, and by the time he got his eyes focused properly he could see that she was staring up into his face as if she was genuinely interested in him.

Louisa May Sigurdson was fifteen years old, the fourth of four more-or-less Doreen Beach Sigurdson daughters, and the only one who hadn't produced a more-or-less Doreen Beach Sigurdson grandchild, though, my mama said, it wasn't for a lack of trying. There were also four more-or-less Doreen Beach Sigurdson sons, and the whole tribe squatted in a log cabin just outside Doreen Beach, a cabin so decrepit even the Indians had abandoned it. The more-or-less Doreen Beach Sigurdsons were casual acquaintances of some other people who knew the Lakustas—no one ever got to be more than casual acquaintances of the more-or-less Doreen Beach Sigurdsons—for they had a reputation, father, mother, four Sigurdsons daughters and four

Sigurdson sons, of stealing anything removable by horse and wagon, or anything that could be led behind a horse and wagon.

The more-or-less Doreen Beach Sigurdsons arrived about an hour after the wedding ceremony, or wedding ceremonies as it turned out, mother, father, the four Sigurdson daughters and three Sigurdson grandchildren in the wagon box, while two Sigurdson boys walked, and two rode double on a thin, sway-backed bay that Sven Bjornson said had been stolen from the Indians over by Lac Ste. Anne.

The more-or-less Doreen Beach Sigurdsons were all white blond and blue eyed, with thin, hatchet faces and furtive eyes, but all Truckbox Al McClintock noticed about Louisa May Sigurdson, once he got his eyes focused properly, was that she had white blond hair, and that there were about a dozen freckles across the bridge of her nose that made him think of a speckled egg, and that she appeared to be genuinely interested in him.

"You the guy's going to Edmonton to play baseball?" Louisa May Sigurdson asked.

Truckbox Al McClintock allowed as he was, noticing as he said so, now that he had his eyes focused properly, that Louisa May Sigurdson was barefoot and had probably been that way most of her life, and that she wore a pink-and-white print dress that had been laundered until the pattern was faded away in most places, making the dress mostly white and very little pink. He could also tell by the way the sun was shining that the faded pink-and-white dress was the only garment that Louisa My Sigurdson was wearing. Wiping her fingers, containing the last of the grease from the piece of fried chicken she had been eating, on the thigh of her dress, Louisa May Sigurdson set her pale blue eyes on Truckbox Al McClintock, who decided then and there, as she was setting her eyes on him, that Louisa May Sigurdson was probably impressed by his reputation as a baseball home-run hitter, his recently acquired nickname, and his new found quality of bigness.

The more-or-less Doreen Beach Sigurdsons, soon after their arrival, had wiped out two platters of fried chicken, a six-quart pot of pyrogies, five dozen cabbage rolls, and a countless number of sandwiches. Now that their stomachs were full, the more-or-less Doreen Beach Sigurdson sons, daughters, and grandchildren were already squirreling away, in their wagon box, bread and cakes and sandwiches and cold cuts and, often as not, were also squirreling away the plates the food came on. At the same time, the father and mother Sigurdson were setting about, on full stomachs for the first time in months, to sample the dandelion wine, chokecherry wine, raisin wine, homemade beer, and Heathen's Rapture, or good old bring-on-blindness, logging-boot-to-the-side-of-the-head homebrew, still managing to keep their eyes open for anything lying loose that could be hauled away in their wagon box, or led away in the dark of night behind their wagon.

"You sure do have big muscles," Louisa May Sigurdson said to Truckbox Al McClintock, placing her long, pale fingers on Truckbox Al's large upper arm, confirming Truckbox Al's theory that she was indeed impressed by, among other things, his new found quality of bigness, while at the same time her touch sent a feeling through Truckbox Al that wasn't a lot different from the time a generator had short-circuited while he was tinkering with it, leaving his arm helpless and tingling. Truckbox Al McClintock remembered that the residue of that short-circuited-generator-tingle had traveled all the way inward to his heart, something the residue of Louisa May Sigurdson's touch also did. Truckbox Al McClintock had an instant fantasy of Louisa May Sigurdson latched onto his arm and remaining somewhat attached there, warm and soft, kissable, and agreeable to the touch, for the remainder of Truckbox Al's life.

"How you gettin' to Edmonton?" Louisa May Sigurdson asked Truckbox Al, who explained to her that since he was going to play baseball against the likes of Bob Feller, Hal Newhouser and Joe DiMaggio himself, he needed to be well fed and rested for the contest. His family, he said, were sending him to Edmonton the Saturday afternoon before the Sunday afternoon game, by means of the eastbound Western Trailways bus that stopped once a day at Bjornsen's Corner. And, he went on to explain, once in Edmonton, The Gateway to the North, he was going to spend the night in a private room at the Castle Hotel on 103 Street, which his daddy assured him, was quite a magnificent place.

"If you was to get me to Edmonton, too, I might do something for you?" Louisa May Sigurdson said to Truckbox Al.

"Like what?" said Truckbox Al, swelling up some with pride, delighted that a pretty girl, even if she was a more-or-less Doreen Beach Sigurdson, was impressed with personally, as well as admiring, among other things, his new found quality of bigness. Truckbox Al remembered that he had almost three dollars in spending money, acquired during the days since the phone call had come from John "The Raja of Renfrew" Ducey inviting him to play baseball for the unimaginatively named Alberta All-Stars; the three dollars had been acquired from well-wishers, a coin at a time: a dime here, a quarter there. Someone might slip a nickel into his beefy, grease-covered hand as he emerged from Fark General Store, or the New Oslo Feed and Grain; a dime might appear magically, along with a tin of Copenhagen Snuff, from the overall pocket of a farmer Truckbox Al was scarcely acquainted with, but a farmer who wanted to be sure Truckbox Al, as the only celebrity the Six Towns area had ever produced, didn't lack for anything on his sojourn in Edmonton.

Louisa May Sigurdson moved closer to Truckbox Al, in fact so close, her thin little lips the color of wild rose petals, were pressed against Truckbox Al's right ear, and her breath on that teacup of an ear, made Truckbox Al acutely aware of his newly acquired quality of bigness.

Louisa May Sigurdson, placing one of her long, pale hands on Truckbox Al's belt, said that in return for Truckbox Al's help in getting to Edmonton she would do something for him. Truckbox Al didn't recognize the term she used, and, try as he might, couldn't picture what it might be; his ability to fantasize ended with Louisa May Sigurdson more-or-less permanently latched onto his arm, warm and soft beside him, kissable, agreeable to the touch, though he guessed, by the way Louisa May Sigurdson pressed herself up close to him and whispered the words hotly into his teacup of an ear, that what she was promising would be something akin to having a generator short-circuit while you were working on it.

Louisa May Sigurdson also said that what she was going to do for Truckbox Al McClintock would both curl his toes and rot his socks, something which made the event sound even more exciting than being zapped by a short-circuiting generator. Louisa May Sigurdson and Truckbox Al McClintock made a bargain, then and there, which Louisa May Sigurdson sealed by pressing herself even closer than she had been before, gripping Truckbox Al's belt even tighter than before, and kissing Truckbox Al right on the mouth, her little pink tongue doing some remarkable explorations, while she urged Truckbox Al to remember what it was she was going to do for him once he got her to Edmonton.

# Chapter Five

**B**esides being the story of how Truckbox Al McClintock almost got a tryout with the genuine St. Louis Cardinals of the National Baseball League, this is also the story of a couple or ten things that happened to me before, and at about the same time as Truckbox Al McClintock was struggling to come to terms with his soon-to-be fame, including my almost getting eaten by a German Shepherd dog the size of the Empire State Building.

My name is Jamie O'Day. James Oliver Curwood O'Day, named for a man who wrote a book called *The Valley of Silent Men*. We had five books and a set of encyclopedias in our house at the end of Nine Pin Road, all acquired in the city of Edmonton, before the Depression, which my daddy said was four books and a set of encyclopedias more than most folks in the Six Towns area. I can name the books: *The Valley of Silent Men*, by James Oliver Curwood; *The Girl of the Limberlost*, by Gene Stratton Porter; *The Desert of Wheat*, by Zane Grey; *The Trail of the Lonesome Pine*, by John Fox, Jr.; and *Tarzan's Great Adventure*, by Edgar Rice Burroughs.

Each and every one of those books had been read aloud to me at least ten times, mainly by my father who liked to read aloud, usually during the winter months, by the light of the coal-oil lamp, the wick ragged at one corner, blackening the lamp chimney, with Daddy eying the damage and saying, "Just one more page and I'll hunt up the scissors," which were brass-colored and shaped like a stork with its wings folded, "and trim the wick."

One of the couple or ten things that happened to me was that the adults of the Six Towns area held a Little Box Social for the children of the Six Towns area, at the Fark Community Hall, after the whist drive, and before the Bjornsen Bros. Swinging Cowboy Musicmakers began playing for the dance.

The idea for the Little Box Social was suggested by Mrs. Edytha Rasmussen Bozniak, the mother of Velvet Bozniak, and was quickly seconded by Mrs. Edytha Rasmussen Bozniak's mother, Mrs. Irma Rasmussen, the grandmother of Velvet Bozniak. These three women were the wife, daughter and granddaughter of Anker Rasmussen, who was a Venusberg Rasmussen and had emigrated directly from Norway, so was no kin to Earl J. Rasmussen, who hailed originally from Norseland, Minnesota, lived alone in the hills with about six hundred sheep, and recited "Casey at the Bat," at the top of his lungs, whenever the opportunity arose.

The idea for the Little Box Social was broached at an informal meeting of the women of the Six Towns area, in our very own kitchen, in the two-story log house, at the end of Nine Pin Road, where the cracks were chinked with straw and manure, where bats lived in the unfinished attic and on summer nights went hurtling across the farmyard as if they'd been catapulted. Nine Pin Road wasn't really a road, but could qualify for most of the year as a trail, or at least as somewhere between a path and a trail, for Nine Pin Road didn't run along any recognized road allowance, but jiggety-jogged along something my daddy and the neighbors called the Correction Line, which I never in my life have learned what it was.

The informal meeting of the women of the Six Towns area, at which the idea for the Little Box Social was broached by Mrs. Edytha Rasmussen Bozniak, was held in conjunction with a Farmers Union meeting, which took place at the same time in our seldom-used living room. The informal meeting of the women, and the more formal meeting of the men, was held on a cool, clear September evening, with the moon bright as a peeled peach, and the Northern Lights running up the sky like green electric wool; I was allowed to stay up late and carry fresh cups of coffee from the blue enameled twelve-cup pot on the cookstove to the men meeting in our seldom-used living room.

To be honest, I was more interested in the women than the men; the men tended to discuss matters that didn't interest me a lot, or that I didn't entirely understand, matters like (a) farm prices: low to nonexistent, (b) who in the Six Towns area had a vehicle in operating condition: Bear Lundquist, Curly McClintock, and possibly the infamous Flop Skalrud, (c) who was getting any on the side: nobody, except possibly the infamous Flop Skalrud.

And they told jokes, mostly ones I didn't understand, though I gathered they were about sex, because when one was finished everyone guffawed, and each time, after the guffawing had subsided, Earl J. Rasmussen brought out the bottle of dandelion wine he had smuggled through our kitchen, hid up the sleeve of his mackinaw, and Wasyl Lakusta brought out the quart sealer of Heathen's Rapture, or good old bring-on-blindness, logging-boot-to-the-side-of-the-head homebrew he'd smuggled through our kitchen under his baggy bib-overalls, and all the men had a drink of dandelion wine and slopped a slug of homebrew into their coffee. Bear Lundquist forgot he had put homebrew in his coffee and added cream, which immediately broke into curds the size of sugar cubes, while everyone guffawed again, as my daddy managed to pry open the west window so they could throw out the curdled cream-coffee-homebrew into the choke-cherry tree whose limbs brushed the window glass all year round, while they sent me to the kitchen to fill Bear Lundquist's cup with fresh coffee.

I preferred to be in the kitchen. The women didn't need any fortification in order to get down to the nitty-gritty. In the living room, the men paid little attention to me, except when they wanted fresh coffee, while the women were concerned about my overhearing their conversations; the women liked to think they were alone when they got down to the nitty-gritty, which made them much more interesting than the men.

Whenever one of the women was saying something particularly vicious about someone who wasn't present, Mama would glance around and say, "Where's Jamie?"

Then, someone else would say, "Little pitchers have big ears," and everyone would nod knowingly.

From my place, out of sight, cuddled up warm as toast between the woodbox and the stove, I could listen to the women, and watch the men through a crack in the door to our seldom-used living room, to see who needed their coffee refilled. I would wonder why the women thought it was only little pitchers who had big ears and not big pitchers or the rest of the team. And didn't at least one of them know I was an outfielder and had no desire to be a pitcher? And besides I didn't have big ears. Truckbox Al McClintock had big ears.

"It's my suggestion that at the next whist drive, which is scheduled for a week from Saturday at Fark Community Hall, we ought to sponsor a box social for the children," Mrs. Edytha Rasmussen Bozniak said when an opportunity presented itself.

The women had just finished demolishing the reputation of the Norman Sigurdson family, none of whom were present, and it was the first chance Mrs. Edytha Rasmussen Bozniak had had to get a word in edgewise for almost half an hour. Among limited company, like if she was one-on-one with my mama, Mrs. Edytha Rasmussen Bozniak was a formidable talker. But it appeared to me that non-stop talking was an art that improved with age, and since Mrs. Edytha Rasmussen Bozniak was the youngest woman present that evening, she was simply a rank amateur, and without the indulgence of the older women would never have got a word in edgewise.

The non-stop talkers were led by Mrs. Bear Lundquist, who had perfected the art of taking a long, deep breath inwards, while the words were still spewing out, so that theoretically she was a perpetual talking device. The widow, Mrs. Beatrice Ann Stevenson, known far and wide for her recitations of Emily Dickinson poems, until she had to unexpectedly switch to Lord Byron, while no match for Mrs. Bear Lundquist, *projected* when she spoke, and in a pinch could out-shout almost anyone, while Mrs. Ibsen (if she had a first name I never heard it), the much younger wife of the Rev. Ibsen, of New Oslo, who didn't have a church anymore but was still called Reverend anyway, and was still called upon in emergencies to christen, or comfort, marry, or bury, though small and shabby, with a pinched face and colorless eyes, was deceptive, and if she managed to get a word in edgewise, was apt to hold the floor for a half hour or more, while my own mama, on a good day and given the right subject, her hatred of Prime Minister Mackenzie King and the Liberal government in Ottawa, being her favorite, could hold her own with, but not surpass, the best talkers in the room.

After demolishing the reputation of the Norman Sigurdson

family, mother, father, plus several Sigurdson sons and several Sigurdson daughters, and at least one Sigurdson grandparent, none of whom were present, and all of whom hailed from between Fark and Magnolia, and were often known as the Red Sigurdsons, or our Sigurdsons, so as not to be confused with the more-or-less Doreen Beach Sigurdsons who I'll tell about later—the one thing the two Sigurdson families had in common, my mama said, was both were white trash, and Mama wondered aloud if their trashiness had to do with their family name.

The women first discussed the fact that the Norman Sigurdsons willingly accepted *relief* yet were still poor, and shiftless, and sorrowful, and ungrateful; they then moved to the subject of Mrs. Norman Sigurdson's latest pregnancy. A stirring debate ensued over whether the latest pregnancy was Mrs. Norman Sigurdson's twelfth or thirteenth, the debate involving a lot of finger pointing, primarily by the widow, Mrs. Beatrice Ann Stevenson, and Mrs. Torval Imsdahl; this was followed by almost everyone in the room engaging in finger-counting of both children and miscarriages; when no definitive total of either could be reached, the women finally moved on to speculation as to who the father might be, *this time.*

And there was *considerable* speculation, some pondering, and even a rumination or two, as to who the father might be, *this time,* though everyone in the room had to be especially delicate and discreet so as not to speculate, ponder, or even ruminate on anyone who was closely related to one of the women present, especially someone who might be married to one to the women present. That eliminated a considerable number of suspects.

The Norman Sigurdsons, like the Venusberg Stevensons, and the more-or-less Doreen Beach Sigurdsons, lived in tents on the road allowance in summer, and in winter, in whatever abandoned shack or ramshackle cabin they could squat in. And they did indeed receive *relief*, which was a dirty word, and receiving *relief*, as far as the women in the room were concerned, was considerably worse than living like Indians in a tent on the road allowance.

"There was no crime in being poor," the women said, frequently, as if they had to impress each other with the wisdom of the observation. But taking *relief*, which was something you had to travel to the Government Subagency in Sangudo to apply for, was a crime, they said, even if the law wouldn't come around and arrest you for doing it. *Relief* was a dirtier word than son-of-a-bitch, and even the swear words with God's name in them, and was, I gathered, a means of getting something for nothing, which everyone in our house at the end of Nine Pin Road, that clear September night with the moon bright as a peeled peach, and the Northern Lights running green up the middle of the sky, considered a crime.

Except for me. Scrunched down, warm as toast, between the cookstove and the woodbox, I couldn't see that getting something for nothing could be all that bad. Not accepting *relief* had something to do with pride, the women said, though pride, I had heard, was a sin in itself, and was said to go before a fall, but apparently there were different species of pride, and the kind of pride that kept my family and most of the other families in the Six Towns area off *relief* was, as far as I could determine, an acceptable species of pride—even though each and every family represented at our house that night was eligible for *relief*, something each and every one of them took almost as much pride in as in not accepting *relief*. Each time the neighbors of the Six Towns area gathered together, whether it was at a Farmers Union meeting, whist drive, box social, community dance, sportsday, or ethnic wedding, the men and women agreed separately, but unanimously, that they would rather starve than accept *relief*.

I decided as I sat behind the woodbox listening to the women, and watching the men through a crack in the door, that *relief* surely involved money, and money to me translated to cellophane bags full of cinnamon-red and lemon-yellow jelly beans. There between the woodbox and the cookstove, I decided that given the opportunity, I would accept *relief* rather than starve.

# THE FULL SCHOLARSHIP ORPHANED GENIUS

# Chapter Six

"**H**aving a Little Box Social for the children will allow them to develop their social skills," Mrs. Edytha Rasmussen Bozniak pointed out quickly, after she managed to get a word in edgewise, and before she could be interrupted by one of the prodigious talkers present.

I could tell that what she meant was the Little Box Social would help her daughter, Velvet Rasmussen Bozniak, develop *her* social skills. Although Velvet Rasmussen Bozniak was a few months younger than me, the only social skill she seemed intent on acquiring was the ability to catch a boyfriend, who would someday evolve into a husband.

Mrs. Edytha Rasmussen Bozniak, who was the youngest woman in the kitchen that clear September evening, was not very old at all, twenty-seven would be my guess, though she talked like a middle-aged lady. She also had a way of condescending to children when she spoke to them, of embarrassing all except her daughter, Velvet, who it seemed both literally and figuratively, did not know the meaning of the word embarrassment.

"And how are you today, my little man?" Mrs. Edytha Rasmussen Bozniak said to me, when she arrived at the meeting; she was a tall, rawboned woman, dressed in a coarse tweed suit, matching coat, and wearing a squashed-looking maroon-velvet hat, a type of hat my mama called a tam, held on by a pearl-handled hatpin. The clothes, my mama said, Mrs. Edytha Rasmussen Bozniak had brought back with her from Edmonton, when she and Velvet returned to live with her parents, the Anker Rasmussens, shortly after World War II began; the hatpin came from Norway and had belonged to her grandmother.

"I'm not anybody's little man," I wanted to say to her, as she extended her long, red hand for me to shake. When I took hold of her hand, which was still cold from the five-mile buggy ride, she leaned down and kissed me, first on one cheek, then the other, like I had seen the President of France doing to a famous general, in a photograph in the *Toronto Star Weekly*. Her face was surrounded by brown sausage curls; she had rouge on both her cheeks, and she smelled of Evening in Paris, the only perfume available at any of the general stores in the Six Towns area, so every mother and grandmother had at least one of the depressing blue bottles on her dresser, or in her medicine cabinet.

"When the women of the Six Towns get together," my daddy said, "it's like the wind was blowing off a lake of Evening in Paris."

I didn't say anything at all to Mrs. Edytha Rasmussen Bozniak, partly because Mama was looking at me out of the corner of her eye with a look that said, Don't you dare embarrass me, and partly because I could hear Mama's voice, earlier that afternoon, talking to Mrs. Lute Magnussen, whose first name was June, about Mrs. Edytha Rasmussen Bozniak.

"The poor thing has to put on airs because she's had so little go right for her in this life."

Another reason I didn't say anything was because I was so relieved that Mrs. Edytha Rasmussen Bozniak had arrived accompanied only by her mother, Mrs. Irma Rasmussen, but not by her daughter, Velvet. All day, I had been dreading the very distinct possibility that Velvet Bozniak might turn up at the meeting, though it was an unwritten rule that, excepting babies who were breastfeeding, children stayed at home with grandparents or older brothers and sisters, while their parents attended meetings such as this.

"So you two charming children can play and develop your communication skills," Mrs. Edytha Rasmussen Bozniak said, the last time she flouted the unwritten rule, and brought Velvet Bozniak to a meeting at our house.

"Since neither of you have brothers or sisters, it's vitally important for you to learn to interact with children of the opposite sex."

I smiled kind of sickly and recalled something else my mama said earlier in the afternoon.

"It's a wonder she don't choke on the language she uses. She ain't been to but half of ninth grade—claims some of her husband's university education rubbed off on her. Ha!"

Velvet Bozniak, who was as tall as me, was slim as a rail, with a dark complexion, blue-black finger curls, black eyes, a frank stare, and a sly smile, owned a Shirley Temple doll that she carried everywhere with her. Whenever she visited our house at the end of Nine Pin Road, Velvet Bozniak always insisted that she and I pretend we were married, and that Shirley Temple was our baby. And, of course, Velvet Bozniak always wore velvet—royal blue, Christmas red, midnight black.

While we were pretending to be married and that Shirley Temple was our baby, Velvet Bozniak claimed to be aware of a lot of things that I wasn't, especially things to do with sex, and she more than once volunteered to show me, among other embarrassing things, how babies got made, which I'm not sure were the communication skills that Mrs. Edytha Rasmussen Bozniak had in mind when she flung us together.

Living on a farm it was difficult not to know how animals reproduced, but I simply wasn't ready to admit that human beings might multiply in the same manner—though I knew deep down it was true, just like I knew for a year or two before I admitted it that there was no Santa Claus, Easter Bunny, or Tooth Fairy—especially any human beings with whom I was acquainted.

"Jamie, don't your mother and father do *it*?" Velvet asked one afternoon.

"No," I said quickly.

Until that moment, the thought had never occurred to me, though I must have known subliminally that my parents were sexual beings. I recalled a joke that they often shared about a fellow from near New Oslo, the infamous Flop Skalrud by name. Sometimes when a group of men would be standing around behind the Fark Community Hall of a summer evening waiting for the whist drive, box social, or ethnic wedding dance to begin, sipping a little dandelion wine, chokecherry wine, raisin wine, or good old bring-on-blindness, logging-boot-to-the-side-of-the-head homebrew, the group, as if on signal would unbutton and relieve themselves into the tall grass and red willow bushes, usually led by Earl J. Rasmussen, or my daddy, John Martin Duffy O'Day.

Whenever the men unbuttoned, and the simultaneous relieving into the tall grass and red willow bushes began, there was bound to be a joke or two made about the infamous Flop Skalrud, unless Flop Skalrud was there, which he usually wasn't, the jokes having to do with the size of Flop Skalrud's relief mechanism, which was variously described, depicted, portrayed, and even on occasion epitomized, as somewhat larger than average.

"In its natural state, if you know what I mean, it just flops about like a five-pound jackfish," said Earl J. Rasmussen, as everyone relieved themselves into the tall grass and red willow bushes. Everyone guffawed, causing many a stream to go crooked for a few seconds.

"Me and Flop were out in the rowboat, fishing on Purgatory Lake one afternoon," Curly McClintock said, "when Flop stood up and went to relieve hisself over the side. Except all that shift in weight tipped the row boat right over, and we both ended up clinging to the underside of the boat for two hours, until Lute Magnussen came down to catch a few jackfish and spotted us floating out there." Everyone guffawed, any streams that weren't exhausted by this time going crooked again.

In our kitchen, at the informal meeting of the women of the Six Towns area, on a cool September night with the moon hanging like a peeled peach above our house at the end of Nine Pin Road, the prime suspect of being the father of Mrs. Norman Sigurdson's latest, be it number twelve or thirteen, something all the finger pointing and finger-counting in the world couldn't establish with certainty, was the infamous Flop Skalrud.

As Flop Skalrud's name came up again, I recalled that the previous winter, when Daddy had manned the county snowplow for four days after a blizzard, getting to plow out everything in the county that was recognized as a highway, road, or trail, but not Nine Pin Road, which wasn't recognized as anything but a path, that after Daddy took the snowplow back to the county office in Doreen Beach, and collected his pay, he arrived home on horseback, straddled our old roan horse Ethan Allen, a heavy canvas sack packed with groceries behind the saddle, one item of which was a roll of bologna that must have weighed ten pounds.

As he was unpacking the groceries, my daddy, who had been away for four days, held that ten-pound roll of bologna against the front of his overalls while he said to Mama, "Reckon this reminds you of anybody you know?"

When Mama and Daddy were talking like that, I knew enough to be absorbed in the cellophane bag of cinnamon-red and lemon-yellow jelly beans I had just been gifted with, cinnamon-red and lemon-yellow jelly beans I was devouring as I sat on a couch next to the cathedral-shaped radio we only used on special occasions, so as to make the big, rectangular black-and-white striped battery that powered it, last longer. I could feel Mama look carefully at me, to see if I was paying any attention to them.

When she saw I wasn't, she giggled real pretty and said, "Flop Skalrud." And she laughed again, in a way that she only laughed with Daddy, and no one else. Daddy laughed too, and then they both allowed as how they were powerful tired, even though it wasn't much past noon, and they excused themselves to go to their bedroom at the back of the house for a rest. And I knew enough to pretend that I hardly noticed and kept chewing on my cinnamon-red and lemon-yellow jelly beans.


Velvet Bozniak, it seemed to me, wanted to take all the fun out of happy times like that; she wanted me to *think* about what was really going on, something I didn't want to do, and couldn't see any reason for doing. Until Velvet Bozniak brought the subject up, I never equated what Mama and Daddy did during their afternoon rests with sex, and when Velvet Bozniak did bring the subject up, I quickly denied any knowledge of the matter, even though I knew deep down, I wasn't being completely honest.

"What do you know about it anyway?" I said to Velvet Bozniak. "You haven't got a daddy anymore," which was as cruel a thing as I had ever said, especially considering what I knew about Velvet Bozniak's daddy, from listening to my mama and her friends gossip. I wouldn't have said such a cruel thing anyway, if Velvet Bozniak hadn't acted so superior, staring at me with her frank, black stare, smoothing down the midnight black velvet bow in her hair, and asking for at least the third time if I didn't want a first-hand demonstration of how babies were made.

But even after I said that cruel thing, Velvet just smiled her sly smile and, as she would do for the rest of her life, didn't let the nasty things anyone said about her bother her for long. Then, still smiling, she put me in my place.

"Before my daddy died a hero in the war, he and my mama used to do *it* every day," Velvet said with authority, silently daring me to call her a lair. "My mama says sex is an expression of love, the nicest thing two people in love can do for each other." Velvet Rasmussen Bozniak of the blue-black finger curls, black eyes, sly smile, frank stare, midnight black hair bows, and sharp tongue, then double-dirty-dared me out loud to call her a liar.

I wasn't ready for a conversation like that, so instead of answering, I picked up Shirley Temple by one leg and dangled her in the direction of the firebox on the cookstove, causing Velvet Bozniak to scream and attract the attention of Mrs. Edytha Rasmussen Bozniak, who smiled and suggested the three of us play Truth or Consequences.

. . .

Unfortunately, everyone at the meeting in our kitchen in the house at the end of Nine Pin Road agreed with Mrs. Edytha Rasmussen Bozniak that holding a Little Box Social would help children develop their social skills, and, for some reason, most of the women present seemed to feel that developing social skills ranked right up there with telling the truth and not having pink eye, ringworm, or cooties.

For the next hour the women discussed, argued, debated, sparred, crossed swords, locked horns, wrangled, bickered and bandied about the details of a Little Box Social. Mrs. Edytha Rasmussen Bozniak made a formal motion that: "At the next whist drive at Fark Community Hall, that the adults of the Six Towns area organize for children sixteen and under, a Little Box Social, in order to develop and enhance the social skills of said children. I so move."

It was my mama who pointed out to Mrs. Edytha Rasmussen Bozniak that while it was all right for her to make a suggestion, or a proposal, or even a recommendation that the adults organize a Little Box Social for the children, that for her to make a motion was unnecessary and uncalled for, because to make a motion there had to be a formal organization with a constitution and elected officers, something this informal group did not have.

Mrs. Edytha Rasmussen Bozniak replied to the effect that parliamentary procedure, like good manners, was never out of place, never unnecessary, and especially never uncalled for.

When, at the end of her speech, Mrs. Edytha Rasmussen Bozniak took a deep breath, her nose rising in the air as she did so, her mother, Mrs. Irma Rasmussen, quickly seconded the motion.

There followed several more minutes of crossed swords, locked horns, wrangling, bickering, and bandying about before everyone realized that they were in favor of having a Little Box Social. But before they came to the realization, it was suggested, I think by Mrs. Lute Magnussen, that they actually create a formal organization with elected officers in order to complement the motion made by Mrs. Edytha Rasmussen Bozniak, and seconded by her mother, Mrs. Irma Rasmussen.

Before the realization that they were all in favor of holding a Little Box Social, they seriously considered the possibility of interrupting the Farmers Union meeting in our seldom-used living room, in order to request that Bear Lundquist, who was an expert on, or at least knowledgeable of, parliamentary procedure, instruct them on how to set up a formal organization, and be their first guest speaker.

The discussion went off on a tangent for some time as they considered names for the proposed organization, names that ranged from The Ladies Auxiliary to the Farmers Union, to The Amalgamated Six Towns Farm Wives. The widow, Mrs. Beatrice Ann Stevenson, then suggested a consolidation with the Fark Sewing Circle and Temperance Society, an organization which already had a constitution and elected officers, though in spite of that its membership had dwindled dramatically in recent years. It was after someone who understood alliteration, perhaps the poetry-reciting widow, Mrs. Beatrice Ann Stevenson, again, suggested the new proposed organization be called the Fark Female Farmerettes, and after everyone had stopped laughing, except my mama, who considered it a cruel joke to live near a town called Fark, the naming of which I'll tell about later, that everyone realized they were in favor of sponsoring a Little Box Social, and if they were going to iron out the details they had better get a move on.

They all raised their hands to show they were in favor of holding a Little Box Social, while no one voted against the idea, except my mama, who didn't vote at all, because even though the motion hadn't been officially passed, and they had not formed a formal organization with elected officers, my mama still saw herself as losing out to Mrs. Edytha Rasmussen Bozniak. Mama just pulled her neck down into her collar an inch or two, and smiled sweet enough to melt sugar in a sugar bowl, as she offered the ladies another round of cinnamon buns and tea.

Mama's especially sweet smile had been aimed directly at Mrs. Edytha Rasmussen Bozniak, with a corner of it aimed at Mrs. Irma Rasmussen, and from my hiding place between the woodbox and the cookstove, I knew, and most of the women in the room knew, that Mama's smile was saying—If I wasn't such a lady I'd bring up the past.

Mrs. Edytha Rasmussen Bozniak's past was exactly what had been brought up at a meeting about six months previous, which neither she nor her mother had been able to attend. The meeting had been held at Mr. and Mrs. Bear Lundquist's, where the men congregated in the seldom-used living room for a Farmers Union meeting, and the women in the kitchen for an informal meeting. I had been personally invited by Mrs. Bear Lundquist, who though she wasn't arthritic, moved like she was, and sometimes played first base for the Sangudo Mustangs baseball team, to pour tea for the women, and coffee for the men, since she had no daughters or granddaughters to do the job.

At the Bear Lundquists', I had no woodbox to hide behind, so in order to eavesdrop on the women I had to settle for sitting on the floor in the seldom-used living room and listening through a crack in the door. The women had chased me out of the kitchen just as they were about to get down to the nitty-gritty, saying, as usual, "Little pitchers have big ears."

Each time I came into the kitchen to refill a coffee cup, or Mrs. Bear Lundquist or my mama called me in, to tour the room refilling cups from the big bone china teapot in its crocheted cozy, the conversation stopped dead, like someone had turned off a radio, or like it did at home when I wandered into the room to find Mama and Daddy discussing Christmas, ice cream, or the infamous Flop Skalrud.

Mama, in the almost ten years she and Daddy had lived in the big, log house at the end of Nine Pin Road, had never missed accompanying Daddy to each and every social event, from wakes and funerals, to christenings, to box socials, ethnic weddings, and Farmers Union meetings, even though, on a number of occasions, she suffered from varying degrees of illness.

Once, when Mama was gravelly-voiced, watery-eyed, and, my daddy said, on the very verge of pneumonia, suffering from a steady cough that sounded like unoiled gears grinding together, my daddy tried to persuade her to stay home from a Farmers Union meeting at Torval Imsdahl's.

"I'm going to go," my mama rasped, coughing and blowing her nose at the same time. "I don't want those biddies to have a chance to talk about me."


During the meeting at Mr. and Mrs. Bear Lundquist's, what with there being no business of any kind to discuss, and with both Mrs. Edytha Rasmussen Bozniak, and her mother, Mrs. Irma Rasmussen, absent, there was presented a perfect opportunity for the women to tell, retell, narrate, report, rehash, recount, recite, depict, and dissect in minute detail, the life of Mrs. Edytha Rasmussen Bozniak, because, as the widow, Mrs. Beatrice Ann Stevenson, said, "Lord knows when we'll get a chance to talk about her again."

The high point of the story, or at least one of several high points of the story, which took the women at least a half hour to get to, because as Mama would say when telling stories at home, certain preliminaries have to be observed, was that the summer before Velvet Bozniak was born, Mr. and Mrs. Anker Rasmussen had employed a hired man, an Indian from down Lac Ste. Anne way, name of Eddie Grassfires, a skinny, mud-colored boy, who rode the nine miles to work each day, bare-back on a walleyed pinto pony.

Eddie Grassfires was the pitcher for the Lac Ste. Anne baseball team, a team that seldom if ever won a game, because Eddie Grassfires was not a very good pitcher, his one saving grace being a passable pickoff move to first base. No one knew it then, but nine or ten years after *that summer*, as the women referred to it, Eddie Grassfires, at the end of his career, would serve up five home-run balls to Truckbox Al McClintock of a Sunday afternoon, on a newly mowed baseball field on the banks of the Pembina River, and Truckbox Al McClintock would hit four of those baseballs into, and one clean across, the Pembina River, thus setting up Truckbox Al's chance for a tryout with the genuine St. Louis Cardinals of the National Baseball League.

All *that summer*, as the women referred to it, while Eddie Grassfires worked the fields for Anker Rasmussen, coiling hay, and later taking a pitchfork and tossing the coiled hay up onto the high, horse-drawn hayracks, where Anker Rasmussen or his neighbor, Torval Imsdahl, built the load until it looked like a giant, mobile loaf of green bread, Edytha Rasmussen, who was sixteen, and as pretty as she was ever going to get, had the job of bringing coffee to the field every mid-morning, lunch every noon, and coffee and pie every mid-afternoon. It was also Edytha Rasmussen's responsibility to see that the cream can, which held drinking water, never got below half full.

In Mrs. Bear Lundquist's kitchen, some of the women spec-ulated, some contemplated, while others pondered, brooded or reflected, on exactly when and how Edytha Rasmussen and Eddie Grassfires got together *that summer*, in order to produce,

between them, what would come to be known as Velvet Bozniak.

"All anyone had to do was put two and two together," Mrs.
Torval Imsdahl said, and Mrs. Bear Lundquist, who wasn't arthritic but moved like she was, said she had to agree that all
anybody had to do was put two and two together.

The women speculated, contemplated, pondered, brooded,
reflected, and finally guessed that one hot evening *that summer*,
Eddie Grassfires only pretended to go home to the reserve, and
that he tied his pinto pony to graze in the lush meadow along
the creek that cut through the back of Anker Rasmussen's one
hundred and sixty acres, and that he crept back to the farm
house, to where Edytha Rasmussen was waiting for him.

The women speculated for some time about whether, on a
certain hot evening *that summer*, Eddie Grassfires came directly
into the Rasmussen house, and whether Eddie Grassfires and
Edytha Rasmussen did what they did right under the noses of
Anker and Irma Rasmussen, so to speak, or whether Edytha
Rasmussen met Eddie Grassfires at the back door, perhaps carrying a blanket, or whether Edytha Rasmussen might have gone
to meet Eddie Grassfires halfway, or even more than halfway,
say in the meadow along the banks of the creek that cut through
the back of Anker Rasmussen's one hundred and sixty acres,
a meadow speckled with yellow buttercups and bordered by
silver and purple fireweed.

It was at Christmas of that selfsame year, the winter after *that
summer*, that Edytha Rasmussen suddenly got an offer from a
friend of a friend of Mrs. Irma Rasmussen's, an offer to go to
Edmonton and babysit that friend of a friend's children. The
*friend of a friend* was actually a couple, the woman being a high
school teacher at Garneau High School in Edmonton, and her
husband being a professor of some intellectual discipline at the
University of Alberta.

Mrs. Irma Rasmussen made the rounds of all her friends and acquaintances in the Six Towns area, passing on the details of Edytha's wonderful opportunity. The high school teacher and the professor of some intellectual discipline, Mrs. Irma Rasmussen said, rented rooms in their large home, close by the University of Alberta, to serious young scholars, one of whom she hoped, might take a shine to Edytha, and wasn't this whole thing just heaven sent, and just the greatest opportunity imaginable?

Everyone Mrs. Irma Rasmussen called on agreed that the whole thing was heaven sent, and was the greatest opportunity imaginable for Edytha, though, my mama said, they sort of winked out of the corners of their eyes when they said it, because they knew that something uncommon was going on, but at the time they didn't know just what, or how uncommon.

Once Edytha Rasmussen got to Edmonton, and all safely ensconced in the home of the high school teacher and the professor of some intellectual discipline, reports flowed back to her mother thick and fast. Mrs. Irma Rasmussen duly revealed that the high school teacher and the professor of some intellectual discipline were the most considerate employers imaginable, the children, two little girls, were perfect angels, and Edytha was happier than any girl her age had a right to be.

Mrs. Irma Rasmussen also duly reported that Edytha was allowed both Saturday and Sunday off, and had found a Lutheran Church within walking distance of the big, brown-shingle house near the University of Alberta. And, Mrs. Irma Rasmussen went on to duly report, Edytha went to a movie each and every Saturday night, at either the Garneau Theater or the Varscona Theater, both of which were close by. And then came the best part of all—Edytha didn't go alone to the movies each and every Saturday night, because, rooming on the second floor of the big, brown-shingle house owned by the high school teacher and the professor of some intellectual discipline, was a tall, dark, and handsome young man named of Arthur Bozniak, a student of engineering at the University of Alberta, and so clever he didn't have to pay a single cent of his tuition, because he was an honor student on a full scholarship.

The second month Edytha was in Edmonton, Mrs. Irma Rasmussen again toured the farms in the Six Towns area, quoting lengthy excerpts from Edytha's letters, and passing on her interpretation of those letters. Mrs. Irma Rasmussen interpreted that Edytha's relationship with the full scholarship honor student, Arthur Bozniak, was getting serious, because the previous week, instead of taking Edytha to the Garneau Theater, or the Varscona Theater, both of which were within walking distance of the big, brown-shingle house where they lived, Arthur Bozniak and Edytha Rasmussen had ridden the Red and White streetcar across the top deck of the High Level Bridge, all the way to downtown Edmonton, where they had taken in a Wallace Beery movie at the Capitol Theater, a theater that had a carpeted lobby, plush velvet seats and genuine stars blinking in the ceiling.

And afterwards, the full scholarship honor student, Arthur Bozniak, had taken Edytha Rasmussen out for Chinese food to the Pan American Café, on Jasper Avenue, the main street of Edmonton, a restaurant where the waiters wore blue vests, and the booths were upholstered in maroon-colored genuine leather.

Only if a young man's intentions were serious did he take a girl out for Chinese food at the Pan American Café on Jasper Avenue, Mrs. Irma Rasmussen reported with authority. She also reported with authority that a certain rumor about the Pan American Café, a rumor that had reached the Six Towns area even before Edytha Rasmussen had been treated to Chinese food at the Pan American Café, a rumor that stated the management of the Pan American Café had been caught substituting diced cat for diced chicken in the chicken chow mein, was libelous and totally unfounded.

She also revealed that the full scholarship honor student, Arthur Bozniak, was an orphan, with no known next of kin in the whole world, and had been raised up in a government orphanage, and was just your average run-of-the-mill orphan with no known next of kin in the whole world, until, in seventh grade, he taught himself trigonometry, and demonstrated an understanding of Einstein's Theory of Relativity.

Arthur Bozniak's seventh grade teacher, a Mr. Paducah, who himself had been an orphan, and who understood only a smattering of trigonometry, and nothing at all about Einstein's Theory of Relativity, took the boy to the head of the Engineering Department, at the University of Alberta, who administered some tests that showed the boy, Arthur Bozniak, orphan with no known next of kin in the whole world, was a genius.

# Chapter Seven

The engagement of Edytha Victoria Rasmussen, and Arthur Bozniak (no second name, his future mother-in-law, Mrs. Irma Rasmussen speculated that for reasons of economy orphans in Alberta were not given second names), was announced at Christmas, exactly nine weeks after Edytha Rasmussen had gone to live in Edmonton and babysit the children of the high school teacher and the professor of some intellectual discipline.

Edytha had, Mrs. Irma Rasmussen duly reported, been swept off her feet by the young orphaned genius, Arthur Bozniak, and they were planning to be married on Valentine's Day, wasn't that romantic, and wasn't Edytha just the luckiest girl in the whole world to go from helping out on her daddy's farm near New Oslo, Alberta, in October, to being engaged to a young orphaned genius engineering student by Christmas time, with a wedding set for Valentine's Day? Everyone agreed that what Mrs. Irma Rasmussen said was true, my mama said, though they still winked out of the corner of their eyes when they said it, because they still suspected that something uncommon was going on, though at that point they didn't know what, or how uncommon.


The women of the Six Towns area gave Edytha Rasmussen a bridal shower in absentia. The bridal shower was held at Mr. and Mrs. Anker Rasmussen's, right after New Year's, so as to give the women of the Six Towns area time, over the Christmas holidays, to knit, crochet, tat, quilt, needlepoint, punchwork, or just plain sew up, a shower present, since most everyone was too poor to afford anything that wasn't handmade.

Edytha was too busy with her babysitting job, and with her wedding plans, to come home for the shower, and the young orphaned genius engineering student, Arthur Bozniak, no one ever called him Art, Mrs. Irma Rasmussen made a point of slipping into almost every conversation, was too busy being a genius at his engineering studies at the University of Alberta, to make the trip to New Oslo. Irma and Anker Rasmussen were simply going to have to wait until the wedding to get a look at their tall, dark, handsome, orphaned genius of a son-in-law.


The shower, my mama reported, was a success, even though the bride wasn't present, and it would have been an outstanding success if the bride's mother hadn't been present, because, with her being there, everyone had to hold their tongues, and there couldn't be even a hint of speculation as to the something uncommon that everyone felt in their bones was going on.

My mama, with pink variegated thread, tatted a two-inch border for a pair of pillow cases that were almost ten years old, left over from more prosperous times, but never used. The widow, Mrs. Beatrice Ann Stevenson, knit a tea cozy with scarlet wool, and slipped it over a teapot, never used, but about the same age as my mama's pillow cases, and inside the teapot she deposited a slim volume of Emily Dickinson poems.

"If she's going to marry a university graduate, she'll have to develop *some* culture," the widow, Mrs. Beatrice Ann Stevenson, confided to my mama. "The Rasmussens, though goodness knows I think kindly of them, consider playing four-handed cribbage a cultural event."

Mrs. Torval Imsdahl arrived at the shower accompanied by a punchwork pillow cover—black velvet, featuring a disconsolate face of Jesus in brown wool, a couple of sky-blue tears, the same color as His eyes, rolling down His misery-ridden face.

Mrs. Bear Lundquist crocheted six antimacassars the thickness and consistency of fish net, while Loretta Cake, who lived in a cabin near Doreen Beach with about one hundred cats, and who no one had invited to the shower because she was thought to be strange, and eccentric, and possibly even dangerous, arrived on foot toting a menacing-looking metal flower. The flower was created by taking tinsnips and cutting an empty can of Quaker State Motor Oil into about one-eighth-inch strips; the strips curled until the object looked a bit like a giant sunflower. The flower, my mama said, could also be used to slice cheese and would amputate the fingers of any curious children who touched it.

Among the other gifts was an assortment of aprons, towels (tea, bath and kitchen), pot holders, items of cutlery left over from better days, and, from Mrs. Wasyl Lakusta, with some apology, though there was no need, a five-pound frozen jackfish from Purgatory Lake.

But, all in all, my mama said, the bridal shower in absentia was a grand success, and on the thirteenth of February, Mrs. Irma Rasmussen, dressed in a well-brushed, fifteen-year-old cloth coat with a fox collar, the fox, all moth-eaten and beady-eyed, with a black pointy nose—set off to attend her daughter's wedding, the moth-eaten and beady-eyed fox staring slyly in the direction of her left breast. Mrs. Irma Rasmussen was accompanied by her husband, Anker Rasmussen, dressed in the same suit he'd been married in in Norway, and wearing, as always, his red-and-black-checkered hunting hat with the earflaps down.

The Rasmussens caught the eastbound Western Trailways bus at Bjornsen's Corner. The bus driver, the youngest Ostapowich boy from Wildwood, a long, boney Ostapowich with thick glasses and a beak of a nose, who had many oil stains on his rumpled and depressing blue-gray uniform, had to pack two large cardboard boxes of shower presents in the luggage compartment underneath the bus before the Rasmussens boarded.

It had been decided that the wedding ceremony would be held in the parlor of the big, brown-shingle house owned by the high school teacher and the university professor of some intellectual discipline, with their little daughters as flower girls, and that the ceremony would be for immediate family only, and since the young full scholarship, orphaned genius, Arthur Bozniak, had no known next of kin in the world, that made for a very small wedding.

The Rasmussens were due back on the evening of February fifteenth on the westbound Western Trailways bus that stopped once a day at Bjornsen's Corner. Mrs. Bear Lundquist spent most of Valentine's Day, and all of February fifteenth, trying to convince Mr. Bear Lundquist that he should borrow Flop Skalrud's Model T Ford in order for the Lundquists to meet the returning Rasmussens in style. Mr. Bear Lundquist pointed out that it being February and the weather having been well below zero for several weeks, and the roads impassable to anything but sleighs and Curly McClintock's dump truck, that attempting to borrow the car would be a waste of time. But Mrs. Bear Lundquist pointed out that she didn't ask for much from Mr. Bear Lundquist, and that arriving at Bjornsen's Corner in a Model T Ford, even if the Model T Ford belonged to the infamous Flop Skalrud, would assure that the returning Rasmussens would ride with them and not any one of the other people from the Six Towns area who might show up, eager to hear the juicy details of the wedding.

Mr. Bear Lundquist, who admitted that Mrs. Bear Lundquist didn't ask all that much of him, on the way to meet the west-bound Western Trailways bus, drove seven miles out of his way to Flop Skalrud's place, only to be told by Flop Skalrud, when he appeared at the door all red-faced, out of breath, and more-or-less glassy-eyed, that the Model T Ford had been up on blocks in the machine shed since October and would stay that way until the snow melted in the spring and the flood that followed the melting snow had receded. Mrs. Bear Lundquist did pick up an interesting piece of information while she was waiting in the sleigh as Mr. Bear Lundquist called on the infamous Flop Skalrud, interrupting him in the midst of the very thing Flop Skalrud was infamous for. Mrs. Bear Lundquist noted that there was a one-horse cutter parked in front of Flop Skalrud's horse barn, a cutter she recognized as belonging to Lute Magnussen, which meant that either Lute Magnussen, or Mrs. Lute Magnussen, or the Lute Magnussens' seventeen-year-old daughter, Anna Marie, was in the house with the infamous Flop Skalrud.

As soon as Mr. Bear Lundquist got back to the sleigh, he announced that Flop Skalrud's Model T Ford was up on blocks in the machine shed until after the spring flood had subsided. He imparted the information in an "I told you so" tone, to let Mrs. Bear Lundquist know that he had known all along that the trip had been a waste of time.

But Mrs. Bear Lundquist hardly seemed to hear that they weren't going to be able to borrow Flop Skalrud's Model T Ford, for all of a sudden her priorities had shifted.

"Who's in there with him?" was the question she asked Mr. Bear Lundquist, to which Mr. Bear Lundquist replied that he had no idea.

"Well, what did he look like when he answered the door? And how long did it take him to answer the door?" Mrs. Bear Lundquist demanded.

Mr. Bear Lundquist began to suspect that Mrs. Bear Lundquist knew something he didn't know. He recalled that in spite of Flop Skalrud's house consisting of only a big kitchen-living room and a small bedroom, and that it was too early in the evening for someone to be in bed unless they were sick or there for purposes other than sleeping, that it had taken over five minutes for Flop Skalrud to answer the door. He then recalled Flop Skalrud's appearance when he had answered the door— all red-faced, out of breath and more-or-less glassy-eyed, and he recalled the fact that in spite of it being February with the makings of a genuine freeze-the-balls-off-a-brass-monkey Alberta blizzard in the wind, that Flop Skalrud, usually a hospitable sort, had not invited him in, but had stood all red-faced, out of breath and more-or-less glassy-eyed, and had done very little other than breathe heavily, stomp his large bare feet on the cold linoleum a few times, clutch his cream-colored GWG underwear at the waist with one hand, and impart the information about the Model T Ford being up on blocks until after the flood.

"He appeared all right to me," Mr. Bear Lundquist replied.

Wishing she had been the one to go to the infamous Flop Skalrud's door, or that she had at least gotten out of the sleigh and examined the one-horse cutter for clues to the identity of the driver, Mrs. Bear Lundquist fired an endless barrage of

questions at Mr. Bear Lundquist as they continued the trip in
their horse-drawn sleigh, all the way to Bjornsen's Corner, even
though it looked like a good old freeze-the-balls-off-a-brass-
monkey Alberta blizzard might be coming up. Mrs. Bear Lundquist insisted she had to be the first to hear about the wedding,
even if it meant risking death in a blizzard, and she was furious
with curiosity about who had been in Flop Skalrud's house, and
she dearly wished that Mr. Bear Lundquist, nice man that he
was, was just a little bit observant when he went to make a
social call.

Along with the Lundquists, the widow, Mrs. Beatrice Ann
Stevenson, was waiting in a horse-drawn sleigh at Bjornsen's
Corner, when the Rasmussens emerged from the westbound
Western Trailways bus. The widow, Mrs. Beatrice Ann Steven-
son, also was there because she felt she had to be the first to
hear about the wedding.

The Rasmussens, just to be on the safe side, had arranged
for Mr. Torval Imsdahl to meet them, and Mrs. Torval Imsdahl
had accompanied Mr. Torval Imsdahl in their horse and sleigh,
because she too felt she had to be the first to hear about the
wedding.

Since there were three vehicles, and only two Rasmussens, a
certain problem arose. Anker Rasmussen, who was not a volu-
ble talker, was the least in demand. The reason he had asked
Torval Imsdahl to meet them was that Torval Imsdahl had the
thickest bearskin sleigh robes in the Six Towns area, and he
was also known to heat rocks in the oven and place them on
the floor of the sleigh so as to keep the feet warm on a long
drive, plus, he probably had at least one bottle of good old
Heathen's Rapture, or bring-on-blindness, logging-boot-to-the-
side-of-the-head homebrew, stashed somewhere in those bearskin robes.

Anker Rasmussen, to no one's surprise, decided to ride with

Torval Imsdahl. That left the Lundquists and the widow, Mrs. Beatrice Ann Stevenson, to fight over Irma Rasmussen. Mrs. Bear Lundquist, and the widow, Mrs. Beatrice Ann Stevenson, were both out of their sleighs and waiting at the side of the road when Irma Rasmussen stepped down off the westbound Western Trailways bus, and both women had been outdoors so long, and were so full of questions, they hardly noticed there was a bitter north wind blowing little pinpricks of snow into their faces, and a genuine freeze-the-balls-off-a-brass-monkey, Alberta blizzard was coming up.

Mrs. Irma Rasmussen, having just stepped out of the fairly warm westbound Western Trailways bus, was quick to notice the little pinpricks of snow being slammed into her face by the bitter north wind, and she had been living in rural Alberta long enough to recognize a good old freeze-the-balls-off-a-brass-monkey blizzard when she saw, felt, and smelled one.

Mrs. Irma Rasmussen allowed rather quickly, before she answered a single question, other than saying that the wedding had been heavenly, as to how she thought she would be warmer riding between Mr. and Mrs. Bear Lundquist, than traveling with the unaccompanied widow, Mrs. Beatrice Ann Stevenson. Then just to smooth things over as best she could, because she knew the widow, Mrs. Beatrice Ann Stevenson, was not going to be ecstatic about her decision, she pointed out how the Lundquists didn't have as far to drive home after delivering her, as did the widow, Mrs. Beatrice Ann Stevenson.

Mrs. Irma Rasmussen climbed up into the Lundquists' sleigh, and settled herself between Bear Lundquist, who was sixty-two years old and arthritic, and Mrs. Bear Lundquist who, though she wasn't arthritic, moved like she was, and they headed off to the north, driving directly into the blizzard. Mrs. Bear Lundquist thought of compensating the widow, Mrs. Beatrice Ann Stevenson, with the news about the Lute Magnussens' one-horse cutter being parked in Flop Skalrud's farmyard, for the widow was an invaluable ally and a bad enemy, but the news was just so wonderful that she couldn't bring herself to do it.

The widow, Mrs. Beatrice Ann Stevenson, feeling genuinely slighted, even snubbed, which everyone knew was worse than slighted, blamed the fact that she found herself going home alone, unaccompanied, unfulfilled, and with no questions about the wedding answered (other than to hear that the wedding was heavenly, something she knew without asking) at least partially on her being a widow, and she considered more seriously than ever before, on her drive west, where the good old freeze-the-balls-off-a-brass-monkey Alberta blizzard blew pinpricks of snow into the right side of her face, whether or not she should marry Earl J. Rasmussen, who lived alone in the hills with about six hundred sheep, and had made it plain on more than one occasion that he was hers for the taking.

# Chapter Eight

At the meeting in the kitchen of our farmhouse at the end of Nine Pin Road, Mrs. Edytha Rasmussen Bozniak busily set out the rules and regulations she felt were necessary to govern all aspects of the Little Box Social. She proposed that the women of the community who had daughters should pack a box lunch for each and every one between, say, five and sixteen years of age, the daughters themselves to decorate the box. The boxes would be put up for auction, where the boys between five and sixteen would bid for the honor of eating lunch with the girl of their choice. The box lunches would be auctioned off by Sven Bjornsen, of the Bjornsen Bros. Swinging Cowboy Musicmakers, or, if for any reason he wasn't available, by Torval Imsdahl's brother, Ture Imsdahl, who didn't have any known auctioneering experience, but had won a hog-calling contest at the Venusberg Pioneer Days and Rodeo in the summer of 1941.

There was no noticeable dissent regarding the rules and

regulations, as proposed by Mrs. Edytha Rasmussen Bozniak, though the widow, Mrs. Beatrice Ann Stevenson, said the mothers should make sure the daughters did actually do the box-decorating themselves, for there was nothing as sad as one or two boxes decorated by children mixed in with a whole bunch decorated by mothers. Everyone present adamantly agreed with that sentiment, though those with daughters all knew in their hearts that they would either decorate their daughter's box lunch themselves, or redecorate it properly after the daughter had made her best effort.

Someone then counted up the number of boys between the ages of five and sixteen, and the number of girls between five and sixteen, and discovered that there were several more boys than girls. There were any number of suggestions to remedy that situation, some downright foolish, before it was agreed that the mothers of the community would pack an extra box of sandwiches, which could be dipped into as required, if more than one boy was eating lunch with a girl.

The bidding structures suggested by Mrs. Edytha Rasmussen Bozniak was that the opening bid be five cents, and increase by one-cent increments, to a maximum of twenty cents, thus, if three boys wanted to each bid twenty cents, all three would each lunch with the girl of their choice, all three filling their stomach with sandwiches from the community sandwich box, once the original box lunch had been disposed of. Mrs. Torval Imsdahl argued that since children didn't have the appreciation of money that adults did, that the bidding should begin at one cent rather than five cents. After fifteen minutes of discussion, it was decided that the bidding would begin at one cent. Mrs. Edytha Rasmussen Bozniak stared carefully around the room after it was decided that the bidding would start at one cent, rather than five, as she had suggested; she briefly considered being insulted, but then decided that she had been neither slighted nor snubbed, which everyone knew was worse than being slighted.

"I just hope there aren't nine or ten boys who want to eat lunch with Velvet," Mrs. Edytha Rasmussen Bozniak said, her nose slightly raised in the air as she said it. "That would surely throw the whole thing out of whack."

"I don't think you have to worry," my mama said, through gritted teeth.

That was as close to saying something genuinely cruel, to someone in the same room, as Mama ever came. But Mrs. Edytha Rasmussen Bozniak allowed as she *did* have to worry, because Velvet was so pretty, and so popular, and she bet that Mama's own little man, Jamie O'Day, would be first in line to spend his twenty cents to buy Velvet's box lunch and the privilege of her company. Fortunately, someone changed the subject, or Mama might have said something genuinely cruel.


In spite of four-foot snowdrifts, and a temperature that hovered around thirty below zero, Mrs. Bear Lundquist toured most of the Six Towns area the day after she and Mr. Bear Lundquist drove Mrs. Irma Rasmussen home from the bus stop at Bjornsen's Corner. In the winter, when the trees were bare, Daddy could see more than a mile down Nine Pin Road from the kitchen window, so he got a good view of Mrs. Bear Lundquist's black horse, King Olav, lunging against the drifts, as he pulled Mrs. Bear Lundquist in a one-horse cutter, which had sleigh runners that curled up like an elf's toes at both front and back.

By the time she got to our house, Mrs. Bear Lundquist's face was the color of a red pheasant's feathers. She started to talk before the sleigh even got stopped in our front yard. Daddy, being the gentleman he was, unhitched her horse, King Olav, walked him to the barn and fed and watered him, while Mrs. Bear Lundquist drank Mama's coffee and talked non-stop.

The first thing Mrs. Bear Lundquist told Mama was that her first stop that morning, though she had had to bypass two closer farms and backtrack to them later, was to visit the widow, Mrs. Beatrice Ann Stevenson, and fill Mrs. Stevenson in on every juicy detail she had missed the night before. Mrs. Bear Lundquist also mentioned that she had found the widow, Mrs. Beatrice Ann Stevenson, still in her housecoat at 9:00 A.M., and that the widow appeared to have suffered a touch of frostbite to her right cheek, and possibly even to the tip of her nose.

The second thing Mrs. Bear Lundquist told Mama was that Mrs. Irma Rasmussen had confirmed that the young, orphaned genius, Arthur Bozniak, was indeed as tall, dark, and handsome as Edytha had reported. She then went on to describe the wedding.

Now, Mrs. Bear Lundquist, who was about sixty years old, and though she wasn't arthritic moved like she was, unlike the tall, dark, and handsome orphaned genius electrical engineering student, Arthur Bozniak, had never been accused of being a genius—Mrs. Bear Lundquist read the *Country Guide* every month, and each issue of the *Western Producer*, and had once had a poem published in the *Winnipeg Free Press and Prairie Farmer*, called "Death of a New Born Kitten," which began, Little kitty cat wherefore art thou?

Mrs. Bear Lundquist went on to confess to my mama, that she had published the poem under her maiden name, Bergquist, so as not to put on airs. What Mrs. Bear Lundquist possessed, whether she knew it or not, was a photographic memory, for she recounted word for word, exactly everything that Mrs. Irma Rasmussen had told her on the drive home in the good old freeze-the-balls-off-a-brass-monkey blizzard the night before. And Mrs. Irma Rasmussen had told her everything, she gloated, unlike Anker Rasmussen, whose sole comment to Mrs. Torval Imsdahl on *their* drive home was, "It was all right," no matter how many questions Mrs. Torval Imsdahl asked.

Mrs. Bear Lundquist described the big, brown-shingle house near the University of Alberta; she described the high school teacher and the university professor of some intellectual discipline, and she described their children. She also described the young orphaned genius electrical engineer, Arthur Bozniak— tall, dark, and handsome in a new blue suit, tasteful tie, and shined shoes; she described Edytha's wedding *ensemble*, and added that an *ensemble* was a polite way of saying the Rasmussens couldn't afford a wedding dress for their daughter, so she got married in a tailored suit, scoop-necked white blouse, and a little squashed-down hat with white feathers.

Thank goodness, Mrs. Bear Lundquist went on, that the young full scholarship orphaned genius electrical engineer groom had seen fit to buy Edytha an orchid corsage, an orchid corsage which all parties were happy to describe as ravishing.

Because the groom had to study hard in order to keep on being a genius, and maintain his full scholarship at the University of Alberta, there would be no honeymoon, but the bride and groom planned a visit to New Oslo just as soon as the orphaned genius, Arthur Bozniak, finished his final exams in electrical engineering, sometime in April.

But even before April, Edytha wrote home to say she was pregnant, so the visit to New Oslo had to be postponed because the young full scholarship orphaned genius, Arthur Bozniak, had to take a paying summer job as a surveyor for the Canadian National Railroad, one of only two summer jobs made available by the Canadian National Railway to University of Alberta engineering students that year, a job which Arthur Bozniak got because he scored 99.9% on his final exams in electrical engineering, the one problem he failed to solve being a trick question, thus assuring himself of being a genius for at least another semester.

The women of the Six Towns area gave Edytha Rasmussen Bozniak a baby shower in absentia, where they all got together at the home of Mrs. Ture Imsdahl, a round-faced woman with round eyes and round glasses, who walked with a cane, though she was never seen to limp, and the general consensus was that she carried the cane in order to whack her children, who were loud and numerous, and had, my mama said, all the manners of heathen baboons.

Velvet Rasmussen Bozniak, weighing in at seven pounds four ounces, was born at the University Hospital in Edmonton, on November fifteenth. In preparation for that great event, Mrs. Irma Rasmussen journeyed to Bjornsen's Corner, where she caught the eastbound Western Trailways bus to Edmonton, carrying two shopping bags full of bonnets, and booties, and bibs, and cute little sweaters. She returned a few days later, radiating baby pictures and a grandmother's pride. The baby pictures showed that Velvet Rasmussen Bozniak was, if not tall, at least dark like her father, and probably handsome, though everyone agreed privately that it was too soon to tell.

As soon as she got home, Mrs. Irma Rasmussen, beating the onset of winter by about twenty-four hours, toured the district expressing her daughter's appreciation to the women of the Six Towns area for the two shopping bags full of bonnets, and booties, and bibs, and cute little sweaters, and said that Velvet's daddy was pleased as punch and twice as proud, and that it was his idea to give the baby a second name, primarily because he had never had one. She went on to say that it was going to be difficult for the three of them to live on the young orphaned genius's full scholarship to the University of Alberta Faculty of Engineering, where he still had two years to go on his degree, though being a genius, he was already considering working toward a master's degree, and maybe even a doctorate, and wouldn't it be funny to talk about my son-in-law the doctor, though he wouldn't be able to doctor anything except electrical transformers, and turbines, and the like?

"That would have been that," my mama said, except for the fact that the widow, Mrs. Beatrice Ann Stevenson, still felt slighted, even snubbed, which everyone knew was worse than slighted, because Mrs. Irma Rasmussen hadn't ridden home with her during the good old freeze-the-balls-off-a-brass-monkey Alberta blizzard, and given her the firsthand details of the wedding.

Mama said that the widow, Mrs. Beatrice Ann Stevenson, was also annoyed because on her lonely, unaccompanied, unfulfilled drive home she had been so mad she hadn't covered her face properly against the bitter north wind and the pinpricks of snow, and had suffered frostbite to the tip of her nose, and in two spots on her right cheek, the one that bore the brunt of the wind.

It wasn't any fault of Mrs. Irma Rasmussen that she wasn't able to split herself in two the night she returned home from her daughter Edytha's wedding, and have one half of her ride between Mr. and Mrs. Bear Lundquist, and the other half of her ride with the widow, Mrs. Beatrice Ann Stevenson, so that both women got a firsthand account of the wedding. Unfortunately, Mrs. Irma Rasmussen had to make a choice, and she chose to ride in warmth and comfort with the Bear Lundquists, or at least as much warmth and comfort as was available on a February night in Alberta when a bitter north wind was blowing little pinpricks of snow into their faces, and a genuine freeze-the-balls-off-a-brass-monkey Alberta blizzard was starting up.

All the time the widow, Mrs. Beatrice Ann Stevenson, was driving home alone, unaccompanied, unfulfilled, and feeling slighted, even snubbed, which everyone knew was worse than slighted, she alternately considered (a) that she might after all marry Earl J. Rasmussen, who lived alone in the hills with about six hundred sheep and had made it plain on more than one occasion that he was hers for the taking, and (b) various ways of making Mrs. Irma Rasmussen, no kin to Earl J., suffer for snubbing her, which everyone knew was worse than slighting her. She imagined that if Earl J. Rasmussen had been perched beside her on the seat of her cutter, that Mrs. Irma Rasmussen would have ridden with them instead of the Bear Lundquists, and that she would have gotten the details of the wedding first. She also imagined herself and Earl J. Rasmussen reciting poetry to each other during the long winter months on Earl J. Rasmussen's farm in the hills, the six hundred sheep safely corralled nearby, she reciting the refined poetry of Emily Dickinson, and Earl J. Rasmussen reciting the less refined poetry of Ernest J. Thayer, and as she thought about that she tried to decide just how long and how many times she could stand to hear Earl J. Rasmussen recite "Casey at the Bat" at the top of his lungs, even if he was her husband, and her thoughts drifted back to ways of making Mrs. Irma Rasmussen suffer for snubbing her.

Unfortunately she couldn't think of anything she could do to Mrs. Irma Rasmussen; she considered starting the rumor that Edytha was pregnant before the wedding, but the wedding was the important thing, so what if she was pregnant, Lord knows being pregnant when you got married was no crime, if it had been four-fifths of the women in the Six Towns area would be in jail. But try as she might, the widow, Mrs. Beatrice Ann Stevenson, couldn't think of a real, solid, hard, tangible thing she could do to take revenge on Mrs. Irma Rasmussen for slighting her, even snubbing her, which everyone knew was worse than slighting.

However, the widow, Mrs. Beatrice Ann Stevenson, was not one to give up, "The Tortoise and the Hare" was one of her favorite stories, she said, whenever Mrs. Irma Rasmussen's name came up in a conversation, and one summer afternoon when she drove by in her horse and cart and stopped in for tea, she said to Mama, "If you wait on the bank of any river long enough the body of your enemy will float by." It was a Chinese proverb, she said ominously, though I don't think Mama knew exactly what she was driving at.

"I have a feeling that there is something rotten in Denmark," the widow, Mrs. Beatrice Ann Stevenson, said, whenever the name of Edytha Rasmussen Bozniak, or Little Velvet Bozniak, or the young, full scholarship orphaned genius Arthur Bozniak, came up. Something rotten in Denmark, my daddy said, was just an expression, and didn't mean a lot around the Six Towns area because there weren't any Danes living nearby. The Rasmussens were Norwegian, and Mrs. Beatrice Ann Stevenson was originally Swedish, though she later became Icelandic by marriage, her husband's family name having been altered by an incompetent immigration official until it was no longer the same as the famous poet Stephan G. Stephanson.

The widow, Mrs. Beatrice Ann Stevenson, was tenacious if nothing else, and having been snubbed, which everyone knew was worse than being slighted, made her more tenacious than ever. When, as a girl, she had attended Camrose Lutheran College, in Camrose, Alberta, she had had a friend name of Mary Gullickson, who married badly but put up a good front, and who, for several years, had lived in Edmonton. The widow, Mrs. Beatrice Ann Stevenson, wrote to Mary Gullickson, and to the other three people she knew who lived in Edmonton, asking each one if they, by any chance, had ever heard of the young orphaned genius full scholarship engineering student, Arthur

Bozniak, or his wife, Mrs. Edytha Rasmussen Bozniak, or their daughter, Velvet Rasmussen Bozniak.

Two of the other three people she knew in Edmonton didn't even bother to reply to her letter, and the third replied she couldn't be of any help, but Mary Gullickson, who had married badly but put up a good front, replied that she, though she didn't need the money, and just did it because she liked to keep busy, worked three days a week at the cafeteria at the University of Alberta, where she would make inquiries about the young orphaned genius full scholarship engineering student, Arthur Bozniak.

A few weeks later, Mary Gullickson, who had married badly but put up a good front, wrote to say all her inquiries had drawn a blank, and that she had gone so far as to drop by the office of the registrar at the University of Alberta, and that there was no one by the name of Arthur Bozniak registered in the Faculty of Engineering, or any other faculty for that matter, and there was certainly no one named Arthur Bozniak on a full scholarship to the University of Alberta.

That Christmas right after Velvet Bozniak's birth, everyone in the Six Towns area had received a Christmas card, postmarked Edmonton, and signed Arthur, Edytha, and Velvet, a card that had the return address printed on it neat as you please. Most everyone had sent a Christmas card in return, and none had been sent back by the post office. The widow, Mrs. Beatrice Ann Stevenson, packaged up an extra pair of pink baby booties she had knitted, and mailed them, not to Mrs. Edytha Rasmussen Bozniak, but to her friend Mary Gullickson, who had married badly but put up a good front. She said in the accompanying letter, that she would pay Mary Gullickson the unheard of sum of five dollars, if she personally delivered the baby booties to Mrs. Edytha Rasmussen Bozniak, being sure to call late of an evening, when she could get a gander at the young full scholarship orphaned genius, Arthur Bozniak.

Mary Gullickson, who had married badly but put up a good front, was apparently ravenous for the five dollars offered by the widow, Mrs. Beatrice Ann Stevenson, for her reply arrived in the next mail. She had taken the bus to the address given, which was indeed a big, brown-shingle house near the University of Alberta, where she was met at the door by a very pregnant girl, who informed her that the owners, the school teacher and the university professor of some intellectual discipline, were engaged in a social situation at another professor's house, playing contract bridge and sipping sherry. The pregnant girl had never heard of Mr. and Mrs. Arthur Bozniak, but, yes, the girl before the girl before her had been named Edytha, and yes, the school teacher and the university professor of some intellectual discipline did forward Edytha's mail to her.

The very pregnant girl volunteered that the high school teacher and the professor of some intellectual discipline were the nicest people in the world, and that they gave her a place to stay for free, and in return all she had to do was babysit their little angel daughters. And when her time came, she went on, she would go to the Fiona McKenna Home for Unwed Mothers, which was located in a big yellow house over in the Forest Heights area of the city, and, yes, the high school teacher and the university professor of some intellectual discipline were both on the board of directors of the Fiona McKenna Home for Unwed Mothers. And, yes, she assumed that is where Edytha had gone when her time had come, which would have been, let's see, last April. Yes, she was sure it was April, and not November, because she had come to the big, brown-shingle house near the University of Alberta, in November, and the girl before her was named Olga, and she had had twins the last week in October at the Fiona McKenna Home for Unwed Mothers.

The very pregnant girl also volunteered to look among the papers on the hall table, and sure enough, she found an address for Edytha Rasmussen, which she passed on to Mary Gullickson.

Mary Gullickson, who had married badly but put up a good front, went on to say that she checked the address for Edytha Rasmussen, which was a room above the Princess Theater on Whyte Avenue, and that someone named Mrs. E. Bozniak lived there, with her baby named Velvet, and that she worked next door at the Hub Cigar Store and News Stand, and was always quick to volunteer to customers at the newsstand, whether asked or not, that her husband, Arthur Bozniak, had been called to Ottawa, the capital of Canada, by his job in the Civil Service, and that he would be sending for her just as soon as he was settled there, though, Mary Gullickson added, no one in the city cared one way or the other about the whereabouts of Arthur Bozniak, or even if there was an Arthur Bozniak, which she was certain there was not.

Well, the widow, Mrs. Beatrice Ann Stevenson, said, people in the Six Towns area cared about the whereabouts of Arthur Bozniak, or if there was indeed an Arthur Bozniak.


The widow, Mrs. Beatrice Ann Stevenson, began talking even before her sleigh pulled to a stop in our front yard. It was a warm March day, the snow was wet, and the smells of an early spring, melting snow, and rising tree sap, were in the air.

We were, the widow, Mrs. Beatrice Ann Stevenson, said, the final stop on her tour. A tour that had taken her all the way from Sangudo, since she was a Sangudo Stevenson, to Fark, to Venusberg, to Magnolia, to New Oslo, to Doreen Beach, and back again, calling on every person who might be a friend, foe, or even a passing acquaintance of Mrs. Irma Rasmussen, her husband Anker Rasmussen, or her daughter Edytha Rasmussen Bozniak, and telling everyone, friends, foes, and passing acquaintances alike, the whole sordid story, as she had personally discovered it. She was, she said, looking forward to heading home, where she planned to gloat for a while, over a cup of rosehip tea.

While the widow, Mrs. Beatrice Ann Stevenson, was traveling from Sangudo to Fark to Doreen Beach and all intermediate points, and back again, informing everyone who might be a friend, foe, or even passing acquaintance of Mrs. Irma Rasmussen, of the truth of the situation as she had discovered it, not only did she recount every sordid detail of what folks came to call the *downfall* of Edytha Rasmussen Bozniak, but she recounted her reason for ferreting out the details in the first place, the fact that she had been slighted, even snubbed, which everyone knew was worse than being slighted, by Mrs. Irma Rasmussen herself.

"What presented itself," the widow, Mrs. Beatrice Ann Stevenson, said to my mama, "was a true dilemma, an impasse, a standstill, a deadlock, even a conundrum. For if that poor, innocent, very pregnant girl at the house of the high school teacher and university professor of some intellectual discipline, was telling the truth, and it certainly looked as if she was, then Velvet Bozniak was really born sometime in April and not in November, and the young orphaned genius full scholarship electrical engineering student, Arthur Bozniak, was a figment of the collective Rasmussen imagination, which meant that if you were able to count even passably on your fingers, that Edytha Rasmussen had been pregnant when she left the Six Towns area, which, so to speak, opened a whole new can of worms."

The widow, Mrs. Beatrice Ann Stevenson, went on to say that at each of her first seven or eight calls, once the shock of her initial announcement had worn off, why some serious speculating, musing, pondering, mulling, brooding, and cogitating then took place—because if Edytha Rasmussen had been pregnant when she left the Six Towns area, then it stood to reason that *someone* in the Six Towns area was the father of the child.

Since Edytha Rasmussen had always been a well-behaved girl, partially because she wasn't very attractive, and didn't get offers to go for a walk in the moonlight while the Bjornsen Bros. Swinging Cowboy Musicmakers were taking their intermission at box socials, whist drives, and ethnic weddings, the list of suspects was narrowed right down.

Someone suggested that it was one of two things, either the infamous Flop Skalrud had been sneaking around, or Anker Rasmussen was the dirtiest old man since Methuselah. It was quickly and unanimously agreed that Anker Rasmussen was not a dirty old man, and then someone pointed out that Flop Skalrud was fair-complected, with hair red as a woodpecker's, while from the baby photographs and from Mrs. Irma Rasmussen's personal accounts, little Velvet Bozniak was dark-haired, dark-eyed, and dark-complected, which, as Mrs. Beatrice Ann Stevenson put it so eloquently, opened *another* whole can of worms.

At our house at the end of Nine Pin Road, after the widow, Mrs. Beatrice Ann Stevenson, had recounted every sordid detail of the *downfall* of Mrs. Edytha Rasmussen Bozniak, and had named each and every person she had called upon, and each and every person she yet intended to call on, Mama said to her, "I reckon you relished stopping in to deliver the details to Irma Rasmussen in person."

"Good heavens, Olivia," the widow, Mrs. Beatrice Ann Stevenson, said to my mama, the indignation just flowing off her tongue, "Irma Rasmussen will certainly never hear a word about it from me."

And not only did Irma Rasmussen not hear a word about the *downfall* of her daughter, Edytha Rasmussen Bozniak, from the widow, Mrs. Beatrice Ann Stevenson, but she didn't hear it from my mama, or Mrs. Bear Lundquist, or Mrs. Torval Imsdahl, or anybody else in the Six Towns area. In fact, she never heard about it at all, and neither did Anker Rasmussen, or Mrs. Edytha Rasmussen Bozniak, or her daughter Velvet.

"Knowing the details ourselves is enough," Mrs. Beatrice Ann Stevenson added, her voice a whole lot less indignant, for she had had time to remember that Mama and Daddy had only lived at the end of Nine Pin Road for less than five years, so were still referred to as newcomers, and as such were to be excused if they didn't understand the true workings of the world in the Six Towns area.

After the widow, Mrs. Beatrice Ann Stevenson, had left, Mama said she understood her reasoning.

"If the Rasmussens found out that everyone knew their secrets and knew they'd been lying through their teeth, why they'd never be able to look anyone in the eye again, and they would almost certainly have to move away somewheres. But the way things are, they'll continue to look us in the eye, and lie through their teeth while they're doing it, and we'll keep on looking them in the eye and pretending we believe them. Everyone will be happy; they'll think they're fooling us, and we'll know they're not fooling anyone one bit."

"I'd think the satisfaction would come from throwing information like that back into the face of the person telling the lies," said my daddy, who had just come in from opening the gate in the barbed wire fence at the end of the lane, so the widow, Mrs. Beatrice Ann Stevenson, could drive on to her next call.

"John Martin Duffy O'Day," said my mama, "everyone knows that a lifetime of smirking behind your hand is a lot better than a few seconds of triumph." Mama sounded so sure of herself that Daddy eventually had to agree with her.

. . .

Late on the evening of the Farmers Union meeting at our house at the end of Nine Pin Road, while I was helping Mama clean up after everyone had gone home, the selfsame evening that Mrs. Edytha Rasmussen Bozniak had been so high and mighty about suggesting and planning the Little Box Social, I said to Mama, "When Mrs. Bozniak gets so high and mighty like she just did, why don't you at least let on that you know some damaging information about her?"

Mama looked at me the way Mrs. Beatrice Ann Stevenson must have looked at her a few years before, and said, "Good gravy, Jamie, folks are *allowed*," which pretty well summed up her philosophy of life.

Mrs. Beatrice Ann Stevenson's discovery, which essentially came about because she had been snubbed, which everyone knew was worse than being slighted, effected no lasting change in the lives of anyone who knew about it. It was just that now, after the discovery, whenever Mrs. Irma Rasmussen finished bringing anyone in the Six Towns area up to date on Edytha and Arthur and Violet, anyone who felt like it could turn away and smirk behind their hand.

Velvet grew up and walked and talked, and she and Edytha came home for Christmas one year. Unfortuntely, they said, Arthur was unable to make it, because he was preparing his master's thesis in electrical engineering. Everyone listened to what Edytha Rasmussen Bozniak had to say, smirked behind their hand, and was careful not to ask Velvet any questions about her father that she might not be able to answer. But they needn't have worried, for Velvet talked freely of her father, as if she really believed he existed, and maybe she did; certainly no one could ask her.

How long Mrs. Edytha Rasmussen Bozniak would have been able to keep up the pretense of having a loving husband who was a young orphaned genius, still on full scholarship, working now toward a doctorate in electrical engineering, is not known, but mercifully for her, World War Two began, and Canada was drawn into it, and Arthur Bozniak, young orphaned genius electrical engineer that he was, was one of the first to join the Royal Canadian Air Force and be shipped off to England, and one of the first Canadians killed in World War Two—his plane went down during a training mission over Scotland, and Arthur Bozniak, hero that he was, helped his co-pilot parachute to safety, but by doing so stayed with the plane too long to escape himself.

Everyone from the Six Towns area sent condolence cards to Mrs. Edytha Rasmussen Bozniak and little Velvet, and Rev. Ibsen, making a rare appearance at the Christ on the Cross Scandinavian Lutheran Church in New Oslo, delivered a eulogy that brought tears to the eyes of a congregation who knew to a person that Arthur Bozniak was a figment of the collective Rasmussen imagination, the reason being, that along with the Rasmussen's, the Ibsens had not been told of Mrs. Beatrice Ann Stevenson's discovery. A few weeks later, the widow, Mrs. Edytha Rasmussen Bozniak, and her daughter, Velvet Bozniak, moved back to Anker Rasmussen's farm not far from New Oslo.

"She is going to try to put her young life back together," Mrs. Irma Rasmussen said, "she'll just have to face the world alone now that World War Two has deprived her of her young orphaned genius electrical engineer husband." And she did just that.

# Chapter Nine

It was at the wedding of the Little American Soldier and the delicately constructed Lavonia Lakusta that I witnessed my first Presentation, a scene and event that I'll never forget. The Presentation is, as far as I know, a rite, or ritual, or ceremony, unique to Ukrainian weddings. The English-speaking people in the Six Towns area, my daddy said, like our family, the Mc-Clintocks, and Mrs. Beatrice Ann Stevenson (even though she had been born Swedish and had become Icelandic by marriage), were called that because English was our first language, and though we were a minority in the Six Towns area, somehow considered our rites, and rituals, and ceremonies, more sensible than anyone else's rites, and rituals, and ceremonies.

As a group, the English-speaking people in the Six Towns area collectively regarded the Presentation as barbaric, and when those English-speaking people got together with the Norwegian-speaking people, who were a majority in the Six

Towns area, they consolidated, amalgamated, and joined their opinions together, to collectively denounce the Presentation as being just one step above dancing half-naked around a campfire.

My daddy said that it seemed to him, and after he pointed it out it also seemed to me, that it would have done most of the English-speaking people, and a majority of the Norwegian-speaking people, a whole lot of good to dance half-naked around a campfire for an evening or two. My daddy's observation was that the English-speaking people he knew, and I think he probably included our family in with them, though he didn't say so in case including our family in with them upset Mama, were generally stuffy, secretive, and often wore too many clothes at all times of the year.

At an English-speaking wedding, my daddy said, the guests tended to arrive bearing very securely wrapped presents. My mama, for her part, was a genuine expert at producing some of the most securely wrapped presents in the history of the world. Mama would place the gift in a cardboard box, the usually breakable gift item swaddled in something called excelsior, which according to our encyclopedia was *fine curled shavings of wood forming a resilient mass, usually used to swaddle breakable items*, though it sure looked like shredded paper to me. The excelsior came in delectable colors, yellows, reds, blues, silvers, and at its best looked like finely cut moonlight.

Mama would first wrap the gift box in white tissue paper, tying the package firmly with white string (I usually got to hold my finger on the knot), then she would cover the white-wrapped package with a layer of brown paper, tying the package firmly with heavy brown string, or binder twine (I would get to hold my finger on the knot again).

The wedding present would then be given its final covering, with whatever colored wrapping paper Mama could recycle from the two shopping bags of used wrapping paper she kept on a top shelf in the closet of her and Daddy's bedroom, even though recycle wasn't a word that had been invented yet. One shopping bag held Christmas wrapping paper, while the other held all other kinds. You never used Christmas wrapping except for Christmas presents, Mama said, but, as circumstances required, it was all right to play mix-and-match with birthday, anniversary, wedding, shower, and baby-gift wrapping paper. Mama would cover the package with bright wrapping paper, tie it with white string again, then tie it with decorative ribbon. After I got to hold my finger on the knots of both the string and the ribbon, the wedding gift was ready to go to the bride's house, or on rare occasions to the wedding reception.

Deep inside the package, down where the gift and the excelsior came together, would be a business-card-sized piece of cardboard, often cut from the side of a breakfast cereal box, with our family name on it, not John, Olivia, and Jamie, but the more formal, Mr. & Mrs. J. M. D. O'Day & family. I was the *and family*.

The wedding presents would be displayed on a table, usually in a bedroom deep in the house, if the bride's family owned a house large enough to have a bedroom deep in the house. The guests would admire the wrappings on the parcels, but the packages were never opened in public, out of a fear, my daddy said, that the poorer friends and relatives would be embarrassed to see the contents of their meager presents displayed.

If the bride and groom were going on a honeymoon, the package opening was delayed until their return. While the bride and groom were away, the bride's family would move the wedding presents to the bride and groom's new home. Even if there was no honeymoon, the packages were moved to the new home where they were opened in private, the cards, which sometimes took a serious search to discover, were stacked carefully for later acknowledgment. The bride and groom would eventually hold an open house at their new residence, where the gifts would be displayed, but no one would ever mention which gifts came from whom, and all but the crassest of guests would refrain from asking.

The Norwegians, who were the majority in the Six Towns area, and most of whom spoke fair to passable English, mainly because English and Norwegian weren't that dissimilar, were more open about wedding-gift-giving, but not much. After a Norwegian wedding there was usually always a wedding dance at the nearest community hall, where the wedding presents, wrapped just as securely as presents for an English wedding, were carried and placed on a table on the stage, beside and behind the Bjornsen Bros. Swinging Cowboy Musicmakers. Everyone got to look at the colorfully wrapped gifts, but they were still carried home to be opened, though Norwegians weren't afraid to say, "That one is from Uncle Valgard," or "The washcloths are from Cousin Ingrid."

The Presentation took place on the second evening of the celebration, moved up from the third because many of the wedding guests planned to travel to Edmonton to see Truckbox Al McClintock play baseball against the likes of Bob Feller, Hal Newhouser, and Joe DiMaggio himself.

"At a Ukrainian wedding no one sleeps," Wasyl Lakusta hollered on more than one occasion, when he detected someone dozing at, or under a table, or simply lying down in the yard catching forty winks.

"Man the guns," shouted Wolfgang Badke, as he woke with a start to find Wasyl Lakusta pouring beer on his face. Wolfgang Badke had fought in World War One, though no one was sure which side he had fought on, and, as my daddy said, discretion being the better part of valor, no one asked.

At one point Wasyl Lakusta rang a cowbell in the ears of the Bjornsen Bros. Swinging Cowboy Musicmakers who were, to a man, sprawled about on the floor of the makeshift stage taking a cat nap.

"Do anything else you want," bellowed Wasyl Lakusta, "but nobody sleeps."

There was a good deal of *anything else you want* going on. At one point I stumbled on the best man, the boy from Mississippi who had an even deeper, deep-south southern drawl than the Little American Soldier; the best man was in the company of the youngest Chalupa girl, and they were occupying a stack of about fifteen gunny sacks behind the hen house, engaged in doing *anything else you want*, which certainly did not involve sleeping. The youngest Chalupa girl had been in the wedding party, and beneath her bridesmaid's dress, she wore about ten heavily starched, pale blue crinolines, which, no matter which way they were pushed, caused a certain amount of interference as she and the best man engaged in *anything else you want*.

"Y'all run along, Sonny," the best man, who had an even deeper, deep-south southern drawl than the Little American Soldier, said to me, when, momentarily distracted from his crinoline shoving, he cast a glance in my direction, where I had been standing for a good ten minutes, learning more about *anything else you want* than I had ever suspected there was to learn. The youngest Chalupa girl was certainly enthusiastic about what she and the best man were doing, loud and enthusiastic, not allowing the gunny sacks beneath her, or the crinolines all around her, to diminish her enjoyment of *anything else you want*, confirming once and for all, the rumor concerning her hot-bloodedness.

At one point, the youngest Chalupa girl shrieked to such an extent, that about a hundred sparrows lifted up out of a cottonwood tree at the corner of the hen house, and I made a note in the back of my mind that, if I ever developed an urge to engage in some *anything else you want* with a girl, something I seriously doubted would ever happen, I would choose a girl as loud and as enthusiastic as the youngest Chalupa.

Apparently, I wasn't the only one to stumble on the best man and the youngest Chalupa girl as they engaged in their crinoline shoving and *anything else you want*, in back of the hen house, because, that very afternoon, Heinrich Badke set out on horseback, leaving directly from the Lakustas by the lake, not even stopping at home to change out of his white shirt, and headed for Stony Plain, some forty miles away, where, when he got there, he tried to join the Canadian Army, demanding as he did so to be sent to Italy, where he said he wanted to fight the fascists, in order to heal his broken heart.

Heinrich Badke was truly disappointed to find that the war in Italy was over, and that Canadian soldiers were now coming home in droves, instead of being sent away overseas. Three days later, he returned to the Six Towns area, still heartbroken, and set to summer-fallowing a forty-acre field on his daddy's farm.

The youngest Chalupa girl and the best man, who had an even deeper, deep-south southern drawl than the Little American Soldier, got married late that fall, an event that was celebrated by another all-out, no-holds-barred Ukrainian wedding, and the two of them moved to Mississippi, where the groom eventually became part owner of a moving and cartage company.


The Presentation came along at an appropriate, and highly opportune time, my daddy said, because after two days of eating and drinking and doing *anything else you want*, some of the guests were getting downright testy, especially those who had been drinking more than they had been eating, and had, either for lack of opportunity or lack of motivation, engaged not at all in *anything else you want.*

In fact, at the very moment that Wasyl Lakusta advised the Bjornsen Bros. Swinging Cowboy Musicmakers to strike up the "Blueskirt Waltz," that particular song being a signal to people who regularly attended Ukrainian weddings, that the Presentation was about to begin, three of the Stefanichin boys who hailed from the vicinity of Wildwood, were fist-fighting the Dwerynchuk twins from over near Stanger; the Dwerynchuk twins were aided by Little Wasyl Podolanchuk, who, because he was a dwarf, probably the only Ukrainian dwarf in Alberta, was allowed to carry into the fight a three-foot piece of two-by-four, which, my daddy said, when properly applied could really clear the sinuses.

After everyone had danced to the "Blueskirt Waltz," including the best man, who had an even deeper, deep-south southern drawl than the Little American Soldier, and the youngest Chalupa girl, both of whom had returned from behind the hen house after their long session of crinoline shoving and *anything else you want*, everyone gathered around the stage, except for several of the more-or-less Doreen Beach Sigurdsons, who thought it an opportune time to see what was lying about loose that could be hauled off in their wagon or led away behind it under the cover of darkness.

Before the Presentation got underway, Grandfather Hewko, Mrs. Rose Lakusta's father, who was ninety years old if he was a day, was helped up onto the stage by Mr. and Mrs. Wasyl Lakusta, where he was bent, folded, and crimped, his extremities rearranged until he was more-or-less seated on a folding chair; he then played the dobro and sang a wedding song in Ukrainian, which a boy about my age, named Bronko Novashewsky, who was about as wide as he was tall, translated for me. The song, Bronko Novashewsky said, wished the bride and groom many children, no leaks in their thatched roof, plenty of wheat, and that their cattle shouldn't get hoof and mouth disease.

Then the Presentation began. At first it appeared no different than the receiving line at an English or Norwegian wedding; the bride and groom stood in front of the stage while all the guests formed a line and each in turn shook hands with the groom, and kissed the bride. Lavonia (*née:* Lakusta), wore, over the top half of her wedding gown, the groom's present to her, which was a red fox jacket, almost the same color as Lavonia's dark red hair, and the envy of every woman at the wedding.

The Little American Soldier, who until the day of the wedding was the only American soldier most of the folks in the Six Towns area had ever seen, was regarded with more than a little awe before the wedding; but after he presented his bride with a red fox jacket, he was regarded with more awe than ever, awe that came a lot closer to reverence than it probably should have, my daddy said.

One of many rumors concerning the Little American Soldier was that he had not only saved his pay all during the war, but had money in the bank in South Carolina before he went into the army. If he could give his bride a red fox jacket as a wedding present, why there was no telling what he might be able to give her when they got back to South Carolina after the war.

To the untrained eye, the first phase of the Presentation didn't appear to be much of a Presentation at all, it consisted mostly of hand shaking, hugging, and bride-kissing, with only a few people handing the bride and groom small packages, which were handed immediately to one of the bride's younger brothers who put them on a table on the stage. Only the English-speaking families, such as ourselves, and a few of the Norwegian families, presented large, securely wrapped parcels.

When the hundred or more wedding guests had all presented themselves to the bride and groom, except for several of the more-or-less Doreen Beach Sigurdsons, who were off casing the farm to see what they could steal now, or steal later, the Bjornsen Bros. Swinging Cowboy Musicmakers once again struck up "The Blueskirt Waltz," and the bride and groom whirled away to the music, the only couple dancing. They twirled slowly around in front of the stage, the bride first taking off her red fox jacket and entrusting it to one of her bridesmaids.

It was then that the true Presentation began, for as the bride and groom danced slowly about on the packed earth in front of the stage, they were approached, first by members of the family, then the remainder of the guests. Usually it was the men who stepped forward one by one, though a few women also took part in the ceremony. Each participant took a tiny silver straight pin from a box on the corner of the stage, and following the slowly twirling bride, caught up with her and pinned paper money to the back of the bride's dress and train.

My daddy had been right in saying that attending a Ukrainian wedding was an unusual and unique experience; I found the first few moments of the Presentation to be a truly magical time; the sun was just beginning to set, turning the western sky Hallowe'en orange, and the shadows of the dancing bride and groom and the shadows of the various people approaching them, stretched long across the farmyard.

It was a duty, my daddy had explained, for those within the Ukrainian community to give the newly married couple a decent start in life, and a decent start in life, whether you were Ukrainian, Norwegian, or English, required money. Consequently, an amazing number of five-, ten-, and twenty-dollar bills appeared from the pockets of very poor people, to be pinned on Lavonia's train, or the back of her dress.

The Presentation was, in many ways, a contest, for relatives

competed with each other to see who could make the largest
gift. In an odd way, the goings-on of the Presentation were the
exact opposite of the English-speaking weddings my family was
used to attending, weddings where securely packaged gifts, our
identities buried deep within them, were presented, the givers
confident that their identities would never be known to anyone
but the bride and groom. While at the Presentation, the bride
and groom never knew who donated how much to help them
start their new life, for the money was pinned to the back of
the bride's dress. The givers knew to the dollar who gave what,
and branches of a family would compete to give their young
people a better start than their neighbors.

As the Presentation went on, some of the English-speaking
people, and a few of the Norwegian people, drifted away, their
noses, if not raised in the air, at least slightly out of joint, but I
was very happy that Daddy had insisted we attend; the custom,
I found, was delightful, simple, direct, and filled with love.

# THE LITTLE
# BOX SOCIAL

# Chapter Ten

When Mama said, "We're hillbillies, though we won't always be that way, unlike some we know," which she said frequently, *unlike some we know*, was generally thought to refer to the Norman Sigurdsons, though my daddy said it could equally well apply to the Venusberg Stevensons, no kin to Mrs. Beatrice Ann Stevenson, who was a Sangudo Stevenson, or to the more-or-less Doreen Beach Sigurdsons, which made Mama wonder aloud if there was something about the name Sigurdson that produced white trash.

Most of the people in the Six Towns area, my mama said, were hardworking farmers who made a marginal living in good times, but were presently mired in poverty because of the Depression. On the other hand, the Norman Sigurdsons, the Venusberg Stevensons, and the more-or-less Doreen Beach Sigurdsons, were all lazy, shiftless, sorry, and ungrateful, and had been mired in poverty even when times were good, and would still be mired in poverty when the Depression ended and times improved.

The Norman Sigurdsons, mainly because of their close proximity, were sometimes called *our* Sigurdsons, to differentiate them from the more-or-less Doreen Beach Sigurdsons; *our* Sigurdsons were also known as the Red Sigurdsons, because both parents, and most of the children, the ones fathered by Mr. Norman Sigurdson at least, those being a majority, had red hair, while the more-or-less Doreen Beach Sigurdsons were known as the White Sigurdsons, because both parents and all the children had white-blond hair, and I suppose it was possible, though I never checked it out, that people who lived in the vicinity of Doreen Beach called the White Sigurdsons *their* Sigurdsons, just like we called the Red Sigurdsons *our* Sigurdsons.

The Red Sigurdsons were lazy and sorrowful, and shiftless, and ungrateful, and when their children came to school, which was seldom, they were sometimes barefoot even after the first snowfall, and often accompanied by lice. The Red Sigurdsons, Mama said, lay about and allowed the county to take care of them; in summer, they lived in a tent on the road allowance, and in the winter either squatted in a cabin so dilapidated it had been abandoned by Indians, or else they broke into a summer cottage down along Purgatory Lake, as soon as the rich folks from Edmonton who owned the cottage had gone back to the city for the winter. The Red Sigurdsons squatted in whatever cabin they chose, until the weather was warm enough for them to live in a tent again.

The White Sigurdsons, who were also called the more-or-less Doreen Beach Sigurdsons, were just as lazy, sorrowful, shiftless, and ungrateful as the Red Sigurdsons, or the Venusberg Stevensons, "Except that they at least have," my daddy said, "initiative enough to steal."

Among the many children of the Norman Sigurdsons, when

those children did come to school at the one-room schoolhouse located just off the abandoned railroad grade between Fark and Purgatory Lake, there was a daughter named Bertha Sigurdson, who was seven years old and in second grade that fall. Bertha, being a Red Sigurdson, and one of the ones everyone agreed had been fathered by Mr. Norman Sigurdson himself, had red-blond hair the color of tiger lilies, and always wore an ill-fitting blue-bell-blue dress, with a pattern of little red star-like flowers growing on it, a dress that had obviously been handed down from an older sister, who had had it handed to her by an even older sister, because it was too big for Bertha, and because it was too big, the hem tended to drag on the ground when she walked.

On the fall days when she came to school to her second grade studies, Bertha Sigurdson was still barefoot, though the brown grasses were silver with frost every morning; she didn't have a jacket or coat either, though her tiger lily-colored hair that came down over her shoulders looked, most days, as if it had been washed occasionally, and combed recently, unlike the other Red Sigurdsons, none of whom looked like either they or their hair had ever been washed.

Though I was a few grades ahead of her, the one-room Fark schoolhouse was so small that Bertha Sigurdson got to sit across the aisle from me, where she smiled shyly as she chewed on the ends of her tiger lily-colored hair, and held her pencil like it was a spear that had been stabbed downward through her clenched fist.

One of the reasons I liked Bertha Sigurdson was that no one else did. The other children had been told too many times that the Red Sigurdsons all probably had cooties, pink eye, ringworm, or possibly all three, so the other children tended not to play with the Sigurdsons at recess, at lunch, or after school. The Sigurdsons, when and if they came to school, tended to congregate together at recess, at lunch, or after school, an awkward, sullen, unsmiling group of shabbily dressed children, whose blue or green eyes looked as if they'd been painted on their faces. I noticed that sometimes the Sigurdsons had no lunch at all, while sometimes one of the older boys carried a collective lunch that consisted of a few slices of homemade bread spread with lard.

I felt protective toward Bertha Sigurdson, a feeling that, my having no brothers or sisters, was completely new to me, but it was a good feeling, like being warmed from the inside out. I remember one recess when all the children except the Sigurdsons were playing a game of some sort, a game where a partner of the opposite sex was needed. I waved aside Little Grendel Badke, and one of the Carlsen sisters, either Emma, or Ena, or Una, all of whom had decided to make me their partner, and instead I made my way across the schoolyard to the sullen circle of Sigurdsons, where I held out my hand to Bertha.

In spite of scowls from several of her green- or blue-eyed brothers and sisters, Bertha accepted my invitation; I wanted to enjoy what little time I had with Bertha Sigurdson, for she and her brothers and sisters didn't come to school very often, and later in the winter I wouldn't attend school for three months or more.

Our house at the end of Nine Pin Road was three and a half miles from the Fark schoolhouse, and once winter set in, and it got to be twenty or thirty below zero for months on end (I wonder if there is any difference between a vertical month and a horizontal month?), there was no way for me to get to school without freezing to death, and right after the snow melted there was a month or more when I couldn't get to school without drowning, for there was always a flood right after the snow melted. I stayed at home, in our house at the end of Nine Pin Road, and Mama ordered my lessons by mail, from Edmonton—correspondence courses, they were called—and what with Mama watching over me like a hawk, and making me copy every lesson out at least three times, before she allowed me to send it away in the mail, that type of studying was a lot harder on me than attending a real school.

After the sullen circle of Sigurdsons reluctantly parted and let me take Bertha away to play whatever game we were playing, all I remember is facing Bertha Sigurdson, joining hands, and swinging her around in a circle, her tiger lily-colored hair in a orange fan behind her, until we both collapsed on the dry September grass, laughing and happy. Afterwards, as we walked together across the school grounds, I fished in my pocket for the remnants of the package of cinnamon-red and lemon-yellow jelly beans my daddy had brought home from Fark General Store with the last order of groceries, and about one-third of which I had saved for just such an occasion as this. The cellophane package had split in my pocket, and the cinnamon-red and lemon-yellow jelly beans were loose, more than a little sticky, liberally coated with lint and a wide variety of grime and tarnish.

That particular day, the Sigurdsons had all arrived at school without lunches, so for every cinnamon-red and lemon-yellow jelly bean I ate I passed three to Bertha Sigurdson, but as I watched her chew them, her enjoyment was so acute, so needle-sharp, that it warmed me through and through to a point where, though I didn't know it at the time, I felt as close to her as I have ever felt to anyone in my entire life. I extended the final half-dozen cinnamon-red and lemon-yellow jelly beans to Bertha Sigurdson; the jelly beans clustered like little nuggets in my palm, each one sticky, feathered with lint, liberally coated with a wide variety of grime and tarnish. Bertha Sigurdson, like the hungry little animal she was, snatched those cinnamon-red and lemon-yellow jelly beans from my palm, and stuffed them all in her mouth at once, then, peering over her shoulder and seeing she was a safe distance from the sullen circle of Sigurdson brothers and sisters, and that the gesture had been unnecessary, smiled at me, her mouth closed, her lips stained by the bright candy. We held hands, our sticky fingers entwined, as we walked in the bright Indian summer sunshine, the remainder of the way to the schoolhouse door.


"The arrival of the box lunches at Fark Community Hall is a ceremony in itself," my daddy said, and he went on to say it was a ceremony I should witness in person at least once in my life. In order for me to witness that ceremony at least once in my life, Daddy arranged for one of the Skalrud boys, a Skalrud boy who was probably, though not necessarily, the infamous Flop Skalrud's nephew, to come by and do the evening farm chores, and when the Skalrud boy arrived about four o'clock, my daddy had our old roan horse, Ethan Allen, hitched to the buggy, and with me sitting up on the buggy seat between Mama and Daddy, we drove off at a brisk pace on the five-mile jaunt to Fark Community Hall.

As Daddy predicted, we were the first to arrive at Fark Community Hall; Daddy unhitched Ethan Allen, and tethered him to graze in the tall grass and red willows at the rear of Fark Community Hall. Since the adults were having just a community lunch that evening, which consisted of plates of sandwiches and cake put out on a long table in front of the stage, first come first served, and since there were no daughters in our family, we didn't have a box lunch to sneak into the hall. Mama just brought a platter full of sandwiches and cake, for the community lunch, the top shrouded by a damp tea towel.

We'd only been there for a few minutes, and Daddy had barely got Ethan Allen tethered properly, when the Einar Carlsens arrived, their vehicle being a wagon pulled by two black horses, one quite a bit larger than the other. With the Einar Carlsens were their four daughters, Emma, Ena, Una, and Gertrude, each girl with her hair in ringlets; the Carlsen sisters had been scrubbed until their faces were the same color as their pink dresses, and each girl carried a package, which obviously contained a box lunch. The box lunches of Emma, Ena, and Una were concealed by brown paper shopping bags, while Gertrude's—some said Gertrude was an afterthought Carlsen, conceived and birthed after the Einar Carlsens had run out of imagination, or at least names that began and ended with vowels—was concealed by a brown gunny sack that had at one time held Netted Gem potatoes.

The next vehicle to arrive was another horse-drawn cart, driven by Mrs. Edytha Rasmussen Bozniak, with her daughter Velvet perched right up on the seat beside her. I had suspected that Velvet Bozniak would be one to arrive early. I had run into her at the Venusberg General Store the week before, and she had smiled at me in that way she had, with her face wide open and her lips curled back from her teeth, like she knew at least two dozen important things about life that I didn't.

"I'm really looking forward to eating lunch with you at the Little Box Social this weekend," Velvet said, which was certainly an invitation, possibly a command, maybe even a threat.

"I only have ten cents to bid with," I lied, and since there was no Shirley Temple doll to dangle by one leg toward the firebox of the cookstove, I headed for the door as fast as I could, meaning I had to miss buying a package of cinnamon-red and lemon-yellow jelly beans with the five cents my daddy had given me to spend as I chose.

Unlike at Farmers Union meetings, or Fark Sewing Circle and Temperance Society meetings, where children, unless they were still breastfeeding, were left at home with relatives, or dropped off at a neighbor's, children of every size and persuasion were allowed and encouraged at the whist drives, box socials, and ethnic weddings. Early in the evening while the whist drive was in progress, the children played at the back of the hall or, if the weather was nice, outdoors. After lunch, whether it was a box social, or just a quick feed at a community table loaded with sandwiches and cake, about the time the Bjornsen Bros. Swinging Cowboy Musicmakers began to tune their instruments, parents began to spread blankets and coats along the back of the stage and the youngest children were put to bed.

The dancing carried on while crawling babies and toddling toddlers, and terrible two-year-olds, who were able to run like lightning but lacked the brainpower to move in a prudent and predictable manner, criss-crossed the dance floor. Children ran and toddled, faltered and wobbled, while all around them polkaing, schottisching, and Virginia-reeling couples thundered, but somehow the children all survived, and I don't remember even one being injured, let alone killed, although killed seemed a very good possibility. As the evening and dancing progressed the children, one by one, retired to the stage, where by the end of the night, wrapped in their bright blankets and quilts, they slept like a variegated border of flowers behind the band.

While the whist drive, preceding the Little Box Social, was in progress, I goofed around with my rabbit-snaring buddy, Floyd Wicker, and some other boys, and tried my best not to have anything to do with, or even glance in the direction of, Velvet Bozniak, who, instead of playing games with the other girls, cruised the perimeter of our circle, and did whatever she had to do to make herself conspicuous.

Once, while I was standing alone, staring out the back door of the Fark Community Hall at the tall grasses and red willows, Velvet floated up and tapped me on the shoulder.

"Do you really only have one dime to bid with?" she asked.

I wasn't used to lying, and I barely remembered that I had lied to her the week before at the Venusberg General Store. I couldn't decide if I really wanted to continue the lie. I paused too long before I said, almost but not quite singing, as I had heard my daddy often sing, "Oh it was whiskey that fed me in my younger days, now a dime on the shelf and the devil to pay."

Velvet Bozniak, taking my ambiguous answer as a Yes, dug in the tiny white clutchbag she carried. She pulled out a dime and slipped it into my hand.

"Now you can bid all the way," she said, and was gone before I could do anything but stare at the bright silver circle in my hand.

The other families from the Six Towns area had arrived, one by one, as darkness fell, and my daddy lit the coal-oil lamps that were bracketed to the walls of Fark Community Hall at about ten-foot intervals, high enough above the floor never to be disturbed by swirling dancers, or unplanned shoving matches that sometimes turned into fist fights, or even altercations, and occasionally became a genuine brouhaha.

The Lakustas by the lake arrived, the Dzubas, the Mc-Clintocks, the Badkes, and a dozen other families, each family guarding their box lunches like military secrets, the boxes disguised by brown paper wrapping, hidden in shopping bags or cardboard boxes, covered in blankets, or robes, encased in grain sacks, sugar or flour sacks, or sometimes just pieces of clothing.

Eventually, Sven Bjornsen of the Bjornsen Bros. Swinging Cowboy Musicmakers arrived, and set about unpacking the box lunches and arranging them in a display on a table on the stage, from which they would later be auctioned. Sven Bjornsen, my daddy said, had developed a discerning eye over the years for fraud. My daddy, and Earl J. Rasmussen, who lived alone in the hills with about six hundred sheep, had once spent all afternoon in our kitchen in the house at the end of Nine Pin Road, preparing and decorating a box lunch; Earl J. Rasmussen had scrambled eggs, while my daddy cut and buttered big slices of homemade bread. Between them, they had baked an apple pie, which was not a spectacular success; they didn't put in enough apples, and added way too much nutmeg, and Earl J. Rasmussen and Daddy both agreed that their pie crust had the consistency of sub-flooring, and they even considered taking out a patent on it for just that purpose.

While they were decorating the box lunch, they shared a bottle of Earl J. Rasmussen's dandelion wine, and enjoyed a few cups of coffee liberally laced with good old Heathen's Rapture, or bring-on-blindness, logging-boot-to-the-side-of-the-head homebrew, the result being that they had to more or less cram the last two slices of pie into the box, which was already full of sandwiches, and a little pie filling trickled down the side of the box and stained the green crepe paper they had worked so hard to attach to the sides of the box, with a paste made of flour and water.

Daddy and Earl J. Rasmussen carried the lunch off to Doreen Beach Community Hall, joking all the way that some poor sucker was going to get the surprise of his life when he purchased their box lunch and had to eat supper with them instead of his lady love. Daddy had borrowed one of Mama's dresses, one that, though ankle-length on Mama, barely came to Daddy's knees, and Mama had loaned another to Earl J. Rasmussen, because he was too chicken to ask the widow, Mrs. Beatrice Ann Stevenson, to loan him a dress, probably, my daddy said, because they were about the same size and shape, and Earl J. Rasmussen thought the dress would fit him too well.

While the box was being auctioned, Daddy and Earl J. Rasmussen planned to slip out the back door, change clothes in the dark, and be ready to sashay back into the hall and eat supper with whatever unlucky fellow bid highest on the box lunch they had created. They had hidden the box in a gunny sack outside the back door of Doreen Beach Community Hall, and sneaked it in when no one was looking. But when Sven Bjornsen, of the Bjornsen Bros. Swinging Cowboy Musicmakers, began to unpack the box lunches and place them on the tables from which they'd be auctioned, he stopped short when he saw the box lunch wrapped in badly stained green crepe paper, hefted it with one hand, sniffed it, stared at it a while longer, then said, "This one ain't legitimate. We'll just set it aside for a spell and see if it ain't."

# Chapter Eleven

While Daddy and I were watching the arrival of the box lunches at Fark Community Hall, sitting in the long grass and red willows a fair distance from the back door, pretending to have no interest in what was going on, I was surprised and very pleased to see, just after Little Grendel Badke had climbed the steps carrying her box lunch carefully hidden in a T. Eaton Department Store shopping bag, to see Bertha Sigurdson put in an appearance. She kind of sneaked up out of the slough grass and red willows, all by herself, and walked, more-or-less sideways, peeking all the time over her shoulder as if she was afraid she was being followed. Bertha's family, the Red Sigurdsons, weren't inclined to attend community events, unlike the more-or-less Doreen Beach Sigurdsons, who, my daddy said, at least had the initiative to steal; the more-or-less Doreen Beach Sigurdsons, he said, came to community events with the intention

of using their initiative, especially while everyone else was dancing, or eating, or whist-playing.

Bertha Sigurdson, as she made her way up out of the long
grasses and red willows, all the time walking sideways and peeking over her shoulder as if she was being followed, headed
toward the back door of Fark Community Hall, carrying a thin
brown paper sack, which, if it contained a box lunch at all,
contained the smallest and scrawniest box and lunch ever sub-
mitted to a box social in the Six Towns area.

Velvet Bozniak's dime was like something live in my pocket;
I envisioned it glowing red through the fabric of my pants,
letting everyone in the Six Towns area know that I had been
bought.

In truth, I had twenty-five cents to spend, not counting Velvet's dime, and as soon as I had watched Bertha Sigurdson
sneak in the back door of Fark Community Hall carrying her
small, thin, brown-bagged lunch, and, a few seconds later sneak
back out and disappear into the tall grass and red willow clumps,
I knew that I was going to do several things, and I'd just have
to wait and see which ones would make me and the people
involved happy, and which wouldn't.

Soon, Daddy and I had viewed the arrivals of all but the very
latecomers, watching from a distance, as they indulged in the
ritual of box-lunch-arrival at Fark Community Hall.

The ritual of box-lunch-arrival somehow reminded me of winter nights when Daddy and I would go owling in the cottonwood
forest to the west of our house on Nine Pin Road. On clear,
cold evenings, when the forest was made bright by a big, yellow
moon, and the Northern Lights ran all green and silver across
the sky, we would walk quietly through the forest, our boots
breaking the snow for the first time. We'd stop in the middle
of the forest, our moonshadows dark and dangerous on the

cotton-like snow, and Daddy would repeatedly make a *who-woo* sound deep in his throat, a sound that if we stood perfectly still, would attract owls, big, tufted barn owls with eyes like saucers, and smaller snowy owls with amber-ember eyes. The owls would glide in silent as shadows, and take a perch at the top of a poplar or cottonwood, sometimes there'd only be one, but usually two or three. We'd watch the owls, though they seldom seemed to be watching us. Daddy said owls actually couldn't see very well, and that they were listening for a repeat of the call that had attracted them in the first place.

When Daddy and I were owling, we'd head on home as soon as our noses and toes got too cold. That same kind of moment took place in the tall grasses and red willow clumps behind Fark Community Hall, there came a point where we both realized we had seen all we had come for, and Daddy wandered off to find Earl J. Rasmussen and see if he'd brought along a jug of dandelion wine, while I skittered off and made my way across the street, actually it was a road, Fark wasn't large enough to have a street, to the Fark General Store, where the owner, Slow Andy McMann, was perched on a stool behind the counter eating the profits, while his body drooped, sagged, deteriorated and slumped, which my daddy described as kind of like a house settling in the night, for Slow Andy McMann weighed at least four hundred pounds.

My daddy, and most everyone else who cared to discuss the matter of Slow Andy McMann, which was almost everybody from around the Six Towns area, said that Slow Andy McMann stayed on that stool for about twenty-three hours a day, his back propped against a wall of coffee cans, the cookies, candy, jams, and canned fruit within arm's reach, though, everyone said, he had to hire one of the Badke boys to come in once a day and rearrange the goodies, unpack new boxes, carry away the empty cans and wrappers.

Fark General Store was at least ten years ahead of its time, because as early as 1941, the year after Slow Andy McMann took up permanent residence on the stool behind the counter, Fark General Store became *self serve* in an era when the term *self serve* was unknown, and wouldn't be known for at least ten years, and wouldn't become commonplace for ten more.

Slow Andy McMann got his name, because when he first tried to run the Fark General Store the way every grocery store in the universe was run, by taking a grocery list from each customer and going about the store with a basket, filling the order from his shelves, which were all off-limits to customers, Andy McMann was so big, and slow, and forgetful, that it could take him up to an hour to fill a five-item order. Folks soon got tired of waiting for an hour for a five-item order, but didn't want to go to another of the stores in the Six Towns area, because if they stopped patronizing Slow Andy McMann, the store would fail, and they would have no choice but to go elsewhere.

Gradually, folks began to say to Slow Andy, as he accepted their list, and began the monumental task of slipping down off the stool and commencing the search for their groceries, "Andy, since there's so few items on my list, why don't you let me gather them up and bring them to the counter?"

And Slow Andy McMann, who, like Truckbox Al McClintock, was never called by his nickname to his face, would let loose another monumental sigh, for which he was famous, and settle back on the stool to eat some more of his meager profit, while his body drooped, sagged, deteriorated, and slumped like, as my daddy said, a house settling in the night.

In spite of there being quite a crowd across the road at Fark Community Hall, I was the only customer at Fark General Store, where Slow Andy McMann sat in the shadows of a single coal-oil lamp, the wick burning high on one corner, blackening the globe. I wasn't afraid of Slow Andy McMann, unlike some of my friends, including my rabbit-snaring buddy Floyd Wicker, who claimed there was some truth to the rumor that Slow Andy had murdered and eaten his parents. It was true that Slow Andy's parents had, a couple of summers before, died within a month of each other, and it was true that they were both tiny people who weighed about one hundred pounds each, and who, folks said, had created Slow Andy, by insisting that he eat everything in sight, *his* gargantuan size somehow making up for their lack of substance.

"What can I get for you, Jamie O'Day?" said Slow Andy, emitting a monumental sigh, his body, which looked like an awkward pile of full flour sacks, or as Daddy said, a stack of dressed-up inner tubes, drooping, sagging, deteriorating, and slumping right before my eyes.

"I only want a couple of things, Andy," I said, "if it's all right with you, I'll just gather them up myself."

Andy sighed, and drooped and slumped, and deteriorated, and sagged right before my eyes, but he also nodded. I walked behind the counter, where I picked out a Wildfire chocolate bar which cost five cents, and was constructed in the shape of a log, about six inches long and an inch or more deep. I moved to the back of the store, where the small produce section was located, and after handling every orange in the orange box, I chose a perfect, round, unblemished, Sunkist orange, the size of my daddy's clenched fist, for which I paid an additional five cents. I paid for my purchases, and carried them, in a brown paper sack, back across the road, Fark being too small to have a street, to Fark Community Hall.

When the whist drive was finally over, the prizes were awarded—Orland Nordquist, who owned the abattoir at Sangudo, and had married the oldest and least bulldog-faced Gordonjensen girl, donated five pounds of pork chops, which were won by the widow, Mrs. Beatrice Ann Stevenson, and her partner, Mrs. Torval Imsdahl; the two women opened up the package and divided up their pink pork chop spoils, right at the card table.

The booby prize for the evening, the prize awarded for finishing dead last, something that took a certain amount of skill and abandon to accomplish, for many of the whist players were old, with vision and hearing problems and language difficulties, went to my daddy and his partner, Earl J. Rassmussen, both of whom had been nipping steadily from a bottle of good old Heathen's Rapture, or bring-on-blindness, logging-boot-to-the-side-of-the-head homebrew. Their prizes, donated by the Fark Sewing Circle and Temperance Society and manufactured by the much younger wife of Rev. Ibsen, unsuccessful farmer, and former full-time pastor of the Christ on the Cross Scandinavian Lutheran Church of New Oslo, who, if she had a first name I never heard it, were two pieces of round green felt about the size of a glass-coaster, with the letter TUIT embroidered on one side of each.

The booby prize, the Rev. Ibsen, unsuccessful farmer and former full-time pastor of the Christ on the Cross Scandinavian Lutheran Church, explained to the assembled crowd, was particularly appropriate, because he had heard both Earl J. Rasmussen and Johnny O'Day say that there were many projects they intended to complete just as soon as they got *around to it*. Well, now he was presenting them each with a round TUIT. The assembled crowd roared. Somehow you had to be there to appreciate how funny it was.

Earl J. Rasmussen soon joined the widow, Mrs. Beatrice Ann Stevenson, and offered to trade his round TUIT for a pair of the center-cut pork chops. The widow, Mrs. Beatrice Ann Stevenson, allowed as how a bachelor, especially one who lived alone in the hills with six hundred sheep, wouldn't know how to properly cook a pork chop, especially a center-cut, but that she would be willing to consider the trade if Earl J. Rasmussen would appear at her door the next evening about supper time, when she would have center-cut pork chops for two, fried to a delicate brown, but soft and tender as a baby's cheek in the center, along with creamed cauliflower, potatoes au gratin, baked tomatoes stuffed with sage dressing, green bean salad with homemade mayonnaise, apple cobbler with whipped cream, and coffee made with a special blend of beans, just like was served to King Olav of Norway, the last time he visited Canada—just her usual Sunday evening fare, the widow assured Earl J. Rasmussen, she wasn't planning on going to any trouble at all.

While the whist drive was in progress, Sven Bjornsen, of the Bjornsen Bros. Swinging Cowboy Musicmakers, had uncovered and unwrapped each and every box lunch, placing the sacks, bags, boxes, and pieces of clothing, which had shielded the box lunches from curious eyes, in a pile on the floor near the back door, so folks could pick up their personal box-lunch-cover as they left for home. Sven Bjornsen then put the box lunches out on display, on two crickety-legged card tables, one green, one red, which sat in the middle of the stage. The largest and most ornately decorated box lunches sat at the front of the table, the less illustrious at the rear, while the downright unappealing were hidden from view almost entirely.

Now it was my turn to be part of the rituals concerned with box socials, just as, before an auction at an adult box social, all the men of the Six Towns area would parade around the tables of box lunches, admiring, occasionally poking and prodding, and trying to guess which lunch might be associated with which female person, so now the boys of the Six Towns area paraded around the two crickety-legged card tables, one green, one red, admiring the more spectacular creations, occasionally poking and prodding, and trying to guess which lunch might be associated with which female person.

My rabbit-snaring friend, Floyd Wicker, walked with me; we admired the more spectacular creations, occasionally poked and prodded, and tried to guess which lunch might be associated with which female person. Floyd, it turned out, had considerably more of a problem discerning which lunch might belong to the female person he was interested in, than I had in discerning which lunch I might be bidding on.

After only one circle of the table, I knew which lunch I was going to bid on, and I knew that my bid would likely be the only one; Floyd, on the other hand, wanted to eat lunch with Una Carlsen, but his problem was that Emma, Ena, and Una Carlsen had apparently produced identical box lunches, or at least there were three seemingly identical, triangular-shaped lunches, each one papered with a different pattern and color of Christmas wrapping paper.

"One of them's got to belong to Una Carlsen," Floyd said, "but which?"

"Ask them for a clue," I said.

Floyd looked at me, his eyes full of genuine terror.

"I can't," he said. "I just can't. I'd fight somebody, though. Anybody. Somebody big like Truckbox Al McClintock, or somebody both big and old, like Ture Imsdahl."


What my rabbit-snaring buddy, Floyd Wicker, said made me recall some of my mama's words. "Box socials," Mama said, as we were bumping over the corduroy road, being hauled toward Fark Community Hall in a cart pulled by our old roan horse, Ethan Allen, "cover every human social situation."

She was answering a question of mine, as to why the adults

couldn't be satisfied to have their box socials, but had to arrange for the children to endure one.

"Box socials are the perfect icebreakers," Mama went on. "They are . . ."

"War," my daddy said. "Box socials promote war. Box socials *are* war. The best military strategists could learn more than a little by studying what goes on at a box social. And, I suppose, at least, the boys need to know about war."

"Box socials teach social skills," Mama said, echoing Mrs. Edytha Rasmussen Bozniak.

"They do," my daddy agreed. "They teach cunning, treachery, cheating, dishonesty; they promote dissension, shoving matches, altercations, fist fights, bent cartilage of the proboscis, blood spots on a Sunday shirt, and on special occasions, a genuine brouhaha. All in all, not bad social skills for any young man to develop."

"That's not what I meant, and you know it," Mama said.

"I've known boys," my daddy said, "who walked ten miles cross-country, and when they finished the ten-mile walk, then had to sneak up to a girl's house in broad daylight, on a Saturday afternoon, crawling on their bellies through sting nettles and raspberry canes, like soldiers or spies behind enemy lines, dodging dogs and little brothers, irate fathers, and an assortment of farm animals, in order to peek in a kitchen window, and catch a glimpse of the box lunch a girl was preparing for that evening. And they endured all that just to get a jump on some other young fellow, who would later accomplish the same thing by paying one of the girl's younger brothers a whole dollar, in a time when a dollar was worth a small fortune, to describe in detail his sister's contribution to the box social.

"And in the event he failed to have a dollar, or even a quarter to bribe the younger brother, he might escort that selfsame younger brother to beyond shouting distance of any place in particular, and make it plain to that selfsame younger brother, that if he wanted to live long and die happy, and not suffer irreparable damage to his physical being, he would provide the information about the size, shape, and style of decoration of his sister's box lunch, for free.

"And I've seen one boy, who knows to the penny how much another has to spend, arrange to have that boy deceived as to which box lunch is which, then bid that boy up until he spends his last cent to buy the lunch of someone he has no interest in, while the one who set up the scheme buys the box lunch of his heart's desire for a fraction of his savings.

"I've seen boys eating the box lunch of their lady love, using two less teeth than they arrived with, the consolation being that the loser of the altercation, fist fight, or on occasion genuine brouhaha, looks worse than they do, and isn't eating lunch with this particular lady love.

"Oh, yes, Olivia," my daddy said, "box socials fill every human social need, mayhem being one of the most dominant social needs."

When the actual auction of the box lunches got under way, with Sven Bjornsen, of the Bjornsen Bros. Swinging Cowboy Musicmakers acting as auctioneer, things started to, as my daddy said, almost immediately go awry, far enough awry that even Mrs. Edytha Rasmussen Bozniak had to admit there were still a few bugs to be ironed out of the plan for the Little Box Social.

"We should have known," the widow, Mrs. Beatrice Ann Stevenson, said, "if having a Little Box Social was such a good idea, one of *us* would have thought of it years ago."

And Mrs. Bear Lundquist, Mrs. Torval Imsdahl, and Mrs. Gunhilda Gordonjensen McClintock were quick to agree with her. My mama agreed too, but she was sitting with Mrs. Irma

Rasmussen, so all she could do was say sweetly, "It appears there's been a thing or two Edytha didn't think of." She said it so sweetly that even Mrs. Irma Rasmussen, mother of Edytha, grandmother of Velvet, that she was, had to agree, at least in principle.

One of the first things to go awry, or amiss, or as Mama said, out of kilter, and show itself up as one of the things Mrs. Edytha Rasmussen Bozniak hadn't thought of, one of the bugs to be ironed out, was that some of the children bidding were five years old, and some of the box lunches they were bidding on belonged to sixteen-year-olds, and vice versa.

When adults held a box social, adults were adults, and often as not husbands bought their wives' box lunches, because the bidding was more or less a formality, the money going to help out someone in the community who was down on their luck, had been burned out, or lost livestock to disease, or were about to be foreclosed on by a bank in Edmonton.

A box social, my daddy said, was a reliable indicator of how happy marriages were. When a fellow stopped bidding on his wife's box lunch, which she always made sure he got a good peek at, either at home or on the drive to the box social, and bought a lunch with which he wasn't familiar, taking a chance that he might acquire a box lunch belonging to one of the un-attached girls in the community, a chance which opened him up to acquiring a box lunch that belonged to a widow ravenous for someone to replace her lost partner, or a box lunch that belonged to one of the fringe people, like Loretta Cake, who lived in an abandoned cabin near Doreen Beach, with about one hundred cats, had no visible means of support, and was considered unusual, eccentric, and even dangerous, Daddy would always remark, on the way home, as we skimmed over the snow, all bundled up in the cutter behind our old roan horse, Ethan Allen, that he guessed the honeymoon was over.

But whoever ended up buying the box lunch of one of the fringe people, like Loretta Cake, who lived in an abandoned cabin near Doreen Beach, with about one hundred cats, was usually always a good sport about it, except for the time Loretta Cake told Matthew McFarlane, a very shy Irish immigrant bachelor, who lived deep in the bush, and seldom spoke to anyone, especially a female, unless he had had several shots of good old Heathen's Rapture, or bring-on-blindness, logging-boot-to-the-side-of-the-head homebrew inside him, that what he thought was a partridge sandwich was really fried cat.

Children, the people of the Six Towns area, and especially Mrs. Edytha Rasmussen Bozniak, soon discovered, were not nearly as tolerant as adults, who weren't very tolerant themselves, and, to add to the situation, the majority of mothers in the Six Towns area had totally disregarded the dictum about allowing their daughters to prepare and decorate their own box lunches.

The first lunch up for auction was a mystery, and as Sven Bjornsen, of the Bjornsen Bros. Swinging Cowboy Musicmakers, held it up over his head, us boys stared at each other, and some of us exchanged whispers, but not one of us had any idea who it belonged to. The box Sven Bjornsen held over his head was not really decorated, but was merely housed in what had once been a five-pound chocolate box; on the box, emblazoned in colors brilliant as embroidery thread, a scene of tropical birds waded in robin's-egg-blue water.

Big Dmetro Wasylenchuk, and Truckbox Al McClintock's kid brother, Gordon Jensen McClintock, bid the chocolate box up to nine cents, at which point Big Dmetro Wasylenchuk bid ten cents, and looked at Gordon Jensen McClintock, who was only about seven years old, with a stare cold as a scythe blade, and the little McClintock dropped out of the bidding. Big Dmetro

Wasylenchuk paid his ten cents, collected the box, which he had hoped belonged to one of the Chalupa girls, and was astonished to see walking toward him, one of the Barkerhouse girls from out near Magnolia.

In that unaccountable way people have of identifying others, the person walking across Fark Community Hall toward Big Dmetro Wasylenchuk, was known to one and all as one of the Barkerhouse girls, even though she had been married for a year to a Kuchera boy from Stanger.

The Barkerhouse girl, Mama said, even though she was eighteen years old, was not smart enough to come in out of the rain, and the Kuchera boy she married, though he was six feet tall and had arms like telephone poles, was himself just barely smart enough to come in out of the rain, but not much smarter, or he wouldn't have married that Barkerhouse girl, who was pale, and wore her mouse-colored hair uncurled, and always wore a green-check mackinaw summer and winter.

The Barkerhouse girl, and the Kuchera boy, had been blessed with a baby about six months after their marriage, and it was that baby the Barkerhouse girl, dressed as always in her green-check mackinaw, carried across Fark Community Hall, and deposited in the ungainly arms of fifteen-year-old Dmetro Wasylenchuk.

"What the hell's this?" said Big Dmetro.

"She owns the lunch. You get to eat with her," said the Barkerhouse girl.

"This here's a baby," said Big Dmetro Wasylenchuk.

"She wanted me to enter for her," the Barkerhouse girl said. "She told me so," and she grinned in a way that was close to scary.

"She ain't nowhere near to five years old," said Big Dmetro.

"What's that got to do with anything?"

"Didn't you read the notice?" asked Big Dmetro.

The Barkerhouse girl, whose right eye was quite a bit bigger than her left, looked at Big Dmetro Wasylenchuk in a way that let him know she had never read anything in her life, wasn't able to read anything, and never would read anything, and had only heard of the Little Box Social second, or third, or fourth hand.

"I'll eat the food, but I ain't gonna eat with her," Big Dmetro said, pointing at the object wrapped in a grayish blanket, that was now propped in the crook of his arm.

The Barkerhouse girl, who, even though she wasn't smart enough to come in out of the rain, was persistent.

"Baby Gloria wants to eat lunch with you," she said. "Baby Gloria thinks you're just about the cutest thing on two wheels."

Then she picked up the gray blob that was Baby Gloria, and poked the topmost portion of the gray blob into the face of Big Dmetro Wasylenchuk, who had straw-colored hair, and even though he was only fifteen years old, was at least 6'2" with most of that 6'2" being muscle.

"Baby Gloria wants to give this big man a kissypoo," said the Barkerhouse girl.

Big Dmetro Wasylenchuk stared at the Barkerhouse girl, and the gray blob that was Baby Gloria, like they had just landed from another planet, as he tried to understand what was happening to him, but he was only fifteen years old, and English was his second language, and this was his first time to bid at a box social, so instead of understanding, his face sort of crumpled up and turned red, and to keep from swatting the gray blob that was Baby Gloria away from his face, and maybe swatting the Barkerhouse girl as well, Big Dmetro Wasylenchuk bolted for the back door, the five-pound chocolate box containing the lunch tucked securely under his arm like a football.

From there on the Little Box Social surpassed awry, and amiss, and went straight down hill.

. . .

My rabbit-snaring buddy, Floyd Wicker, paid ten cents for the
first triangular-shaped box lunch decorated with Christmas paper; the giggling girl who appeared to claim him was not Una
Carlsen, the Carlsen sister Floyd Wicker was interested in, but
Emma Carlsen, one of the three Carlsen sisters Floyd Wicker
wasn't interested in. Floyd Wicker was small for his age, slight-
built and skinny as his daddy, Bandy Wicker, who had brought
his family to Alberta from Odessa, Texas.

Floyd's daddy, Bandy Wicker, was a smiling, good-natured
little man, who, my daddy said, had more accidents and dis-
ablements visited on him than should be permissible for just
one man. Bandy Wicker was forever having a saddle horse fall
while he was on its back, or a wagon roll its steel-belted wheel
over his toe, or an ax find his foot instead of a piece of firewood,
or a car he was cranking would backfire and break his wrist.

Floyd, like me, was barely as tall as my dog, Benito Mussolini, who, if the light was right, looked as if he had a long bald
head, and though Floyd wasn't as accident-prone as his daddy,
events at the Little Box Social made it look as if he might be
just as unlucky.

Floyd paid as little attention as possible to Emma Carlsen
hanging on his arm, and when bidding began on the second
triangular box lunch decorated with Christmas paper, he, having some savings from trapping muskrats, and collecting the
bounty paid at the Government Sub-Agency at Sangudo for coy-
ote tails and crow and magpie legs, was able to bid again,
successfully, on the second triangular box lunch wrapped in
Christmas paper, this time having to go to sixteen cents to outbid one of the Lakustas by the lake, a boy with a ferret face
and crooked teeth.

"I mean, how long can the odds stay against me," Floyd

said, his accent as Odessa, Texas, as his daddy's, though he had lived all his life in Alberta.

But the odds remained against him, for the second triangular box lunch decorated with Christmas paper belonged to Ena Carlsen, another Carlsen daughter in whom Floyd Wicker wasn't interested. When the third triangular box immediately came up for auction, Floyd, paying as little attention as possible to the Carlsen daughters he wasn't interested in, one hanging on each arm, set about to bidding again, and this time he had to go all the way to seventeen cents, to outbid the same Lakusta by the lake, who in the meantime, in order to raise the bid, had begged, borrowed or stolen another penny.

To Floyd's dismay, the third triangular box lunch decorated with Christmas paper once again did not belong to Una Carlsen, the Carlsen daughter he was interested in, but to Gertrude, the afterthought Carlsen daughter, born after the Einar Carlsens had run out of imagination, or at least names that began and ended with vowels.

There stood my rabbit-snaring buddy Floyd Wicker, forty-three cents poorer, paying as little attention as possible to the three Carlsen sisters, who clung to various parts of his anatomy, and in possession of three triangular box lunches decorated with Christmas paper, none of which he was greatly interested in. Floyd Wicker now had only seven cents left to bid with, and had no idea in the world which of the remaining box lunches belonged to Una, the Carlsen daughter he was interested in, and who was interested in Floyd Wicker, and had accordingly packed a box lunch completely different in size, shape, and contents, from her three sisters, in order to make it easier for Floyd Wicker to be her partner, and eat lunch with her at the Little Box Social.

"Why didn't you ask me what my box lunch looked like?" Una Carlsen said, appearing at Floyd's side and trying to find a portion of his anatomy that one of her sisters hadn't attached herself to.

"I didn't think you'd tell me," said Floyd dumbly.

One of the Blankenship boys from Doreen Beach bought Una Carlsen's box lunch for fifteen cents, and though my rabbit-snaring buddy Floyd Wicker offered to trade him three Carlsen sisters and three triangle-shaped box lunches for one Carlsen sister and one box lunch, the Blankenship boy wouldn't make a deal.

# Chapter Twelve

Truckbox Al McClintock, was, at the time of the Little Box Social, already recognized as a pretty good country hardball player, a boy able to hit home runs frequently and play a passable right field for the New Oslo Blue Devils, but Truckbox Al was several months away from becoming a celebrity, the only one in the history of the Six Towns, his status as a celebrity coming about because, after hitting five home runs in five times at bat, four into and one clean across the Pembina River, he was invited by John "The Rajah of Renfrew" Ducey, to play baseball at Renfrew Park, down on the river flats in Edmonton, Alberta, against a team of Major Leaguers featuring the likes of Bob Feller, Hal Newhouser, and Joe DiMaggio himself.

The night of the Little Box Social, Truckbox Al McClintock had an eye for the beauty of, and a severe hankering to eat lunch with, the youngest Chalupa girl, who was rumored to be hot-blooded. Unfortunately, Truckbox Al McClintock's chief competition for the box lunch and affections of the youngest Chalupa girl was Heinrich Badke.

Heinrich Badke was one of the Adolph Badkes, who lived south of Fark, about half-way to Bjornsen's Corner and the Edmonton-Jasper Highway. Heinrich Badke's daddy, Adolph Badke, was a broad-backed man with a huge nose the color and texture of a red potato, a man with a truly guttural voice, who sounded, when he was speaking, as if he was engaged in constant throat-clearing. One had to be in Adolph Badke's presence for several minutes before the throat clearing could be translated into speech patterns. Adolph Badke's favorite expression was "Eeeya Christus," something that was not really a swear word, but punctuation. Just as some people worked "you know" into every sentence, Adolph Badke worked "Eeeya Christus" into every sentence.

The Badkes had emigrated from Germany, and since Canada was presently at war with Germany, some German families, even though they chose to keep a low profile, and especially our neighbor, Hopfstadt, who kept no profile at all, were regarded with suspicion, even distrust, which with little or no provocation, could turn directly to animosity, bypassing unfriendliness, malice, and even rancor.

Adolph Badke, in spite of being named Adolph, which was a favorite name in the Six Towns area for large, egg-sucking dogs, mean bulls, and unridable horses, was not affected in the least when it came to the suggestion that just because he was German he might be an enemy agent, or even a full-fledged enemy, or just plain downright disloyal. The widow, Mrs. Beatrice Ann Stevenson, said that Adolph Badke was pure as the driven snow. An endorsement from the widow, Mrs. Beatrice Ann Stevenson, my mama said, took a lot of pressure off everyone else in the Six Towns area.

This was the same widow, Mrs. Beatrice Ann Stevenson, who spread unseemly rumors about Hopfstadt, and another German family in the Six Towns area, so one had to assume that she had tried her level best, but had been unable to find anything to generate suspicion, or distrust, let alone animosity, malice, or rancor, when it came to Adolph Badke.

In spite of being German, Adolph Badke kept a high profile in the community, and was the kind of man, my daddy said, who would get up at four A.M. and walk five miles in a good old freeze-the-balls-off-a-brass-monkey Alberta blizzard, in order to do the farm chores of a sick neighbor: split the wood, stoke the stove, cook breakfast for the neighbor, and feed him if necessary, before walking five miles home in the good old freeze-the-balls-off-a-brass-monkey Alberta blizzard, in order to do his own farm chores.

Even Mrs. Sven Bjornsen, whose first name was Viola, and who believed that anyone who was not a Holy Roller was going straight to hell, said that the Lord would probably make an exception for Adolph Badke, because, even though he might be German, and Lutheran, and generally misguided, he had a kind and loving heart.

At whist drives, box socials, community dances, or ethnic weddings, my daddy, and Earl J. Rasmussen, who lived alone in the hills with about six hundred sheep, would share a bottle of dandelion wine, chokecherry wine, raisin wine, homemade beer, Heathen's Rapture, or good old bring-on-blindness, logging-boot-to-the-side-of-the-head homebrew, with Adolph Badke, who after a few shots would slap Daddy on the back, say, "Eeeya Christus," and wonder aloud how he came to miss Daddy in the Big War. In World War One, Adolph Badke had fought for the Kaiser, while Daddy, being from South Carolina, had fought for the United States, and he and Adolph Badke found, by comparing notes, that they'd been in some of the same battles during the war, and may indeed have, on more than one occasion, taken a pot shot in each other's direction.

Hopfstadt, as near as anyone could determine, had not been in the war; Hopfstadt was not at the Little Box Social, and he did not attend community dances, whist drives, or ethnic weddings, even ones he was invited to, though he probably hadn't been invited often. To many of the people in the Six Towns area, Hopfstadt was only a rumor; he lived in a converted granary on a farm so isolated the closest road was a mile away, and it made Nine Pin Road, which was little more than a trail, look like a highway. My daddy told me that Hopfstadt had taken over the farm of a mysterious family named Starr, who had, one summer, sort of melted back into the bush, the same way they had come out of it a few years earlier. My family probably knew Hopfstadt better than anyone, and we didn't know him at all, my daddy said. We had put Hopfstadt up for a week or two one winter, after his unpainted farm house, that had once belonged to the mysterious Starrs, had caught fire, and burned to ashes, in the middle of a bitterly cold January.

The last day Hopfstadt stayed with us was the the day that Hopfstadt's new stove was unloaded from the box of Curly McClintock's dump truck onto the front step of Fark General Store. On the trip to Fark, Daddy and I rode along in Hopfstadt's sleigh, where Daddy and Hopfstadt sat up on the seat at the front, and shared a small bottle of Earl J. Rasmussen's raisin wine, while I sat in the back of the sleighbox, with my dog Benito Mussolini, wrapped in horsehide robes in about a foot of green-smelling alfalfa hay.

At Fark General Store, Daddy and Hopfstadt wrestled the huge black stove into the sleighbox, and when we got back to Hopfstadt's farm they wrestled it out of the sleighbox and into the granary that Hopfstadt was going to use as his new home.

Daddy climbed up and, using a keyhole saw, cut a hole in the roof of the granary; he and Hopfstadt then shoved a length of stovepipe through the hole; they stuffed the stove with wood and fired it up; the inside of the granary smelled of burning metal, but the whole place, considering it must have been twenty below outside, quickly warmed up until we couldn't see our breath anymore. Hopfstadt was ready to live on his own again.

He had been a carpenter in the Old Country, just as my daddy had been a carpenter in the City of Edmonton. Being a carpenter didn't prepare you for being a farmer, my daddy said, so he sympathized with Hopfstadt, who, he said, would never have two dimes to rub together as long as he farmed that rocky, muskegy quarter section.

Hopfstadt had framed a couch, to replace his bed that had been burned up, padded it with potato sacks and stuffed it with green-smelling alfalfa hay. After the fire, my folks and several other neighbors donated kitchen utensils, and blankets, and now, in the room full of odors of burning metal and heating stovepipe, Hopfstadt pointed to a large, sand-colored German Shepherd dog, a dog that rumbled like an earthquake whenever someone other than Hopfstadt got what the dog considered too close to it. The dog had just rumbled at me, and I was standing with my back pressed against the inside of the granary door, which was held closed by a new silver latch. Hopfstadt hissed a few words at the dog, almost smiling, and though I didn't quite catch the words, the dog seemed to smile back. Eventually, I understood that Hopfstadt was joking with Daddy about the dog keeping him warm if the fire went out at night.

"This is three-dog weather," my daddy said, "you need either two more big dogs or a wife to keep you warm," but Hopfstadt only smiled, clearly not understanding.

Even during the time Hopfstadt stayed with us we barely saw him; he would be up and gone before dawn, a chunk of bread and a slab of cheese tucked in the pocket of his mackinaw, and he would return to our farm at the end of Nine Pin Road, long after dark. He would sit sideways at the end of our kitchen table and shovel food into his mouth with quick, efficient movements; he would thank my mother for the food, or he would at least hiss a few words very fast, smiling at the oilcloth table cover, words that we assumed were thanks. Hopfstadt was probably around forty years old, slightly built, with blond hair that bristled every which way, and eyes that were a very pale blue.

"He works like a demon, from dawn to dusk," Daddy said to me, "too bad his land is so stony and useless. He'll never make a go of it. There isn't much land in the Old Country, and folks, when they learn they can afford to buy one hundred and sixty acres in North America, for a reasonable price, jump at the chance; they don't realize you can starve on six hundred and forty acres over here, the same as you could on one or two acres in the Old Country."

Over a year later, Daddy decided that I was old enough to, at least during the summer months, walk the five miles to Fark General Store and post office and pick up our mail. We didn't get much mail, an occasional letter from daddy's sisters in South Dakota, or a card from my grandfather, Mama's daddy the mining engineer, who worked at a diamond mine in South Africa. But what we did get was the Saturday edition of a big city newspaper, the *Toronto Star Weekly*. I taught myself to read on the *Toronto Star Weekly*. Each week, there were many pages of colored comics, a photo section, five or six short stories, plus a complete novel, a novel that, at least in the winter months when farm work was slack, Daddy read aloud in the evening. I was willing to engage in a ten-mile walk, any time, when the reward was an edition of the *Toronto Star Weekly*, the fact that it was often three weeks old by the time it reached us, not mattering at all.

Daddy walked with me the first time, in order to show me the short cuts; it was easier to walk cross-country, following the banks of a nameless creek that flooded in the spring, grew green and slimy by summer, and dried right up entirely by fall. Daddy suggested we should give the creek a name, Dead Indian Creek, or Nine Pin Creek, after the road we lived on, or Creak Creek, just to confuse map makers.

"How about Jamie O'Day Creek?" I suggested, modestly.

Daddy said he didn't see why not, that it would be nice for me to have something named after me, even if we were the only people who knew about it.

Following the snake-wiggle that was Jamie O'Day Creek not only brought us out within sight of Fark General Store, but, on the way, took us close by Hopfstadt's farm. We collected Hopfstadt's mail from Slow Andy McMann at Fark General Store, one thin purple air-mail letter, addressed in almost unreadable script to Herr Eberhardt Hopfstadt, and delivered it on our way home.

I understood virtually nothing that Hopfstadt said during our brief visit, but on the way home Daddy said that the letter was from Hopfstadt's sweetheart in the Old Country, a sweetheart who had been all set to join him in Canada, when she had been trapped in Germany by the war. She was now trying to get to Switzerland, where it would be easier for her to emigrate to North America once the war was over.

I made the weekly jaunt all that summer and the next. I would collect our mail, and Hopfstadt's, from Slow Andy McMann, and deliver Hopfstadt's on my way home, sometimes seeing him, sometimes not. I always hoped he would be there, because of the dog. I hated the dog, that large, snarling, rumbling German Shepherd, tethered in front of the granary by a heavy chain. The dog, who looked as large as the Empire State Building, would bark and lunge whenever I approached. If Hopfstadt was there, he would quiet the dog by speaking softly to him and calling him by a strange, gutteral name, one that I was never able to catch.

The widow, Mrs. Beatrice Ann Stevenson, though she had only been told about Hopfstadt's dog, nicknamed it Der Fuehrer, a name that caught on with virtually everyone in the Six Towns area. She speculated that Hopfstadt was probably a German spy, writing down the number, make, model, and nationality of each aircraft that droned over the Six Towns area on the way to Edmonton—the Six Towns was beneath the flight route of planes coming in from Alaska and even Russia—and somehow reporting that information to the Germans, possibly by two-way radio, the widow, Mrs. Beatrice Ann Stevenson, theorized.

My daddy pointed out to the widow that Hopfstadt didn't even have a one-way radio, that he didn't subscribe to any magazines, and that the only mail he ever sent or received was from his bride-to-be. An unfortunate statement for Daddy to make, because the widow, Mrs. Beatrice Ann Stevenson, was quick to point out that the bride-to-be, if such a person existed, was probably a first cousin, or even closer relative to Heinrich Himmler, Joseph Goebbels, or even Der Fuehrer himself, and that the bride-to-be was almost certainly a staunch defender of the Third Reich, who was not planning on coming to North America to marry Hopfstadt, but was merely using him to obtain vital military information.

I loathed Der Fuehrer, and my worst fear, each time he loomed up large as the Empire State Building, was that he would break his chain and attack me. I was used to my dog, Benito Mussolini, who when the light was right, looked as if he had a long bald head. Benito Mussolini was a devout coward of a dog, who was bullied by cats and chickens, and was happiest when fawning on the ground in front of me or Daddy, hoping to be petted or fed, or both. Benito Mussolini sometimes accompanied me on my walk, but I was afraid for him, for he was a fainthearted dog, who would cower, tongue lolling, against my side when he heard a twig snap in the undergrowth, or when a raucous blue jay screeched overhead, and when we reached Hopfstadt's, would suddenly find serious rabbit tracks that led him in the direction of home, while he left me to creep into Hopfstadt's yard alone, to deliver the mail.

If Hopfstadt was not in the fields when I made my delivery, he would speak a few words that would silence Der Fuehrer, then hiss a few words at me that I seldom understood, though I intimated that the words were asking me to wait. Hopfstadt would then disappear inside the granary that was his home, and reappear with a small horehound candy; he would slip the amber circle into my hand, pat me on the head and whisper, "Iss gute boy," and sometimes a few other words that I didn't understand. I would then hurry off to catch up with my cowardly dog, Benito Mussolini, who would be peering around the corner of a clump of red willow a quarter mile down the trail.

Hopfstadt owned a tractor, a huge, steel-wheeled monster that usually sat in a shed-machine shop near the gate. One day, as I approached, I could hear the motor sputtering spasmodically, and I discovered Hopfstadt cranking the tractor; the motor caught just as I arrived. Daddy owned no tractor, or car, or anything with a motor; I must have been wide-eyed with curiosity.

"Rhide?" said Hopfstadt, taking hold of me under the arms and lifting me up onto the iron beast, which had once been painted boxcar red but was now mainly rust colored. The tractor backfired several times and somewhere outside the fence I could hear Benito Mussolini yap as if he had been shot.

Four times we circled the small plowed field behind Hopfstadt's granary-house, the harrows dragging behind the tractor; there was a brisk wind blowing, and by the time the fourth round was finished we were both choked with dust. On the last trip round the field, Hopfstadt let me hold the wheel while we lumbered down the straightaway, and he guided my hands, helping me to turn the huge wheel, as we left the field and parked the vehicle in the yard. After shutting off the tractor, we shared a dipper of water from Hopfstadt's well; then, following his example, I cupped my hands under the mouth of the pump and washed the dust from or at least rearranged the dust on my face with the clear, cold water. Those were some of the happiest moments of my life.

That summer, in the scrub pines north of the granary, near to where Starr's farmhouse had originally stood, there emerged a large, comfortable looking cabin, but even when it was far enough along to appear habitable, Hopfstadt continued to live in the granary, apparently saving the cabin for his bride when and if she managed to get out of Europe.

There followed a long period of time, one that must have stretched to nearly two months, when no mail arrived for Hopfstadt, though Slow Andy McMann once mentioned that on Hopfstadt's infrequent visits to Fark General Store, he still posted letters to his sweetheart. Then, one day, a dozen of Hopfstadt's letters to Germany and Switzerland were returned in a bundle, the name of Hopfstadt's sweetheart crossed out, and a few words in German printed in red ink written across the top of each letter.

When I approached the farm all was quiet; it was a sun-struck summer afternoon and the only sounds were bees buzzing lazily and a few birds twittering. As I left the stack of letters on the steps of the granary, Hopfstadt and Der Fuehrer were nowhere to be seen, then, allowing as how it had been a long time since my last visit, I walked around to check what progress had been made on Hopfstadt's cabin. The door was unlocked, in fact it had no lock; I pushed the door open and looked inside.

Never had I seen anything like it. The interior was in complete contrast to every home I'd visited in the Six Towns area—most kitchens, which were always the main room in the house, contained an overbearing black and chrome cookstove, a few shelves bracketed to wallpapered or calcimined walls; Torval Imsdahl made rough, but servicable cabinets, and a few kitchens boasted them, but Torval Imsdahl's cabinets were made of plain lumber and usually painted an apple-green or sky-blue. Hopfstadt's kitchen had a full set of cabinets that took up a whole wall; they were made of some exotic, golden wood, every inch handcarved in the most elaborate manner imaginable.

Tiptoeing across the kitchen, I peered into the living room, which was furnished with chairs, tables, cabinets, bookcases, each piece lovingly carved, stained and varnished, putting to shame even the few pieces of *city furniture* my family had managed to hang onto. I moved on to the bedroom, where I found a large, elaborate, four-poster bed, trees and a river carved on the headboard, and beside the bed a cradle with kitten faces carved on either end. The kittens appeared so real that I had to bend and touch them just to be sure.

A low, rumbling sound caused me to turn, and there in the doorway stood Der Fuehrer; he was about the size of the Empire State Building, his yellow eyes burning, saliva dripping off his fangs. I froze. Der Fuehrer growled again, growing a couple of stories higher as he did so. I looked around desperately in hopes of seeing Hopfstadt, wondering at the same time what it would be like to be chewed to death by a big, ugly dog like Der Fuehrer, and having been to a funeral earlier that summer, I pictured Mama crying over an open grave, as my coffin was lowered, and Daddy in his shiny city suit, his shoulders stooped, standing beside her, an arm around her waist.

I wished I knew the dog's real name so I could appeal to him in some way; I wondered how to say Rover, or Spot, or

Fido, in German. My tongue was clotted in my mouth and my feet were rooted to the floor as Der Fuehrer advanced on me, head thrust forward, fangs dripping, tongue lolling. In spite of my fantasizing it, Hopfstadt did not magically appear to save me; Der Fuehrer reached me all too soon, but to my surprise, instead of seizing me by an arm and flinging me about the cabin like a rag doll, he licked my paralyzed hand—the dog was gentle as his master.

A moment later, Hopfstadt did appear, the package of purplish air-mail letters clutched in his hand. He had obviously come from the fields, and I could see that his dusty cheeks were stained with tears; he looked at me in silence, then, realizing that I didn't entirely understand what was happening, he tousled my hair, as he had done on other occasions, whispered, "Iss gute boy," along with a considerable number of words in German that I didn't comprehend, though he repeated the words over and over, his voice so plaintive, so yearning, that, as he hugged me to him briefly, I found myself on the verge of crying, too.

Hopfstadt was strong and he smelled like work, and I wanted to share his sorrow; I knew that something terrible had happened, that somehow his whole life had been altered. I knew, too, that at that moment, side by side, we could have fended off the whole world. In that moment I loved him, but the words of comfort and courage did not come.

Hopfstadt repeated a phrase, over and over, in German, followed by what I assumed to be the equivalent words in English, though I had to hear the English several times in Hopfstadt's rapid, hissing voice, before I could make them out. As I slowly came to understand, I could feel my throat constrict, and I knew I was about to burst into tears. Hopfstadt took a deep breath, pushed me away gently, and slipped out the door of the cabin.

A moment later, as I walked by the granary, on my way to

the path and home, Hopfstadt appeared from inside the granary, clutching the remainder of the bag of horehound candies, which he handed to me in silence.

A hundred yards into the forest I was joined by my cowardly dog, Benito Mussolini. I cried all the way home, and when I got there I didn't tell Daddy or Mama, either about the letters, or what Hopfstadt had said to me; somehow his words were too personal even to share with my parents.

"A son like you," was what he had said to me, over and over, "a son like you . . ."

# Chapter Thirteen

One of the many problems arising at the Little Box Social was that Truckbox Al McClintock and the youngest Chalupa girl were under sixteen, while Heinrich Badke, who fancied himself in love with the youngest Chalupa girl, was over sixteen, so Heinrich Badke, even though he felt he had a lot more interest in the youngest Chalupa girl than Truckbox Al McClintock, and certainly had a lot more experience with the youngest Chalupa girl than Truckbox Al McClintock, and had reason to *know*, rather than merely speculate, about the youngest Chalupa girl being hot-blooded, was not allowed to bid on her box lunch.

Neither Heinrich Badke nor Truckbox Al McClintock had the initiative, foresight, or plain common sense, to have walked a few miles cross-country and sneaked a peek in the window of the Chalupa kitchen, in order to determine the exact size, shape, and coloring of the youngest Chalupa girl's contribution to the Little Box Social. Truckbox Al McClintock, taking after the Mc-

Clintock side of the family, wasn't inclined to think about much that didn't have to do with baseball, grease, oil, or truck parts, his interest in the youngest Chalupa girl being pure instinct. When he thought about the youngest Chalupa girl's box lunch, which he did in a hazy sort of way, fantasizing himself eating lunch with her, while afterwards, she would put her arms around his neck and kiss him full on the mouth, Truckbox Al simply assumed that he would recognize the youngest Chalupa girl's box lunch when he saw it. It would, he thought distractedly, be a hot-blooded box lunch, much like its owner.

Heinrich Badke, on the other hand, having reason to *know* that the youngest Chalupa girl was hot-blooded, fantasized also, when he thought about it at all, which he did in a considerably more graphic way than Truckbox Al McClintock, that after eating lunch with the youngest Chalupa girl the two of them would go for a walk in the moonlight and end up in a wagonbox well stocked with robes and green-smelling alfalfa hay, where they would engage in some serious rubbing together of their private and personal body parts.

Heinrich Badke also figured that he, too, would recognize the youngest Chalupa girl's box lunch because it would appear to be a hot-blooded box lunch. What Heinrich Badke did think somewhat clearly about was the way that he could eliminate the competition, the competition being Truckbox Al McClintock. In order to do that, he first had to make promises he never intended to keep to his twelve-year-old brother, in order to get the brother to do his box lunch buying for him.

Truckbox Al McClintock, who was slow, but not comatose, kept one eye on the twelve-year-old Badke brother, whose name was Helmut, because, he figured wrongly, Heinrich Badke probably knew which box lunch would lead to the arms of the youngest Chalupa girl. As the number of boxes on the table diminished, Truckbox Al, keeping watch out of the corner of

his eye on Helmut Badke, was pleased to see that, as Sven
Bjornsen, of the Bjornsen Bros. Swinging Cowboy Musicmakers,
moved closer to a small box wrapped in green paper, Helmut
Badke began fidgeting until he went through perturbed, and
distracted, directly to a state of genuine agitation.

When the small, green-wrapped box lunch went on the auction block, Helmut Badke immediately opened the bidding at
eighteen cents. Truckbox Al looked over his shoulder, and what
he saw, right there on the edge of the crowd, a lot closer to the
youngest Chalupa girl than he liked to see him, was Heinrich
Badke, looking every bit as if he, too, had passed through fidgeting, perturbed and distracted, directly to genuine agitation.

"Twenty cents," shouted Truckbox Al McClintock, loud
enough so that everyone in Fark Community Hall who wasn't
engaged in something downright carnal behind the blue curtain
at the back of the stage stopped to look at him.

Both Badke boys slapped their hands together in simultaneous gestures of disgust, as if they had been outfoxed.

"Sold," said Sven Bjornsen, of the Bjornsen Bros. Swinging
Cowboy Musicmakers.

But as Truckbox Al McClintock paid his twenty cents to Sven
Bjornsen, instead of the youngest Chalupa girl making her way
forward to claim the box lunch, and team up with Truckbox Al,
he was joined at the spot where the small green-wrapped box
lunch met the auction table, by one of the Oxendine girls from
near Sangudo. The Oxendine girl, whose first name may have
been Chloe, was an Oxendine girl who had a mole the size of
a cat's paw just to the right of her nose, and one eye that tended
to, at all times, look at the ceiling in the furthest corner of the
room.

When, a few minutes later, a white shoe box with a couple
of pink crepe paper bows, came up for auction, the youngest
Chalupa girl moved a little closer to Heinrich Badke, and slip-

ping one of her small pink hands into the back pocket of his jeans, she pinched, allowing Heinrich Badke to, all in one second, bypass fidgeting, perturbed, and distracted, while moving directly to a state of genuine agitation. In his state of genuine agitation, Heinrich Badke attracted the attention of his twelve-year-old brother, Helmut Badke, to whom he had made promises he did not intend to keep, by slapping him alongside the head, hard enough that if twelve-year-old Helmut Badke hadn't been kept on his feet by Earl J. Rasmussen, Heinrich Badke, due to his state of genuine agitation, could have been credited with an eight-count knockdown.

"Twenty cents!" shouted twelve-year-old Helmut Badke, as soon as his head cleared, and the youngest Chalupa girl, her small pink hand still in the back pocket of Heinrich Badke's jeans, pinched again, and since he had bypassed fidgeting, perturbed, and distracted, and was already in a state of genuine agitation, he allowed the agitation to increase to all-out pleasure, as he began salivating at the thought of tasting both the youngest Chalupa girl's box lunch, and the youngest Chalupa girl.

"Twenty cents!" shouted Truckbox Al McClintock, loud enough so that everyone in Fark Community Hall who wasn't engaged in something genuinely carnal behind the ragged blue curtain at the back of the stage was forced to pay attention. Between the time he had purchased the box lunch of the mole-faced, starey-eyed Oxendine girl, and all the while the pinching, and agitating, and slapping-alongside-the-head, had been going on, Truckbox Al McClintock had been making promises he never intended to keep, to his daddy, Curly McClintock, in fact promising to make one complete circuit of the Six Towns area with his daddy, in his daddy's dump truck, during which circuit Truckbox Al would personally lift up every full cream can and place it carefully in the truck; he also promised that when they got to Edmonton, he would personally unload each and every cream can at whatever dairy they were to be unloaded at, and he would load up the empty cream cans from the previous trip, and the groceries from the wholesale, and he also promised to unload those same items when they got back to the Six Towns area, all in return for the loan of twenty cents, with which he could buy the box lunch of the youngest Chalupa girl.

Curly McClintock punched my daddy on the arm, and said he reckoned boys nowadays seemed to know a lot more about girls than he did at that age, and he recalled that he had been twenty years old and married before he discovered what it was that homely girls tried hard at on their honeymoon. My daddy said for Curly to speak for himself about what he knew and when he knew it, but also said Curly should give the boy twenty cents to buy his sweetheart's box lunch, which Curly did, just in time for Truckbox Al to get in his bid.

"Sold!" said Sven Bjornsen, of the Bjornsen Bros. Swinging Cowboy Musicmakers, and both boys stepped forward to pay their money. Truckbox Al McClintock deposited two dimes in Sven Bjornsen's hand, while Helmut Badke deposited a quarter in Sven Bjornsen's hand, and when he got his nickel change, he accidentally-on-purpose sent it skittering across the stage onto the floor of Fark Community Hall, where it rolled to safety under one of the benches along the wall.

"Hey, Al, if you want to pick it up you can keep it," Helmut Badke said to Truckbox Al McClintock. And Truckbox Al, taking him up on the offer, scrambled down off the stage, lumbered across the hall, and dug around under the bench, where he retrieved the nickel. Unfortunately, by the time he had retrieved the nickel, there was no sign of Heinrich Badke, the youngest Chalupa girl, or the white shoe box with the two pink crepe paper bows on it. Truckbox Al McClintock, holding the nickel in his large hand, stared out the back door of Fark Community Hall into the blue-black of the night for several minutes, before returning to the side of the mole-faced, starey-eyed Ox-endine girl. He hoped there were at least two pieces of home-made pie in her box lunch.

There were about five or six box lunches left on the table, along with the sad little brown-bagged package that interested me, when Velvet Bozniak's lunch was auctioned. There was never a lot of doubt about who that particular box lunch belonged to; it was three-tiered, like a wedding cake, and on the front of the third tier was a Christmas-red, velvet bow identical to the ones Velvet Bozniak sported on either side of her head, in among her blue-black finger curls.

As Sven Bjornsen, of the Bjornsen Bros. Swinging Cowboy Musicmakers, hefted the box and prepared to start the bidding, I tried very hard not to look at Velvet Bozniak, but I failed, and when our eyes did meet—Velvet was standing, white-stockinged-ankles crossed, black patent leather shoes glistening like jewels in the lamplight, against the ragged blue curtain at the side of the stage—Velvet smiled and wriggled like a puppy about to be petted. Her shiny silver dime burned like a hot coal in my palm.

A couple of little boys, their shirt tails out, faces pink from roughhousing in the tall grass and red willow clumps behind Fark Community Hall, opened the bidding, one calling out "One cent," and the other raising the bid to two. The little boys couldn't have cared less about who the box belonged to; they were bidding for the largest lunch on the table. But even the largest lunch on the table couldn't entice anyone else into the bidding.

The little boys pushed and shoved each other between bids, and ran the total, penny by penny, toward twenty cents. At eighteen cents, I again looked helplessly at Velvet, who was still staring at me and smiling as sweetly as Velvet Bozniak could.

She was still expecting me to bid; she thought I was just letting the bid run up so I would pay the maximum for her lunch which she, without question, thought was surely worth the maximum.

One of the little boys bid twenty cents, and the other followed suit; Sven Bjornsen looked about and asked if anybody else wanted to make it a threesome. I remembered something Mama had said to me once, something about small gestures making people happy, and how I should make such small gestures whenever possible. I considered just how happy my bidding twenty cents would make Velvet Bozniak, which was really happy. But I couldn't bring myself to do it.

I thought of Velvet slipping the dime into my hand, and what she expected from me in return, and I suddenly knew why Mama and Daddy and most of the people in the Six Towns area would rather starve than accept Relief. And at that moment I reevaluated my opinion on the matter, and decided that I, too, would rather starve than accept Relief. Sven sold Velvet Bozniak's box lunch to the two little boys, one of whom was an Ostrander from New Oslo, while the other might have been a more-or-less Doreen Beach Sigurdson, or not.

Velvet Bozniak stared at me like I was covered with open sores.

The two little boys paid their two dimes each, then took a side of the lunch box apiece, and headed for a bench to spread out and consume their bounty.

"Is this yours, lady?" the one of them, who may have been a more-or-less Doreen Beach Sigurdson, said to Velvet Bozniak, as they walked by her, hefting their cargo.

As Velvet dejectedly followed the two little boys down off the stage, I made my way to her side. I couldn't think of a thing to say, but I held out the dime to her, between thumb and finger, as if it might burn me if I retained it.

Velvet Bozniak slapped at my hand, and the dime went rolling across the rough board floor of Fark Community Hall, where it lay under a bench against the wall for several minutes, until one of the more-or-less Doreen Beach Sigurdsons, who, as my daddy said, at least had the initiative to steal, picked it up, after looking carefully around several times, and stuffed it in his hip pocket.

The Dwerynchuk twins, who, my daddy said, shared enough sibling rivalry to supply the whole Six Towns area, each set their sights on a flat wooden box that had once held peaches; the box was only partially wrapped but had a large silver bow on the top middle of it.

When I asked what sibling rivalry was, my daddy said to be thankful I didn't have any brothers or sisters, and if I wanted a first-hand lesson just to watch the Dwerynchuk twins, who folks had given up trying to tell apart years ago. The Dwerynchuk twins, whose names people said, were Wasyl and Bodhan, the English equivalent of William and Robert, or Bill and Bob, were, as far as anyone could tell, completely interchangable; they were fifteen years old, blond and blue-eyed, with brushcut hair; they were of identical height, and both were solid and muscular, wearing jeans and white shirts, open at the neck, with the sleeves rolled to one turn beyond the elbow. They each had a missing tooth on the right side of their face; Wasyl had knocked out Bodhan's, and Bodhan had knocked out Wasyl's. They had each broken the small finger on their left hand by getting it tangled up in the potato cultivator, and each break had left the second joint of the finger bent crooked, so that each Dwerynchuk twin looked as though he was holding an invisible teacup in his left hand.

Neither Dwerynchuk twin had any idea who the wooden peach box with the silver bow belonged to, and neither cared a lot; it looked to them like it contained a plentiful supply of food, and the fact that one twin was interested in it was good enough for the other one.

"One cent," said Twin One.

"Two cents," said Twin Two.

"Three cents," said Twin One.

"Four cents, said Twin Two.

The bidding rolled right along until Twin Two, who, because Twin One wasn't imaginative enough to raise the bid more than one cent at a time, reached twenty cents. Twin Two stared at Twin One and said, "Buy your own lunch, you son-a-ma-bitch." Twin One raised his bid to twenty cents, and just as the last word was escaping his mouth, Twin Two slammed him across the ear with an open hand.

When Twin One got up off the floor of Fark Community Hall, he got up in the shape of a battering ram, his head doing the battering, and body doing the ramming, as he charged, with his head buried in Twin Two's belly, until Twin Two hit the log wall of Fark Community Hall. Sven Bjornsen, of the Bjornsen Bros. Swinging Cowboy Musicmakers, was left holding the wooden peach box with the silver bow, while the twins fought, and everyone in the hall gathered around to watch, and cheer, and clap in rhythm to the blows.

It was generally agreed that what we were witnessing was a genuine brouhaha, one that had immediately bypassed disagreement, shoving match, and altercation, to get to that state, though Bear Lundquist argued with Ture Imsdahl, that a genuine brouhaha needed at least three participants, and that a fight with only two participants could never be classed as more than an altercation, no matter the scope, carnage, or entertainment value.

Ture Imsdahl, who had been bear Lundquist's best friend for thirty years, said that if Bear Lundquist wasn't sixty-two years old and arthritic, he would show him what a two-person brouhaha was all about. Bear Lundquist countered that it was not Ture Imsdahl talking but a combination of raisin wine, dandelion wine, chokecherry wine, and Heathen's Rapture, or good old bring-on-blindness, logging-boot-to-the-side-of-the-head homebrew, that was speaking. Ture Imsdahl wanted to continue the argument, but he couldn't recall clearly what Bear Lundquist had just said, so he settled for sliding slowly off his bench and having a short nap on the floor of Fark Community Hall.

Twin One broke Twin Two's nose with a right-hand shot; Twin Two broke Twin One's nose with a left-hand shot. Both bled considerably, their white shirts developing interesting patterns as the fight progressed, and they splattered indiscriminately on spectators, the walls, and floor of Fark Community Hall.

After ten minutes or so, my daddy and Earl J. Rasmussen stepped in and declared the fight, or brouhaha, which was generally agreed to have bypassed disagreement, shoving match, and altercation, and moved directly to whatever it was at that moment, a draw. The Dwerynchuk twins, having exercised their democratic right to relieve their tensions and increase their appetites, by beating each other senseless, shook hands, paid their twenty cents each, and carried the wooden peach box with the silver bow to a far corner of the hall, where they would have another short, angry exchange, over who got to slice the blueberry pie, all the time completely ignoring Little Grendel Badke, who had made the sandwiches herself, while her mother had baked the blueberry pie and decorated the box.

There were only two other box lunches left on the table when Sven Bjornsen, of the Bjornsen Bros. Swinging Cowboy Musicmakers, held up the thin brown paper sack that was exactly the size of one sandwich, and on the outside of which was a small sprig of red excelsior, attached by a bent bobby pin.

I could see Bertha Sigurdson sitting on the far edge of the stage with her legs dangling, toying with the ragged blue curtain, sort of covering and uncovering herself with it.

Sven Bjornsen could think of nothing to say about the sad little package.

"Here we have . . ." Sven said, and faltered. Several people in the audience laughed.

"Ten cents," I shouted.

"We have a ten-cent bid," said Sven Bjornsen, relieved. "Do I hear fifteen?"

"Fifteen," I said.

More people laughed.

"You just raised your own bid, Jamie O'Day," said Sven Bjornsen.

"That's all right," I said. I stood awkwardly for some time, as Sven Bjornsen tried to extract a higher bid; everyone in the hall knew he wasn't going to get it, but he felt, as auctioneer, that each box lunch deserved approximately the same time and effort.

"Sold to Jamie O'Day, for fifteen cents," Sven finally said.

I paid for and collected the small package. I couldn't keep from looking to the far corner of the room where the Ostrander boy was tossing chicken bones at what may or may not have been a more-or-less Doreen Beach Sigurdson, while Velvet Bozniak sat nearby, delicately munching on a sandwich with its crusts trimmed off.

Lunch in hand, I made my way to Bertha Sigurdson, though she had made no move to join me.

"This is yours, isn't it?" I said.

She nodded shyly, still sitting on the edge of the stage, playing with the ragged blue curtain. We adjourned to a bench, as far away from Velvet Bozniak and her companions as possible.

When we were settled, Bertha stared at me because I made no move to open the brown bag I had purchased. Finally I handed it to her.

"I've eaten already," I said. "You go ahead."

Bertha tore open the brown bag which contained, not a sandwich, but a single slice of homemade bread spread with bacon fat; the fat having stained the bottom side of the brown paper bag, but not before she detached the little sprig of red excelsior, and slipped it into the single pocket in her skirt.

"That looked nice," I said, pointing to the pocket where the crinkly red excelsior had disappeared.

"I found it in the garbage behind the Venusberg General Store. It's the only pretty thing I've ever had." Then, "You're sure?" she said, pointing to the sandwich. I indicated I was sure. Bertha Sigurdson then began eating the sandwich, greedily, hardly stopping for breath, staring out of the corners of her eyes as she did so, alert, afraid that someone might snatch the bread from her.

I watched her, my heart quickening with affection. When she had finished I extracted the orange from my pocket and extended it to her.

"This was left over," I lied. She took it from me, and I believe her hand was trembling as she did so. She bit into it, swallowing quickly, peel and all; if there were any seeds she ate them also.

When the orange was gone, she wiped her hands on her skirt, and smiled at me.

I withdrew the Wildfire chocolate bar from my pocket and handed it to her. She did not attack it as ravenously as she had the orange. She unwrapped the purple, red, and yellow wrapper, took a large bite off the end of the log-like bar, then offered to share it with me. I lied again, by saying I wasn't hungry. She ate silently for a moment.

"It must be nice to be rich," Bertha said.

I stared at her, incredulous.

"You always get enough to eat." It was a statement, not a question.

I nodded. I had never been hungry. I had never even thought about being hungry.

"I bet you have your own bed, with blankets, not gunny sacks."

She licked the chocolate from her lips. She tipped up the wrapper of the Wildfire chocolate bar; cornering a few crumbs of chocolate, she picked them out one at a time, with the tip of her tongue. Her fingers were sticky from the warm chocolate; she reached out tentatively and touched the back of my hand with an index finger, touching me slowly, inquiringly, as if I wasn't quite real to her.

I had never felt so protective, so heated from the inside out; I wanted to run to Mama and Daddy and beg them to let me bring Bertha home with us, to our house at the end of Nine Pin Road, where it was warm, where we always had enough to eat, and where she'd have her own bed with blankets, and on cold winter nights, a smooth five-pound stone heated in the oven and slipped in the foot of the bed an hour before bedtime.

# Chapter Fourteen

Around the middle of November there was a terrible winter storm, or as Daddy always called it, a good old freeze-the-balls-off-a-brass-monkey Alberta blizzard, with drafts that buried all but the tops of Mama's caragana hedge, and turned the fields into scalloped tundra. The mercury on the thermometer that advertised Lifebuoy Soap, a soap that was red, the same color as a block of iodized cattle salt, stayed at about twenty below zero until January, and the only way my daddy could get to town, was to saddle up our old roan horse, Ethan Allen, and point him into the drifts.

Our house at the end of Nine Pin Road was three and a half miles from the Fark schoolhouse, so, like other winters, as soon as the weather got cold, and we got snowed in, I stayed home and I studied my lessons by correspondence, with Mama checking up to see I did my assignments, making me copy each lesson out at least three times before she'd let me mail it off to Edmonton, and saying she'd never seen anyone with as sloppy a handwriting, and that I'd better buy me a typewriter as soon as I could afford one, since nobody would ever in a hundred years be able to read anything I wrote by hand, and generally being twice as hard on me as Miss Chillibeck the teacher at Fark schoolhouse had been.

The weather warmed up in mid-March, but then everything flooded, and the only way Daddy could get to town was to saddle up Ethan Allen, and ride along the banks of what we now called Jamie O'Day Creek, pointing Ethan Allen into the current at the shallowest spots, which Daddy said was just this side of Fark, where Jamie O'Day Creek was about a mile wide, but only a couple of feet deep.

It was the middle of April before I attended school again. The one person I was looking forward to seeing at school, other than my rabbit-snaring buddy, Floyd Wicker, and the reason, even though the weather was warm, that I wore the hand-sewn, red vest Mama had made me for Christmas, was Bertha Sigurdson, with her hair the color of tiger lilies. I wasn't surprised that there were no Sigurdson children at school the day I returned, because the Sigurdson children only came to school occasionally, usually after somebody from the School Board Office in Sangudo stopped in at whatever cabin they were squatting in, and laid down the law to the whole Red Sigurdson tribe, parents and children alike.

But when I got to school, on a day when the first purple crocuses were pushing up out of the hillside in front of the schoolhouse, Floyd Wicker, my rabbit-snaring buddy, told me something that really surprised me, the entire Red Sigurdson tribe had moved away, just at the time the weather broke, but before everything flooded. Just up and gone in the night, Floyd Wicker said, no one knew where, no one cared where. They had been squatting in a one-room, slant-roofed cabin, on the

shores of Purgatory Lake, about three miles down the abandoned railroad grade in the direction of Magnolia. And then
Floyd Wicker told me the worst news of all, cushioning the blow
by, even though it wasn't even nine in the morning, giving me
a large raisin and walnut cookie from his lunch bag. Bertha
Sigurdson, Floyd said, had died during the winter, of the pneumonia, though, he pointed out quickly, wanting, as my rabbit-
snaring buddy, to give me some hope, that no one knew Bertha
Sigurdson's death to be the absolute truth, because no one had
actually seen the Red Sigurdsons leave the district, and, as a
family, they were known to be secretive with strangers, and
didn't have any friends.

The school year ended, and now, when Mama said, "We're
hillbillies, but we know we're hillbillies, and we won't always
be that way, unlike some we know," which she said frequently,
the *unlike some we know*, now referred only to the Venusberg
Stevensons, and the more-or-less Doreen Beach Sigurdsons.

On a Sunday afternoon in the middle of June, maybe even
the selfsame Sunday that Truckbox Al McClintock was busy
hitting five home runs, four into and one clean across the Pembina River, off a skinny Indian pitcher name of Eddy Grassfires,
who was near the end of his career, and whose only saving
grace was a passable pickoff move to first base, I packed two
pieces of fried chicken, and a couple of squares of shortbread,
in the waxed paper from a box of Kellogg's Corn Flakes, and
set out to walk the four miles or so, mainly cross-country to the
one-room, slant-roofed cabin that was the last place the Norman
Sigurdsons had lived.

I didn't tell Mama or Daddy where I was going, because they
wouldn't have let me. I knew what it was that I was looking for,
and I was scared to death that I'd find it.

The summer flowers were in bloom, rocky mountain colum-
bine, bluebells, violets, cowslips, and except for the strangling
sound of an occasional crow, or the burble of a meadowlark,
there was total silence as I walked, and the silence seemed to
grow deeper as I approached the cabin which sat back from
Purgatory Lake a good fifty yards, in a stand of scrub poplar.
The cabin had no glass in its window; the window had been
covered with potato sacks during the cold weather, but the sacks
had been ripped away, and now hung raggedly down over the
unchinked logs like an evil stain. A rusting Roger's Golden
Syrup pail lay near the door, which dangled by one twisted
hinge, a can of Aylmer's Tomato Soup, brimming with rain-
water, its dark green label intact, sat upright a few feet from
the door.

The inside of the cabin smelled moldy and scary, and cold;
the only furniture left was a rusting oil-barrel stove with a piece
of bluish stovepipe leading to the ceiling. A few pieces of flow-
ered wallpaper dangled from the back wall. Behind the cabin I
found an ash pile, half-burned cans, bottles, a section of broken
plate in the Blue Willow pattern, the kind of dishes everyone in
the Six Towns area owned, because they were given away in
boxes of soap flakes; fireweed and raspberry canes were already
pushing up through the ashes. The land dropped off sharply to
Purgatory Lake, which though it was close by couldn't be seen
because of the summer foliage; to the left was a muskeg where
blueberries and low-bush cranberries grew wild; the sinister
odor of groundfire filled the air.

Behind the ash pile was a makeshift shed, makeshift because
it was constructed by nailing slabs of young poplar trees to form
a five-sided structure with a brush roof. The shed had been
used to store firewood; the shed door had fallen off and was
propped at an angle, partially covering the entrance. I touched
the rough slabs of the door, trying to see into the darkness of

the shed, all the time thinking of what I'd heard from Floyd Wicker and the other boys at school.

"Bertha Sigurdson died in the winter," they said, "of the pneumonia."

"There's no place to bury a body in the winter," they said.

"The Sigurdsons laid out her body in the woodshed, on top of the cords of wood," they said, "and they had to prop the door closed with a heavy piece of firewood, to keep the animals away."

One of the Osbaldson boys, and Ture Magnussen, claimed they had skated down Purgatory Lake, then crept up the hill and had a look at Bertha's body, where it lay frozen in the woodshed. But the Osbaldson boy was a known liar, and Ture Magnussen was a coward, so I didn't necessarily believe them.

I could imagine Bertha's body, dressed in her long blue dress, with the little red flower-like objects on it, and I could imagine her lying there across the cords of split white poplar, like a large doll, a doll with a pale freckled face, and hair the color of tiger lilies. That picture of her haunted my dreams, and because of that picture, I hated to go alone to my room at the back of the house on Nine Pin Road, and I liked to stay on the couch in the warm kitchen, a couch my daddy had framed with lengths of left-over two-by-four, and my mama had finished by stuffing gunny sack cloth with sweet red clover, until I fell asleep. And I would try not to wake up as my daddy carried me to my bed, and Mama said to Daddy as he hefted me up, "Honestly, Johnny, I don't know what to do about that boy; he's awful old to be developing a fear of the dark."

I don't know what kind of evidence I expected to find in the shed behind the Sigurdsons' cabin, but whatever I was looking for, it wasn't there, for the woodshed was as empty as the house, nothing there at all but a few chips of firewood. I rubbed my fingers down the crude slab wall, hoping perhaps for some confirmation, a few tiger lily-colored hairs, a swatch of the sad blue dress Bertha always wore, hoping at the same time not to find them, which I didn't.

Somewhere down in the muskeg a groundfire burned, between the scrawny and crippled tamaracks a thin spume of bitter smoke drifted up and flattened out over the marshy ground. I picked my way among the fireweed, and red willow slips, avoiding the tall sting nettles, the edges of their dark green leaves serrated like knives. Then I saw it, a few steps ahead, in the mossy belly of the hillside, earth turned up and over, a long rectangle of it. I could hear what my mama would say if she saw it: "Those Sigurdsons are so lazy and sorrowful they couldn't even dig an honest grave." And I agreed with my mama as I skidded a few feet down toward the grave, the serrated edge of a sting nettle leaf slashing across my cheek and nose.

I stopped at the very edge of the grave, though I didn't want it to be a grave; I wanted it to be anything else, but it wasn't; it was a grave. The earth had been piled high and some deadfall laid across it to keep animals away, but the earth was sinking now, in a few weeks there would be nothing but a gentle mound, and by fall the place would be grown over, unfindable. Fireweed, a few bluebells, swamp grass, were already pushing up, wild, healing the wounds made by the shovel. Among the fresh growth, one bright object, like a cardinal flashing across a thicket, a few strands of the same red excelsior that had graced Bertha's box lunch last fall; that excelsior, the final confirmation I had sought, and feared to find.

I felt in my pockets, but I had brought nothing to leave, and I knew I wouldn't come back, couldn't come back. Then I remembered Bertha's words, her statement as we sat at the Little Box Social, she licking the chocolate off her lips, her sticky finger touching the back of my hand as though I wasn't quite real to her.

"You always get enough to eat," she said, her hair the color of tiger lilies, her tongue exploring the inside of the Wildfire chocolate bar wrapper.

I took from my pocket the lunch I had packed inside the waxed lining of a Kellogg's Corn Flakes box. The packet was crushed flat in my pocket, the chicken warm from the sun and my body heat, the shortbread crumbled. I realized suddenly, as I tore the waxed paper, as the odor of the fried chicken reached my nostrils, that I was ravenously hungry. But instead of eating, I laid the lunch down next to the few strands of red excelsior, and as I did so for some reason I remembered some of my daddy's words, him sitting sideways at our kitchen table in the house at the end of Nine Pin Road, just finishing a long tale about the times he had growing up in South Carolina: "Jamie, you'll retell my stories until you live a few of your own." I decided, as I turned away, my fingers tracing the nettle welts on my cheek, that this was my story, that I'd lived it, and someday I'd tell it, but not too soon, for right now it would hurt too much. Perhaps by the time I got home, I thought, I might have some idea of what it was like to be really hungry.

# BOB FELLER, HAL NEWHOUSER, AND JOE DIMAGGIO HIMSELF

# Chapter Fifteen

As far as Truckbox Al McClintock was concerned, it was decided, in one of those decisions that is arrived at without a vote, but unanimously, and involved not only his family but his friends and neighbors in and around the Six Towns area, that since Truckbox Al McClintock needed to save all his energy, both physical and mental, for playing baseball against Bob Feller, Hal Newhouser, and Joe DiMaggio himself, that, on the Saturday before the Sunday he was due to play, he should travel to Edmonton on the eastbound Western Trailways Bus which stopped once a day at Bjornsen's Corner on the Edmonton-Jasper Highway, a highway which was sometimes called the Jasper-Edmonton Highway, depending on which direction you were traveling.

Just like at the Presentation, after the wedding of the Little American Soldier and the delicately constructed Lavonia Lakusta, of the Lakustas by the lake, money mysteriously emerged from many and various pockets, a dime here, a dollar there, until the bus fare was paid for and money provided for a hotel room at the Castle Hotel, on 103 Street, in downtown Edmonton, which my daddy said was a somewhat elegant place with a sink in every room and a bathroom on every floor, not to mention a desk clerk on duty twenty-four hours a day, and genuine leather arm chairs and divans in the lobby, which was sprinkled with squat brass spittoons that got emptied at least once a day, every day, all year long. Curly McClintock, as he promised his friends he would do, on one of his forays into Edmonton in his inherited dump truck, carried along a load of his favorite car parts, motorcycle parts, and a goodly portion of his generator collection, which he sold at an auto wreckers in Edmonton, in order to come up with enough money to buy Truckbox Al a new glove, and a pair of size thirteen cleats. Curly had already been gifted with the proceeds from the oldtimers' baseball game, which were to be used to buy the boy a new baseball uniform.

Curly McClintock purchased the baseball equipment at the Marshall-Wells Wholesale on 104 Street, in downtown Edmonton, buying it in the name of Fark General Store, a gift from Slow Andy McMann, which enabled him to get the equipment for half of retail, which was a good thing, because by the time he counted out the handful of change he'd received from the auto wreckers for his auto parts, motorcycle parts, and generator collection, there was only seventy-five cents left, just enough to buy gas for the truck so it would definitely get him back to Bjornsen's Corner, where he knew the Bjornsens kept a five-gallon jerry can of purple gas in their machine shed, possibly as far as Doreen Beach, where his credit was good for several gallons of gas, or, if he was lucky, all the way to Fark, where he had the key to Slow Andy McMann's gas pump.

Fark, the name of the town closest to where we lived, was, I gathered, a somewhat unusual name for a town, or anything at all for that matter. Fark was a name which my mama said was a cruel joke, and she felt it was some kind of punishment, divine or otherwise, that we had to live in relatively close proximity to, and have a place called Fark as a mailing address.

"Being hillbillies is one thing, but living near a town with a name that sounds like a curse word is entirely another," my mama often said. And our relatives in South Dakota didn't help the situation, for they never failed to mention the unusualness of the name *Fark* every time they wrote us a letter, which was no more than Christmas and my daddy's birthday, but always printing the word FARK on the outside of the envelope in capital letters, often in red pencil. My daddy would write back to say that living near a town called Fark was no worse than living near the capital of South Dakota, P-i-e-r-r-e, which he said was spelled like the name of a waiter in a fancy French restaurant, but was often pronounced *pear*, like the fruit, or *pair*, a mediocre poker hand, or *père*, like somebody's French father, and was other times pronounced *peer*, like an equal, or *pier*, like a place where you tied up an ocean liner, or *peer*, like what you did when you stood on tippety-toe and stared over the fence at your neighbor's garden. And he would explain to his relatives, in great detail, as if Daddy knew any other way, how Fark came to get a name like that.

In the days when there was a railroad, and when that railroad decided to build a station house at a certain location on the line, there came a time for that location to be named, christened as it were, and it was the responsibility of the station agent for the railway to find a suitable name.

It was, therefore, my daddy said, not a coincidence that a vast number of towns, villages, and hamlets, located along railroad lines and ex-railroad lines in Alberta, and everywhere else where there were railroads, were named for railway station agents.

The station agent at the location that was to eventually become the hamlet of Fark, was named Farquharson. When Mr. Farquharson was asked to name the new railway depot and possible city, town, village, or hamlet that might spring up there, he was sent a form to fill out and return, to whatever government department was responsible for approving the names of new towns, their job being to see that nothing suggestive or obscene was slipped in as a town name, and that there weren't a dozen Smithvilles, Jonestowns, Johnson Cities, and Williamsburgs on each and every provincial map.

Mr. Farquharson, the station master at the as yet unnamed place, that would eventually become Fark, took his responsibility seriously; he filled out the form, in triplicate as required, and suggested that the new town be named Farquharson City, Alberta, and a certain thrill ran through his blood as he printed the name in block capitals, as the form requested, stuffed it into an envelope and mailed it to the government department in charge of naming new towns.

The government department in charge of naming new towns wrote back, in triplicate, saying that, in their opinion, there had been too many two-word towns named recently, and asking Mr. Farquharson to cut the name to one word. Mr. Farquharson studied the situation for a week or two, and eventually decided that if he had to choose between the two words, *Farquharson* and *City*, he would choose Farquharson rather than City, so he wrote to the government department in charge of naming new towns, in triplicate as requested, his letter stating that if he was only going to be allowed one word, he would be right pleased to have the new town called Farquharson. A certain lesser thrill ran through his blood as he printed the name in block capitals, and got the letter ready for mailing to the government department in charge of naming new towns.

The government department in charge of naming new towns,

wrote back, not saying *in their opinion*, which might have given Mr. Farquharson a leg to stand on, but stating as fact, that brevity was in and long names were out, and the government department in charge of naming new towns pointed up the fact that Farquharson contained eleven letters. Would Mr. Farquharson be good enough to come up with a short and succinct name for the new town?

Mr. Farquharson's first inclination was to write back to the government department in charge of naming new towns, in triplicate as requested, and tell them that he was fully aware that *Farquharson* had eleven letters, but Farquharson was his name, and that was the name he wanted his railroad depot, and whatever city, town, village, or hamlet happened to grow up there, to bear. He considered adding that since Farquharson was a good solid eleven-letter Scottish name, neither suggestive nor obscene, that the government department in charge of naming new towns should stop harassing him and get on with more important matters. However, Mr. Farquharson reconsidered his first inclination, and having a desire to keep his job, he went ahead and considered some alternatives.

Mr. Farquharson considered F-a-r, and Mr. Farquharson considered F-a-r-q, and Mr. Farquharson considered Q-u-h-a-r, and, using his initiative to become unusually inventive, and by so doing, taxing his imagination to the maximum, Mr. Farquharson considered Q-u-a-r, and Mr. Farquharson considered S-o-n; Mr. Farquharson even considered A-l-e-x, which was his first name, but he couldn't decide on any of them. The form, in triplicate, eventually got pushed to the back of the rolltop desk in the station house, and only after three reminders from the government department in charge of naming new towns, did Mr. Farquharson decide on F-a-r-q-, which he printed out in block capitals, though no thrill of accomplishment ran through his blood as he did so.

But the government department in charge of naming new towns was still not satisfied. They pointed out to Mr. Farquharson, that F-a-r-q didn't sound like much of anything, and that $Q$ was, as far as the government department in charge of naming new towns was concerned, always followed by $U$, which, if put into practice, would make the suggested name even stranger than it already was.

By that time, Mr. Farquharson was sick of the whole idea of naming a town, and ignored the three additional reminder letters that came at one-month intervals from the government department in charge of naming new towns. The fourth reminder letter that arrived stated that since Mr. Farquharson had apparently lost interest in naming the new railroad depot, the government department in charge of naming new towns had decided to take it upon itself to simplify the last suggestion, and, henceforth, the railway depot, plus the soon-to-be post office, and whatever city, town, village, or hamlet would spring up there, would be called FARK.

Soon after that, Mr. Alex Farquharson quit his job as station agent with the railroad, moved to Edmonton, and got a job driving a horse-drawn lumber wagon for the M.D. Muttart Lumber Company, where he gradually improved himself until he was a regional sales manager, though, to his dying day, he regretted not having a railroad depot and town called Farquharson City, named after him.

On the second day of the wedding celebration for Lavonia Lakusta and the Little American Soldier, Curly and Gunhilda McClintock forcibly removed Truckbox Al from the Lakusta farm. He was more vague and distracted than he usually was, and slower to answer questions than he ever was, and he stared at his mother and father as if they had asked him to write an essay on a subject unfamiliar to him, something they would never have dreamed of doing. In spite of his lackadaisicalness, Curly and Gunhilda McClintock (*née:* Gordonjensen) carried Truckbox Al home to New Oslo, to the old Gordonjensen place, scrubbed him up, saw to it that he slept for a few hours, and then they carried him to Bjornsen's Corner where he was to be placed on the eastbound Western Trailways bus to Edmonton, Alberta, and a major league baseball career.

There was a genuine farewell party at Bjornsen's Corner, where the eastbound Western Trailways bus stopped once a day. There were a considerable number of people present to contribute to Truckbox Al's sendoff, though not nearly as many as would have been there if the wedding of the Little American Soldier and the delicately constructed Lavonia Lakusta had not been going on at the Lakustas by the lake, but the gathering at Bjornsen's Corner was still large by Six Towns standards.

Two of the Osbaldson boys played a harmonica duet, after which Little Grendel Badke sang "Red Sails in the Sunset," accompanied by her little brother, Kaiser Wilhelm Badke, on the recorder. Brother Bickerstaff, who was waiting for the Western Trailways bus in the other direction, condescended to offer a prayer for Truckbox Al McClintock's safe journey, a prayer which went on for several minutes, and did not seem to have a lot to do with Truckbox Al McClintock, but mentioned Sodom and Gomorrah, evil and temptation, dancing, baseball, and banned books, none of which were mentioned in a positive light. The prayer was finally interrupted by the sound of the airbrakes of the Western Trailways bus, the sight and sound of the bald bus tires grasping gravel, and the sight, sound, taste, touch, and smell of a cloud of grayish dust enveloping Brother Bickerstaff and the entire farewell party.

The eastbound Western Trailways bus was driven by one of the Ostapowich boys from Wildwood, a long, bony Ostapowich, with thick glasses and a beak of a nose. Truckbox Al McClintock was sent on his way wearing a new pair of lime-green suit pants from the Goodwill Store in Sangudo, and a red and yellow plaid shirt sewn by hand by his mother, Gunhilda McClintock, that came pretty close to fitting him. Truckbox Al McClintock had a suitcase filled with his brand new baseball uniform, his brand new baseball glove, and his brand new, size thirteen baseball cleats; he also had enough money to pay for the hotel room at the Castle Hotel, on 103 Street in Edmonton, plus nearly three dollars' spending money, and a map of how to get from the Western Trailways Bus Terminal to the Castle Hotel, even though the hotel was less than two blocks from the bus depot.

Truckbox All was also accompanied by two huge baskets, each one containing enough food to feed a dozen people; the food came mainly from the Lakusta wedding, sent with the blessing of Wasyl and Rose Lakusta, the Little American Soldier and his delicately constructed wife, Lavonia, and the whole wedding party.

The bus had only progressed a mile toward Edmonton when it was flagged down at the next crossroad by a thin, blond girl, barefoot and wearing a faded pink dress. As the thin, blond, barefoot, pink-dressed girl climbed on, she stared toward the back of the dark bus where Truckbox Al McClintock, his heart pounding like the exhaust on his daddy's dump truck, was climbing over the two baskets of food on the seat next to him, and making his way toward the front of the bus, where he counted into the long, bony hand, of the long, bony Ostapowich from Wildwood, the exact change for the thin, blond, barefoot, pink-dressed girl's one-way fare to Edmonton.

During the ride to Edmonton, Louisa May Sigurdson kept one of the baskets of food on the dusty blue velvet seat between her and Truckbox Al McClintock, but occasionally, as she rested after eating pieces of fried chicken, cold cabbage rolls, slices of chocolate cake, and cinnamon rolls, Louisa May would reach over and stroke Truckbox Al's arm, remarking each time she did so on how big his muscles were, and how strong he must be, and how far he must be able to hit a baseball, which was enough attention to keep Truckbox Al in a state of genuine agitation for the entire ride to Edmonton.

When they arrived in Edmonton, at the Western Trailways Bus Depot, Truckbox Al McClintock, after studying the map his father had given him, spreading it out on one of the wooden benches in the bus depot to do so, was able to devise a route to the Castle Hotel on 103 Street, which was only a block from the bus depot anyway. Louisa May Sigurdson tagged right along with him each step of the way, each of them carrying a half-full basket of food, and staring up at the unbelievably tall buildings, one of which must have been all of seven stories. Truckbox Al, his suitcase, and the food baskets checked into the hotel, while Louisa May Sigurdson waited on the sidewalk, then he and Louisa May Sigurdson walked downtown, which was all of another two blocks, where they planned to see a movie. Truckbox Al sounded out a sign that said T. Eaton Co. Department Store, and another that said Belmont Café.

"Think that might be a theater?" Truckbox Al asked, pointing at a place with about a thousand lightbulbs out front.

"Can't read," said Louis May Sigurdson, clutching tightly to Truckbox Al's arm.

Truckbox Al eventually sounded out Rialto Theater, and the two of them sat in the dark on red velvet seats, and watched a color movie about Buffalo Bill. Late that night, after seeing the movie about Buffalo Bill, and eating two caramel sundaes each at the Hollywood Inn Café, Truckbox Al sneaked Louisa May Sigurdson into his room at the Castle Hotel, on 103 Street, and Louisa May Sigurdson proved not to be a piker, for she did to Truckbox Al McClintock exactly what she had promised she would do, when she first approached him at the Lakusta wedding.

On the bus ride to Edmonton, and at the movie about Buffalo Bill, and while eating two caramel sundaes at the Hollywood Inn Café, Truckbox Al McClintock had experienced several varieties of deep-down stirrings, achings, and longings, whenever he looked at Louisa May Sigurdson, but he had no idea that what she promised him at the Lakusta wedding consisted of what it consisted of, and when she did to him what she did, it did indeed curl his toes, though when he checked the next morning he couldn't see that it contributed to rotting his socks any.

Louisa May Sigurdson, though she had fulfilled her obligation to Truckbox Al McClintock, she being the only more-or-less Doreen Beach Sigurdson who apparently possessed a sense of honor, had decided that she would go and watch Truckbox Al play baseball, exploring while she did so the possibility that Truckbox Al was as big a baseball star as he claimed, and if baseball stars made as much money as Truckbox Al said they did, why she might just stick with him—because she liked sleeping in a genuine bed in a truly warm room, at the Castle Hotel on 103 Street in Edmonton, sitting in comfortable seats in the dark to watch a movie about Buffalo Bill, and eating two caramel sundaes at the Hollywood Inn Café—and not go looking for someone rich and handsome who could buy her pretty clothes and see that she ate three times a day.

After breakfast at the Hollywood Inn Café, two doors down from the Castle Hotel, Truckbox Al McClintock put on his brand new baseball uniform, his brand new size thirteen baseball cleats, and slipped his brand new baseball glove on his hand. After asking directions, he and Louisa May Sigurdson headed for Renfrew Park, down on the river flats, which was right down the hill from the Rialto Theater, where they had sat in the dark and seen the color movie about Buffalo Bill.

Truckbox Al had wakened up with the very same stirrings, achings, and longings as he'd had the day before, deep-down stirrings, achings, and longings, which had been satisfied so eloquently by Louisa May Sigurdson, and he suggested that she do again what she had done before.

"Not until after the game," Louisa May Sigurdson told Truckbox Al. She went on to say that if he happened to hit one of the home runs he talked about so much, why she would do to him what she had done before, and she would show him a couple of other tricks that would curl his hair, as well as curling his toes, and rotting his socks.

When they got down onto the river flats, Truckbox Al Mc-Clintock and Louisa May Sigurdson stood out front of Renfrew Park, in the parking lot, where Truckbox Al sounded out the words Renfrew Park, and sounded out the words ticket booth, and sounded out the word concessions, and sounded out the words no exit, before sounding out the words player's gate, which he decided, was the place he should report.

At Renfrew Park, down on the river flats, in Edmonton, Alberta, in the summer of 1945 or '46, John "The Raja of Renfrew" Ducey wasn't allowed to charge admission to Sunday games, so a silver collection was taken at the gate, which meant that adults, who ordinarily paid seventy-five cents, got in by giving a quarter, and kids, who ordinarily paid a quarter, walked in free.

Truckbox Al McClintock gave Louisa May Sigurdson a quarter for her admission, and fifty cents in case she wanted some refreshments, and told her that he'd be looking for her during the game, though he wanted to tell her he was going to dedicate his first home run to her, he simply couldn't find the words, so he just scratched his large, round head, and looked as if he'd been asked to write an essay on a subject unfamiliar to him, and lumbered off toward the player's gate. Louisa May Sigurdson told Truckbox Al she'd be watching him, too, and to be sure and hit at least one home run if he wanted her to do to him again what she had done to him the night before.

The motorcade from the Six Towns to Edmonton, Alberta, and Renfrew Park, down on the river flats, was composed of only three vehicles, one 1929 Model T Ford, owned and operated by the infamous Flop Skalrud, with two people in front, one being the infamous Flop Skalrud, and the other being Christine Annamarie Magnussen, Lute Magnussen's oldest girl, a situation that would ordinarily have created enough gossip to keep the Six Towns area humming for several days, but was overshadowed by the excitement of the trip to Edmonton to see the Six Towns' only celebrity in history play baseball against Bob Feller, Hal Newhouser, and Joe DiMaggio himself.

A couple of Flop Skalrud's nephews and one of Christine Annamarie Magnussen's younger brothers were squashed into the rumble seat of that 1929 Model T Ford; the other Ford in the Six Towns area, in spite of having the chickens chased out of it, its oil pan welded on, and its battery charged, in preparation for the journey, had died of excitement that very morning.

The second vehicle was Bear Lundquist's 1941 Pontiac Silver Streak, with Mr. and Mrs. Bear Lundquist in the front seat and, miracle of miracles, our family, the John Martin Duffy O'Days, in the back. It seems that, unknown to me, and possibly even unknown to my mama who had a sharp eye for such things, Mr. Bear Lundquist had, of a bitter winter, borrowed from my daddy four heaping wagonloads of hay for his cattle, and had not as he was supposed to repaid that hay the next summer. Daddy had called in an old debt—in return for transportation to and from Edmonton, the debt would be canceled.

Daddy had somehow come up with enough money for the three of us to stay at the Castle Hotel, on 103 Street in Edmonton, for one night, and eat two meals, supper and breakfast, the former at the Belmont Café on 101 Street, and the latter at the Hollywood Inn Café, two doors down from the Castle Hotel on 103 Street in Edmonton.

The rest of the motorcade consisted of Curly McClintock's dump truck with four people in the cab, and twenty-six people in the truck box. At the last minute, Daddy, who always had a soft heart, allowed as how we could find room for the widow, Mrs. Beatrice Ann Stevenson, in the back seat with us, which meant that I got displaced, and had to sit on my daddy's bony knee all the way to Edmonton, which wasn't too bad, once we got to the Edmonton-Jasper Highway, that part of the trip taking only two-and-a-half hours, with Bear Lundquist's 1941 Pontiac Silver Streak having to be pulled out of mud holes, by his son, Ole Lundquist, and his team of bays, only six times.

The Wasyl Lakustas, along with whatever local wedding guests were sober enough to travel, were in the box of the dump truck. The Little American Soldier and his delicately constructed bride, Lavonia (*née:* Lakusta), had driven west on the Edmonton-Jasper Highway in the Little American Soldier's camouflage-brindle, two-ton truck, where they planned to spend some of the proceeds from the Presentation to stay a night or two at Jasper Park Lodge, a place so ritzy that Bing Crosby and Bob Hope were said to visit there twice a summer to eat venison steak and play golf.

At Renfrew Park, down on the river flats, at least an hour before the game was to begin, everybody from the Six Towns area was settled in their seats, seats that had been chosen by my daddy and Earl J. Rasmussen, and which were a goodly distance down the right field line, the only place Daddy and Earl J. Rasmussen could find forty seats together, somewhere close enough to right field so Truckbox Al McClintock would be able to hear the occupants of those seats cheering.

Most of the people from the Six Towns area had never been to a genuine baseball park even once in their life, and they were so busy rubbernecking that many of them failed to take advantage of batting practice to see the likes of Joe DiMaggio himself and his teammates hit baseballs out of Renfrew Park. The park held maybe three thousand people, and a good half of the three thousand were American soldiers, who had been bussed in from Namao Airport, after most of them had been flown in in flying boxcars from somewhere way up on the Alaska Highway. Everyone, my daddy said, was glad to have made the effort, for they knew in their hearts, that, to a man, the American soldiers would build a better highway, and, if called upon, fight a better war, because they had been properly entertained.

There was a certain amount of disappointment, especially to the American troops, and to Daddy, and Earl J. Rasmussen, and Bear Lundquist, all of whom knew a little bit about baseball, when it was announced over the public address system that Joe DiMaggio himself was not going to play. He had to fly back to the United States to take part in a very important charity event which was raising funds for the war effort, the public address announcer said.

There was considerably more disappointment, mainly just to Daddy, and Earl J. Rasmussen, and Bear Lundquist, all of whom knew a little about baseball, when after studying the baseball program, which had a colored photo of Joe DiMaggio himself on the cover, Daddy discovered that Hal Newhouser was not only not going to play, but as far as he could determine, had never been on the squad at all. Daddy did take consolation in pointing out to me Bob Feller of Cleveland Indian fame, where he was warming up on the sidelines.

"Listen for the sound of the ball smacking into the glove," Daddy said. "Bob Feller," he went on, "can pitch a baseball one hundred miles per hour." And Daddy explained that he could back up his facts because he had read in the *St. Louis Sporting News*, that Bob Feller's fastball had been clocked at one hundred miles per hour, and the *St. Louis Sporting News* was seldom known to print falsehoods.

My daddy, Earl J. Rasmussen, and Bear Lundquist, each of whom knew a little about baseball, experienced considerably more disappointment, when, after studying both the baseball program and the players on the field, they ascertained that the Major League All-Stars were made up primarily of minor league players. Mostly refugees from Triple A, my daddy said. Other than Bob Feller, the only genuine Major Leaguer on the squad was a fellow named Cookie Lavagetto, at third base, a fellow who had had a fairly average career with the Brooklyn Dodgers before he joined the United States Army.

It came as a shock, and a surprise, and a downright disappointment, not only to my daddy, Earl J. Rasmussen, and Bear Lundquist, each of whom knew a little about baseball, but to most of the fans from the Six Towns area as well, that Truckbox Al McClintock wasn't in the starting line-up for the unimaginatively named Alberta All-Stars.

Surveying the situation, my mama said, "There is a lot of chagrin in these here stands, not to mention vexation, rankling, smarting, and downright annoyance."

My daddy, who was the only fan from the Six Towns area who had played genuine semi-professional baseball—though Earl J. Rasmussen might have played at least semi-professional baseball if his mother hadn't stopped him from attending a tryout with the Washington Senators baseball club of the American League—even if Daddy's semi-professional baseball had been played in Florida and California in the United States, had to restrain several of the Six Towns area baseball fans from going down on the field and giving the manager of the unimaginatively named Alberta All-Stars a piece of their mind, or worse.

"Somebody has to be available for reserve duty," my daddy pointed out logically. But several fans, including the widow, Mrs. Beatrice Ann Stevenson, still wanted to go down to the dugout and point out Truckbox Al McClintock's good qualities to the manager of the unimaginatively named Alberta All-Stars, while establishing at the same time if Truckbox Al was hungry, or thirsty, or needed to find a washroom.

Fortunately, before the fans became too chagrined, vexed, rankled, or downright annoyed because Truckbox Al McClintock was not in the starting line-up, they were distracted by the pre-game ceremonies, which went on for an endless period of time, and consisted partially of the Mayor of Edmonton, followed by the Premier of Alberta, a Bible-thumper with slicked-down hair and gold-rimmed glasses, who actually had a Sunday morning radio show called "The Back to the Bible Hour," which ran more than an hour, saying a few words.

As we all know, there is not a politician in the world who can say only a few words. A half hour later, after The Old Strathcona High School Drum and Bugle Corps, and a quartet of Shriners in fuzzy yellow hats, had murdered both the American and Canadian national anthems, things being quite a bit less sophisticated than they are today, our own Earl J. Rasmussen was called upon to deliver his rendition of "Casey at the Bat." And to give the performance an international flavor, Earl J. Rasmussen was introduced as Earl J. Rasmussen, of Norseland,

Minnesota, and New Oslo, Alberta. During Earl J. Rasmussen's performance the widow, Mrs. Beatrice Ann Stevenson, wondered aloud several times why, if Earl J. Rasmussen could recite "Casey at the Bat" at the top of his lungs for three thousand people, she couldn't provide a little refinement to the occasion by reciting a trio of Emily Dickinson poems to the assembled multitude.

Truckbox Al McClintock didn't get into the game until there was one out in the last of the sixth inning, when he was sent in to pinch hit for the right fielder. When Truckbox Al finally got himself squared away in the batter's box, he wiggled his bat and stared over the crook of his elbow at the one and only Bob Feller, of the Cleveland Indians baseball club, of the American Baseball League.

As Truckbox Al dug in at the plate, everybody from the Six Towns area stood up, and my daddy, who had played some minor league baseball in Florida and California, and had attended many a Major League baseball game in his day, and liked to tell the story of how, at a minor league game in Palm Springs, California, where he was a spectator, rather than a player, a young pitcher named Tony had been struggling for his life until my daddy and a few of his friends stood up, well fortified by red-hots and draft beer, and chanted, "Pour it on 'em, Tony!" every time the troubled pitcher went into his windup, until the pitcher named Tony began to gain confidence with every pitch, went on to win the game, and later, to have a fair-to-middlin' career in Triple A baseball.

My daddy led the forty or so fans from the Six Towns area in chanting, "Pour it on 'em, Truckbox," most of the fans fortified by hot dogs, and, as beer was not sold at Renfrew Park, down on the river flats, a few snorts of Heathen's Rapture, or good old bring-on-blindness, logging-boot-to-the-side-of-the-head homebrew, a jug or two of which had been left over from Lavonia Lakusta's wedding to the Little American Soldier, and transported along in the box of Curly McClintock's dump truck, in case it was needed.

Bob Feller, of Cleveland Indian fame, went into his wind-up and fired a fastball. The only way Truckbox Al McClintock knew that the fastball got from Bob Feller's hand to the catcher's mitt was by the sound that eventually reached his ears, and the cloud of dust that eventually emanated from the catcher's mitt. The umpire's right fist went up in the air to signal strike one.

Truckbox Al McClintock, who no one would ever accuse of being in the genius category, must have been just on the verge of realizing he had one strike on him, when he had two. For while he'd been listening to the fading sound of the ball hitting the catcher's mitt, and watching the cloud of dust emanating and dispersing from the very same catcher's mitt, Bob Feller, of Cleveland Indian fame, had wound up and pitched a second fastball, and there had been a second sound like a gunshot as the ball hit the catcher's mitt, and a second cloud of dust emanating from the very same catcher's mitt, and the umpire's right fist had gone up in the air to signal strike two.

"Pour it on 'em, Truckbox!" yelled my daddy, and the forty or so people from the Six Towns area, plus a few of the American soldiers who had been flown in in flying boxcars from way up on the Alaska Highway, plus a few of the ordinary citizens who were seated around us, and who were standing up because we were standing up, and slightly excited because we were a lot excited. But all Truckbox Al McClintock heard, if he heard anything at all, were the two gunshot-like sounds of the two fastballs hitting the catcher's mitt, and all Truckbox Al saw, if he saw anything at all, was the residue of two clouds of dust from the catcher's mitt dispersing into the late afternoon air.

Truckbox Al McClintock was still contemplating the second emanation of dust, when the third fastball passed by, and the umpire's right fist went up in the air for the third time. While the Major League All-Stars were whipping the ball around the infield and getting it back to Bob Feller, of Cleveland Indian fame, the next batter for the unimaginatively named Alberta All-Stars approached the plate, gently nudging Truckbox Al out of the batter's box as he did so.

"Y'all only get one at-bat at a time," the catcher said to Truckbox Al's back.

"Huh?" said Truckbox Al, as the new batter gently turned him around and pointed him toward the dugout, which wasn't a dugout at all, but a green-painted bench along the third base bleacher.

Truckbox Al McClintock, while sitting on the bench among the unimaginatively named Alberta All-Stars for six innings, had eventually been able to spot Louisa May Sigurdson sitting on the first base side of Renfrew Park, right in the midst of about two dozen American soldiers, who were dressed in their snazzy gabardine uniforms and genuine military caps, that made each and every one of them look like Smilin' Jack. But by the time he got sat down on the bench, after his strike out, and his mind had cleared enough for him to look for Louisa May Sigurdson again, he was just able to catch a glimpse of her leaving the ballpark, with at least one, and maybe two or three, American soldiers.

Louisa May Sigurdson was never seen around the Six Towns again, and, my mama said, someone eventually told the Little American Soldier that she married a softhearted lieutenant from Missouri, who didn't mind his wife being barefoot and illiterate, mainly because he had all the time expected to marry a barefoot and illiterate girl, and was both surprised and pleased as punch to find one at a baseball game in a place like Edmonton, Alberta, of the same Sunday afternoon he got to see Bob Feller, of Cleveland Indian fame, pitch in an exhibition baseball game.

As Truckbox Al McClintock was called out on strikes, everybody from the Six Towns sat down, and you could almost hear the simultaneous exhalation of breath, an exhalation of breath that would have blown a foul ball fair, if Truckbox Al McClintock had been able to get his bat off his shoulder to hit a foul ball. Casey's fans in Mudville weren't any sadder.

"When is he gonna hit the ball?" the widow, Mrs. Beatrice Ann Stevenson, asked.

"Not this time," my daddy said. But then Daddy, who was known to look on the bright side of things, added, "All we have to do is get a couple of men on base and Truckbox Al will get to bat in the last of the ninth, when the outcome of the game might very well be on the line."

The part about the outcome of the game being on the line was truly wishful thinking, which my mama accused my daddy of nearly every day of the year, for the unimaginatively named Alberta All-Stars were already seven runs behind, and the prospects for the final innings were that they would fall further behind, not close in on the Major League All-Stars, or Triple A All-Stars, as my daddy said they deserved to be called.

The sad truth was that Truckbox Al McClintock never got a second at-bat. He did go in to the play right field, and as he did so we all applauded and whistled and stomped appropriately. And he did get to handle a three-hop single, scooping it up without incident, in his new glove from Marshal-Wells Wholesale, and, when the runner took a wide turn at first, firing behind the runner, just like a professional outfielder would do. We all cheered at Truckbox Al's expert handling of the ball, and the baseball savvy it took for him to recognize a situation where it was appropriate to fire behind the runner. But we had to stop in mid-hurrah, because, as soon as Truckbox Al committed himself to throw behind the runner, the runner took off for second base, and had enough time to tell his life story to the second baseman before the ball, relayed from Truckbox Al to the first baseman, and then to the second baseman, got there.

The unimaginatively named Alberta All-Stars did not get another man on base, and Truckbox Al, and Truckbox Al's dreams of a Major League career, died, as my daddy put it so eloquently, in the on-deck circle.

That game, which might have been Truckbox Al's big break, was, though not one of us realized it at the time, an end to an era, and a beginning to a new one. The rapidly improving economy soon made it possible for ordinary folks in the Six Towns area to own cars, and once they owned cars they traveled, and once they traveled things were never the same again. There was work in the cities, and people, including our family, the John Martin Duffy O'Days, eventually moved to the city where there were fine houses to be built, and money, and color moving picture shows, and where *everybody* owned a radio. The Saturday night box socials, whist drives, and country dances dwindled and faded, and in another decade had all but disappeared, as did some of the towns.

This story, in fact, is part memory and part imagination, told after I have had many years, and many miles, to distance me from the events I've written about. A year ago, when I visited Alberta, I took a leisurely drive around the Six Towns area. Five of the towns are still in existence, changed very little from 1945 or '46. Only Fark and Bjornsen's Corner are gone. Bjornsen's Corner is still there, but the big white house with the green trim that at one time belonged to the Bjornsens was gone, so thoroughly gone, that I couldn't even find the spot where it used to be.

Instead of trails, there are now oiled roads, and graveled roads, and the Edmonton-Jasper Highway is paved, but there are still a few dirt roads, and one of them leads to the farm where I grew up, and another heads into a light growth of poplar and birch saplings and red willow, and would eventually lead to Fark, if there was a Fark for it to lead to. Somebody who knew said the general store and community hall were gone, the store torn down and the hall sunk into the ground, and, if you could find Fark, as this person did while partridge hunting a few years ago, all that was left was the shell of the gas pump, leaning at a forty-five degree angle, and flaking rust onto the sting nettles and the occasional bluebell that grew low in the tangled grasses.

The day after the big game between the Major League All-Stars and the unimaginatively named Alberta All-Stars, at Renfrew Park, down on the river flats in Edmonton, Alberta, summer of 1945 or '46, John "The Raja of Renfrew" Ducey, announced at a press conference—Edmonton, like certain other North American metropolises, being a two-newspaper city, even in 1945 or '46—that he had used his influential contacts inside Major League Baseball to arrange for a brand new and exciting league which would start the next spring, and which would be peopled with players from the farm organizations of several Major League teams. It would be an Inter-City League, and would feature two teams from Edmonton, the New Edmonton Hotel Eskimos, and the Edmonton Motors Chevrolet Cubs, and two teams from Calgary, the Calgary Brewing Company Buffalos, and the Calgary Purity 99's Oilers, none of the sponsoring organizations being shy about their business names appearing in the title.

The next spring, Truckbox Al McClintock got a tryout with the New Edmonton Hotel Eskimos, but was one of their first cuts. As it turned out, Truckbox Al couldn't hit the curveball. He settled for playing a half-dozen times a summer at sportsdays, and picnics, where he occasionally hit a ball far over the centerfielder's head, so far that if he'd been playing against an all-Indian team from Lac Ste. Anne, at a ballfield on the banks of the Pembina River, batting against a skinny Indian pitcher whose only saving grace was a passable pickoff move to first base, the ball would have gone directly in the drink, and bobbed away downstream, getting smaller and less white as it did so.

**ABOUT THE AUTHOR**

W. P. Kinsella is the author of two novels, *Shoeless Joe*, for which he won the Houghton Mifflin Literary Fellowship Award, and *The Iowa Baseball Confederacy*, as well as eleven highly acclaimed short story collections. He lives in the Pacific Northwest, where he and his wife, Ann, are card-carrying scouts for the Atlanta Braves.